Bolan brought the binoculars back up to his eyes

He scanned the eastern horizon. A craft was coming around the far side of the Japanese atoll.

"We have company."

"What kind?"

Bolan adjusted the magnification and looked at the flag on a small commercial vessel slightly larger than *Scrappy*. The flag featured a red, rayed ball on a white background. It was the flag of the Rising Sun.

The Japanese flag of w̶

Bolan lowere̶ ̶nd."

MACK BOLAN ®
The Executioner

DON PENDLETON'S
EXECUTIONER®
THE
BLOOD OF THE EARTH

A GOLD EAGLE BOOK FROM
WORLDWIDE.

TORONTO • NEW YORK • LONDON
AMSTERDAM • PARIS • SYDNEY • HAMBURG
STOCKHOLM • ATHENS • TOKYO • MILAN
MADRID • WARSAW • BUDAPEST • AUCKLAND

First edition June 1999
ISBN 0-373-64246-6

Special thanks and acknowledgment to
Chuck Rogers for his contribution to this work.

BLOOD OF THE EARTH

Printed in U.S.A.

Aggression unchallenged is aggression unleashed.
—Lyndon B. Johnson

Sometimes, anger can be the best source of courage.
—Mack Bolan

THE
MACK BOLAN®
LEGEND

Nothing less than a war could have fashioned the destiny of the man called Mack Bolan. Bolan earned the Executioner title in the jungle hell of Vietnam.

But this soldier also wore another name—Sergeant Mercy. He was so tagged because of the compassion he showed to wounded comrades-in-arms and Vietnamese civilians.

Mack Bolan's second tour of duty ended prematurely when he was given emergency leave to return home and bury his family, victims of the Mob. Then he declared a one-man war against the Mafia.

He confronted the Families head-on from coast to coast, and soon a hope of victory began to appear. But Bolan had broken society's every rule. That same society started gunning for this elusive warrior—to no avail.

So Bolan was offered amnesty to work within the system against terrorism. This time, as an employee of Uncle Sam, Bolan became Colonel John Phoenix. With a command center at Stony Man Farm in Virginia, he and his new allies—Able Team and Phoenix Force—waged relentless war on a new adversary: the KGB.

But when his one true love, April Rose, died at the hands of the Soviet terror machine, Bolan severed all ties with Establishment authority.

Now, after a lengthy lone-wolf struggle and much soul-searching, the Executioner has agreed to enter an "arm's-length" alliance with his government once more, reserving the right to pursue personal missions in his Everlasting War.

PROLOGUE

Skip Porter thought he heard a noise.

He sat up in bed and listened in the darkness. The island was stiflingly hot. Everyone had been hoping all day for a cool breeze, but no wind came off the beach. The humid heat held everything still. Porter stared at the illuminated numbers of the clock radio on the nightstand. It was 4:02 a.m. He had managed to doze off only an hour ago, and now he was wide awake again. He sighed and sagged his wiry frame back onto the bed. It was nothing. Probably one of the hundreds of feral cats that infested the islands and were decimating the tropical bird and lizard populations. Porter shook his head. This job consulting in the islands for the oil company was supposed to have been more of a vacation than a job.

Porter bolted upright in bed.

He craned his neck and peered into the blackness. He couldn't tell if he had actually heard anything, but that didn't matter. The sweat on his skin had gone clammy. Longer ago than Skip Porter cared to think about, he had been a combat engineer in Vietnam with the 56th Engineering Demolitions Team. His cherry status as a college recruit and his bantam weight physique had earned him the job of company tunnel rat. When the infantry discovered a VC tunnel complex, Porter and others like him were the first men down. Armed with little more than a .45 automatic pistol and a flashlight, he had ferreted the Viet Cong out of their own underground lairs. Porter had excelled at the job, and he had been decorated numerous times. In those claustrophobic tunnels and frantic point-blank firefights, Porter had earned uncanny instincts the hard way. The war had ended for Porter many years ago, but those instincts still survived, and they were screaming at him now from the pit of his stomach.

Someone was in the house.

Porter slid his hand between the mattress and the headboard, and his fingers curled around the grip of the same type of government issue .45 he had carried so long ago. Firearms were strictly forbidden in the Pacific Trust Islands, but after the incidents on the islands began, Porter had sent his wife back to Oregon and she had sent his pistol back in a box marked stereo components.

The .45's safety flicked off silently in Porter's gun hand, and his left pulled the miniflashlight off the nightstand. He slid out of bed noiselessly and crouched in the darkness. The red glow of the clock's numerals was the only source of light in the room. Porter cursed himself. He had left the windows open in the hope of a breeze. For a split second he debated closing them, but instead he moved slightly and knelt with his pistol ready.

Almost imperceptibly, the knob to the door of his room made a noise.

Porter swung the .45 by memory to the middle of the door and fired three times. The roar of the heavy pistol was deafening in the stillness, and the flare of its muzzle-blast sent pulsing bursts of color across his vision. He felt the floorboards beneath his feet flex from behind him and whirled the automatic around and punched on the flashlight.

He only saw the flash of the heavy blade as it chopped into him. The flashlight tumbled from his hand and clattered to the floor. It spun for a moment, sending its cone of light revolving at ankle level. Porter sagged as the blade came out of him, and he tried to raise the .45. His arm barely obeyed him, and the pistol seemed to weigh as much as a mountain in his nerveless hand.

Skip Porter never felt the second blow or the others that followed.

Hal Brognola was ushered into the Oval Office without ceremony. The President looked anxious. Brognola recognized the secretary of state, standing off to the left looking at a wall-sized map of the Pacific Ocean, and he didn't look terribly pleased. The big Fed also recognized the assistant director of the CIA as the man raised an eyebrow in acknowledgment at him. A tall thin man in a blue suit whom Brognola couldn't place sat to one side with his hands steepled before him. Probably the Pentagon. A three-star Marine general sat next to him, and the two men studiously ignored each other. The President waved Brognola in.

"Come in, Hal, have a seat."

Brognola sat in the nearest chair. "Thank you, sir. How may I be of assistance?"

"Frankly, we have a situation."

Brognola nodded. This wasn't the first American President who had begun a conversation with him using those exact same words. "What kind of situation?"

The President looked at the secretary of state. "I guess we're all here, Jim. Why don't you start?"

The secretary nodded and tapped a point on the wall map with his finger. "What we have is a small, very ugly situation developing in the Pacific. Americans have been killed."

Brognola's face tightened. He had watched the news, and he knew what the man was talking about. "The Pacific Trust Islands."

The diplomat nodded. "Exactly."

The general folded his arms across his chest and looked about the room sternly. "I hate to beat a dead horse, gentlemen, but with one Marine Expeditionary Force I can have the whole situation under complete control in forty-eight hours."

The President smiled. "I know, Earl, but it's a little more complicated than that."

The general shrugged. He was totally aware of the political situation, and it turned his stomach. He was a soldier, and American citizens were being wantonly killed. The man from the State Department looked scornfully at the old Marine, then turned to the President. "Sir, I don't like whipping dead horses either, but I feel I must remind everyone present that the Pacific Trust Islands are currently cogoverned by their own provisional government and the United Nations, and that they are about to receive full sovereign nation status."

The assistant director of the CIA was a short man with thick curly gray hair. He ran a hand through it and sighed as he sank deeper into his chair. "As much as I hate to admit it, he's right. The United Nations will never sanction a U.S. invasion of the islands, and, on a more personal level, neither will our friends, the French or the Japanese."

Brognola shrugged. "Why not a joint venture? International friendship and cooperation during a crisis always looks good."

The President sighed wistfully. "I wish it were that simple. Unfortunately, the French and the Japanese aren't exactly our allies in this."

The Justice man frowned. "From what I've read, the killings and the rioting are by a native terrorist group that wants to keep foreigners and foreign development out of their islands. They've reportedly killed French and Japanese nationals, as well. You'd think they'd want us to go in."

The secretary nodded. "One would think so on first examination. However, there is another factor involved, and that factor is oil. Recent exploratory drillings offshore along the islands' undersea plateaus suggest there might be very large oil deposits in the island chain."

Brognola's eyes narrowed. Both France and Japan were

poor in oil resources, and both countries were constantly trying to improve their petroleum resource base. Neither France nor Japan would allow an American military force to control the islands while the development rights to the oil were up in the air. Brognola took a deep breath before beginning. "I gather the local provisional government hasn't signed over the oil development rights to anybody."

The CIA man sat up in his chair. "That's exactly right. As a matter of fact, they seem quite happy to let the American, French and Japanese bicker and match bribes over who will get the deal. They're making quite a profit, and it will drive up the final price." The man tapped his finger on the arm of his chair. "Also, the local government wants to stay when the Pacific Trust Islands gain full nation status next year. It doesn't seem willing to do anything that might get its homegrown terrorists angry at it. The local government isn't taking any action on the murders or the riots beyond lip service. Frankly, it's turning a blind eye to the whole thing."

"Who's got the most clout?" Brognola asked.

The secretary frowned again. "That's an interesting question. The United States was instrumental in helping the people set up the provisional government after World War II. But most of their immediate trading neighbors are the French-influenced islands. The local police use French weapons, and most of the cars, mopeds, appliances and the like are of French manufacture. France has some economic clout in the islands. The Japanese were in the islands during World War II, but they didn't exactly make any friends during their occupation. However, enough yen under the table can smooth over a lot of old animosities. I don't think anyone has a lock on the islanders' sympathies, and the Native Isolationists Movement wants all of us out. I'm forced to agree with the Central Intelligence Agency. The islanders are waiting to see who is going to come out on top."

Brognola grimaced. "What kind of military do the islands have?"

The Marine general shrugged. "Not much. They have a

constabulary of about a hundred and fifty men, mostly armed with French-made rifles and submachine guns. They have a couple of small obsolete armed patrol boats. That's about it.'' The Marine grinned. ''Like I said, given the word, I can make those islands the fifty-first state in the Union in about forty-five minutes.''

There was some laughter around the room.

The President put his hands on the tabletop. ''Gentlemen, I would like the United States to acquire the oil development rights in the Pacific Trust Islands, but that isn't my major concern here. Our priority is American lives. Our civilians are being murdered, and something must be done about it. I don't want to buck the United Nations and invade the islands, and our relations with France and Japan are strained enough as it is without getting into a saber rattling with either one of them. But I won't sit by while American civilians are being killed. I want something done about it, and I want it done now.''

The man from the Pentagon unsteepled his fingers. ''There is one other factor to be considered. Someone is arming the native terrorist faction. It wouldn't surprise me if it was one of our two competitors doing it to curry favor with the islanders. We should keep in mind that someone outside the islands is actively working against the United States and has no qualms about seeing American civilians killed.''

The Oval Office was quiet for a moment as the group mulled over the situation. The President finally spoke. ''Gentlemen, I have a press conference in fifteen minutes. I would like to reconvene this meeting at one o'clock. I'm hoping for some suggestions by that time.''

The most powerful men in the United States rose silently and left the Oval Office. The President beckoned to Brognola. ''Hal, could you stay for a moment?''

Brognola sat back down and waited until he and the President were alone. The Man took a breath and let it out slowly. ''Hal, I was wondering if you might have a suggestion about this situation you might have wanted to make privately.''

Brognola took a deep breath himself. ''Frankly, sir, I agree with the general. Send in the Marines. They're good at these kind of things.''

The President sighed heavily. "God knows I'd like to, but an invasion is a last-resort option, and the fallout with the United Nations and two of our ally nations in particular would be enormous.'' The President paused and looked hard at Brognola. "I'd like another option.''

Brognola nodded. "I believe we have one.''

2

Mack Bolan walked off the air-conditioned plane, and the thick tropical heat hit him like a wall. The Executioner walked down the boarding ramp with a large, black nylon carry-on over his shoulder. The airport was little more than a tower, one tarmac long enough for airliners and a couple of corrugated steel hangars for small planes and helicopters. The islands were a series of volcanic mountains that stuck up out of the water from a long undersea plateau. From the plane, the main island suddenly appeared, rising almost straight into the air. Several of the smaller islands were visible as lushly green lumps across the electric blue of the Pacific Ocean.

At the bottom of the ramp a tall, lanky man with crew-cut red hair stood in an aloha shirt and khaki shorts holding a hand marked sign that read, Mr. Belasko. Bolan walked up to the man and stuck out his hand. "I'm Belasko. USO Oil security consultant."

The man looked the Executioner up and down and grinned as he pumped his hand. "Well, I was hoping for the U.S. Marines, but damn if you don't look like you might be up to the job, anyway. I'm Redland. Howard Redland, but everyone calls me Red. I'm the new chief of operations with USO Oil here in the islands. Pleased to meet you, Belasko." He jerked his thumb behind him. "I've got a jeep at the other end of the tarmac. Why don't we get the hell out of here?"

Bolan glanced around. Palm trees sagged in the humid heat. Even the ocean seemed completely still. "Are we in a hurry?"

"No, not particularly, I guess," Redland said, frowning. "I

suppose they already knew you were coming, and I suppose they've already spotted you, too. But hell, we might as well get you out of the sun.''

Bolan's eyes narrowed as they walked toward an old Army jeep. ''Who's 'they'?''

''The French, the Japanese, the Coconuts. It's like a damn demilitarized zone around here.''

Bolan raised a questioning eyebrow. ''The Coconuts?''

Redland shrugged sheepishly as he climbed behind the wheel. ''The Native Isolationist Movement. It's not exactly politically correct, but it kind of makes them seem a little less threatening. But don't let that fool you, the Isolationists are stone killers.''

Bolan nodded. ''You say you're the new chief of operations?''

Redland's expression turned bitter as he started the engine. ''Yeah. I got a promotion. Skip Porter was our old chief.'' Redland's lips twisted with anger. ''The Coconuts cut Skip into fish bait a week ago. He was a good man, and he had a family back stateside. He didn't deserve to go out like that.''

The jeep pulled out in a spray of gravel. The wind was a welcome relief from the heat as they sped along the shore road. To their right was thick green forest, and to their left was a thin strip of beach and the ocean beyond. Redland reached under his seat and pulled out a rolled towel. ''Here, take this.''

Bolan took the towel and unrolled it. He examined the four-inch .357 Magnum revolver in his lap. Some of its blue finish was worn and the grips were smooth from use, but the gun seemed to have been well maintained. Next to it was a cardboard box half full of jacketed hollowpoint bullets. Redland glanced over at Bolan.

''You know how to use one of those?''

The Executioner almost smiled. Under his tailored khaki shirt rode a snub-nosed .38 Smith & Wesson Centennial revolver. His Beretta 93-R machine pistol and his .44 Magnum Desert Eagle hand cannon were in his carry-on, and both were locked and loaded. Grenades of several varieties were stowed in the bag as well, along with a thin aluminum briefcase.

Bolan shrugged at Redland as he opened the revolver and checked the loads. "I'm familiar with them." The Executioner snapped the cylinder back into place. "But as I understand it, owning private firearms is strictly illegal in the islands."

Redland nodded. "It is, and if you're caught with one, you're fined heavily and thrown out of the islands. But it sure as hell beats being cut into dog food. I'd keep that handy if I were you." The man suddenly looked at Bolan guiltily. "Not that I'm trying to tell you how to do your business or anything like that."

Bolan smiled. "I appreciate the concern, Red. Thanks."

The man grinned as he tooled the jeep along the coastline. "No problem. We should be okay once we get to the compound. When we're there I'll show you—"

The Executioner pointed a finger ahead while his right hand curled around the revolver's grips.

Redland snarled. "Damn!"

The one-lane road ahead was blocked by several fallen palm trees. Bolan spoke quietly as he unzipped the bag at his feet. "Floor it. Don't stop."

Redland gunned the engine and accelerated straight at the roadblock. There was only the ocean to their left, and Bolan kept his eye on the overgrown hillside to the right. A piercing war cry erupted from the bushes near the roadblock. Bolan raised the .357 Magnum revolver in a hard two-handed hold and fired.

A large Polynesian man leaped out of the brush brandishing a machete and firing an automatic pistol. The man's face was twisted into a rictus of rage as he extended the gun and fired continuously as he charged. A bullet shrieked off the hood of the jeep as Bolan put the front sight of the revolver on the big man's chest and pulled the trigger. The big weapon recoiled in Bolan's hands, and the man staggered as the Magnum hollowpoint shot hit him in the chest. The revolver bucked twice more, and the man went down. A shotgun roared from the bushes, and the jeep fishtailed as its right rear wheel buckled in on itself. The vehicle hit the fallen palms head-on and bounced brutally as its front wheels gripped the tree trunks and tried to climb. The shotgun roared again, and the front fender twisted and crumpled under the impact of the buckshot. The jeep bounced again, but the deflated left tire gave no support as the chassis lurched down. The drivetrain screamed as the rear axle snapped.

Bolan emptied the revolver's remaining rounds into the tree line and grabbed his bag as he rolled out of the crippled jeep. "Move!"

Redland dived out of the vehicle. The palm trunk nearest Bolan's head erupted into pulp as it took a pattern of buckshot. The Executioner rose into a crouch with his Beretta 93-R machine pistol leveled. The shotgun roared again, and the weapon's muzzle-flash gave away the ambusher's position as it shook the bushes. Bolan fired a 3-round burst into the spot and heard a man scream.

Redland crouched with his .38 Colt revolver in his hand. "Christ! It's like we're in Indian country!" Bolan suddenly twisted and fired as an automatic rifle snarled at them and ripped wet holes into their palm trunk cover. Bullets buzzed past the two men and dug into the dirt behind them. The palms were no defense against high-powered rifle bullets. Redland fired his revolver and ducked as the rifle answered back in a long burst. Bolan caught sight of the rifle's strobing muzzle-flash in the thick bushes above them and put two quick bursts from the Beretta into the spot. A clump of bushes shuddered, and the soldier put a third burst directly into it. The rifle fell silent, but more war whoops sounded up the road ahead of them.

Bolan glanced around quickly. "The hardmen up the road were waiting for us if we had swerved onto the beach to avoid the roadblock. I'd bet there are at least two who let us pass by but are supposed to take us if we turn back. If our friends here had spotters or backup higher on the hill, they'll be coming too."

Redland swallowed with difficulty and looked at Bolan with an unhappy but determined look. "All right. What do we do?"

Bolan looked Redland over critically. The man was pale, but he wasn't panicking. It was obvious this was his first experience in combat. "We take the road and go right down their throats. It's the only way to break an ambush. If we wait around here, they'll flank us and pick us off at their leisure. You stay behind me and to the left, Red. Don't do anything until I do, then shoot anything that isn't me."

Redland nodded grimly. "Okay. Let's do it."

The Executioner drew a pair of spare magazines for the Beretta and stuck them into his waistband and slung his bag over his shoulder as he moved through the tree line along the road. The whooping was getting closer. He reached back into the bag and pulled out a fragmentation grenade. Redland's eyes grew wide. Bolan nodded. "By the way, Red, when I tell you to get down, hit the ground fast."

Redland nodded vigorously and fell back several paces to Bolan's left as they moved out. It was only seconds before they had company. Bolan crouched as three men came running into view down the side of the road. They were large, powerful looking men. All of them had elaborate, green tribal tattooing covering much of their legs and torsos. Their long black hair flew back as they ran effortlessly through the trees. They would have looked like a primeval war party out of the past except for the lethally efficient modern weapons they carried in their hands. Two of the men had AK-47 rifles, while the other easily held a French 9 mm MAT-49 submachine gun in his fist hand like a handgun. The Executioner pulled the pin on the grenade and threw the bomb. The approaching men nearly ran over the grenade before they saw it.

"Down!" Bolan yelled at Redland.

Redland threw himself to the ground, and Bolan slid behind a thick palm. The grenade detonated with a boom, and the charging men twisted and fell. Lethal metal fragments hissed through the brush overhead. The Executioner rose with the Beretta leveled and ready. There was no need. All three men had been well within the ten-yard killing radius of the grenade's shrapnel. Redland stared at the bloodied corpses in shock as wisps of white grenade smoke hung in the still air above them. Fragmentation grenades didn't lend themselves to clean kills, and Redland's face was quickly taking on a greenish cast. Bolan shook the man's shoulder. There were more shouts coming from the hillside behind them.

"Reload."

Redland nodded absently. "Um, right." He broke open his revolver and replaced the spent shells with rounds from his pocket.

Bolan slid a fresh magazine into the Beretta. "How far is the compound?"

"About a mile, mile and a half up the road."

"Can you run it?"

Redland was pale, but he smiled weakly. "I used to jog it every morning, until the trouble started."

"Good. I'll race you." The Executioner broke into a steady, loping run and heard Redland dig into stride behind him. Farther back, the war cries had turned into howls of rage as the enemy found the corpses by the empty jeep. Bolan picked up the pace. Redland matched his stride as they ran down the middle of the road.

The Executioner had been in the islands less than twenty minutes, and already he had been marked for death.

3

Howard Redland sat in the USO Oil compound's conference room surrounded by most of the exploration crew and breathlessly retold the story of the ambush and the firefight for the third time. It was the first time any Americans had come out alive in an encounter with the Isolationist natives, and the rest of the crew couldn't hear it often enough. The men stole respectful glances at Bolan during the telling. He sat back and let Redland do the talking. It was an exciting story, and it was getting better every time the Texan told it. Bolan spoke quietly.

"Is there someplace where I can have some privacy?"

The USO Oil compound was little more than a couple of corrugated iron sheds around a wooden pier that was fenced off from the landward side. They had a single helicopter pad of packed and leveled sand, and two small exploration craft on either side of a dock facing a tiny lagoon.

Redland stopped in midstory. "Well, there's the storage shed. What do you need?"

"To communicate privately with the States."

A tall sandy-haired man whose nameplate read Nelson shrugged. "I doubt the Coconuts have any spies among us.

Bolan shrugged. "We have problems other than just the Isolationists."

Redland suddenly understood. "You think the compound may be bugged?"

A small, wiry-haired young man with a beard raised his hand. Redland laughed at him. "We're not in school, Chris.

You don't have to raise your hand.'' The young man flushed red under his deep tan. Red waved a hand toward him. "This is Chris Racine, our new underwater geologist.''

Bolan looked at Redland, and the Texan knew his question without being asked. "Our old geologist, Tom, well, he got lucky.''

The Executioner raised an eyebrow. "How so?''

"He went home alive.''

"What happened?''

"Tom went out by himself to get some supplies in town, which was a pretty dumb maneuver. He was also friendly with a local girl, probably why he went and left the compound by himself. Anyway, he sort of got lucky. The French got hold of him before the Coconuts did.''

"What did the French do?''

Redland shook his head ruefully. "They beat the living bejesus out of him. Broke his nose, his jaw, six of his ribs, gave him a concussion, detached the retina of his left eye, busted a bunch of his fingers and tore a kidney. His face needed about fifty stitches by the time they were through with him.''

"But they didn't kill him?''

Red shrugged. "No, they aren't killing anyone yet, not that I know of. But they sent Tom stateside on a stretcher. Dr. Tutarotaro said it was a very professional beating, and Tom's not the first guy they've jumped. The French are playing rough.'' Redland paused. "You know, you should visit the doc. He's a local, but he's a pretty cool customer and treats everyone who comes in pretty much equally.''

Bolan filed that away. "How are the French able to throw their weight around?''

"The French have a small test derrick off the sister island, and they have their own roughnecks working the rig. They're some pretty rough customers, and they're like a private goon squad when they're on shore. They'll pick a fight with anybody who isn't French, and their policy is to jump anyone who works for a rival and make them wish they were dead. Now that everyone is carrying guns illegally, they're being more careful about the strong-arm tactics, but you still better be damn careful around them. About two weeks ago, they got hold of one of the Japanese down by the harbor and beat him half to death right in front of one of the local constables. The cop just grinned and watched the whole thing. Didn't lift a finger to help the poor bastard.''

Bolan nodded. "I'll keep that in mind. What do you know about the Japanese contingent?''

Redland's frown grew quizzical. "Pretty damn little. They keep to themselves on one of the smaller coral islands they've leased. They only come into town once in a blue moon, and they come in squads, do their business and leave. The French act like they own the place, and the Japanese are like ghosts. They act spooky, but you hardly ever see them.''

He suddenly remembered Chris Racine and jerked a thumb at him. "Anyway, after Tom went home, the company sent us college boy over here." Redland grinned. "Frankly, we were hoping for someone a little bigger.''

Bolan looked at Racine. "You had a point about possible bugs, Chris?''

Racine nodded at the Executioner sheepishly. "Well, Mr. Belasko, if you're worried about bugs, you can go down by our pier. It's sheltered from the land by the shack. There's a little bit of beach around it, and I doubt anyone is bugging the ocean yet.''

"An excellent idea. Thank you. Pardon me, gentlemen.'' Bolan took the thin aluminum briefcase out of his bag and strode from the room. Outside the sun had risen to full noon, and it beat down with brutal, midsummer intensity. He found a small strip of sand shaded by the pier and crouched over his case. He flipped the locks and opened the case to reveal the satellite link to Stony Man Farm. Bolan unfolded the small antenna, aimed it at the proper spot in the sky, plugged in the headset and punched in the codes on the small keypad. The signal shot up from the island to a U.S. communications satellite and was relayed halfway around the world to the Farm in a fraction of a second.

Barbara Price answered almost immediately. Her voice was so clear she could have been sitting next to Bolan on the sand, watching the ocean with him.

"Good morning, Striker."

"It's noon here."

"How is it?"

Bolan squinted at the glare coming off the still water. "Hot."

"What's the situation?"

"Four confirmed kills. Apparently native Isolationists." Price paused. "That was fast."

"They were waiting for me. Is Aaron around?"

"He's waiting here next to me."

Aaron Kurtzman's voice came crystal clear across the satellite comm link. "So things are getting rough early?"

"I was ambushed five minutes down the road from the airstrip. It was fairly well planned, though the opposition seemed more enthusiastic than skilled with their small arms. I doubt whether they were expecting any resistance. Their weapons were a hodge-podge of rifles, submachine guns, handguns and shotguns."

Bolan could hear Kurtzman's finger tapping meditatively on a tabletop. "Did you get hold of any of them?"

"No time, and it was a low priority. The bad guys had friends, and I was already loaded down with equipment. I also had a citizen to get back to the compound."

"Do you think they suspect you're anything more than a security consultant?" Price asked.

Bolan smiled as he thought of Redland back in the conference room. He was probably on his fifth rehash of the firefight. "At the moment they think I'm the greatest thing since indoor plumbing. Apparently, they were feeling pretty lonely and abandoned out here. I can see why. According to the USO Oil crew, the main island has become Dodge City. Weapons are outlawed, but everyone is armed. The natives are killing any nonnative they can get their hands on, there's no sheriff in town, and the rest of the world seems to be sitting on their hands and waiting to see what happens."

The Executioner glanced across the water at the small coral island a few hundred yards offshore. "Speaking of the rest of the world, what's the situation with the United Nations? It's supposed to be cogoverning the area."

Kurtzman sighed. "Right now its members are debating a resolution to form a coalition subcommittee to investigate the situation that was introduced by Sweden."

A ghost of a smile crossed the Executioner's face. "Let me guess. France and Japan are stalling."

Kurtzman laughed. "Give the man a cigar. But what about you, Striker? What kind of fallout can we expect from your activities this morning?"

Bolan considered. "From the local government, none. The Isolationists knew I was coming as a security consultant, and I broke their ambush and killed some of their gunners. I suspect they'll be coming back for blood. I've had no contact with the French or the Japanese elements on the island, but I'm willing to bet they know an American named Mike Belasko is in the islands."

"You be careful around the French and the Japanese, Striker. They're not our friends on this one."

Bolan scooped up a handful of sand and watched it sift through his fingers as he made a fist. "So I've heard. What can you give me on them?"

"Not as much as I'd like, but I'm working on it. Other than stalling in the UN, France is being very quiet, which I don't like. The French are pretty single-minded in these kind of situations. The Action Directorate branch of the Direction Générale de la Sécurité Extérieure has never been known to play around, and with French civilians being killed, I'd bet anything French Intelligence is going to want blood, and no one is going to worry too much about collateral damage to anyone who gets in the way. The DGSE has some real cowboys, Striker. If they're in the islands, there's going to be fireworks. I'd be careful around anyone with a French accent."

Bolan understood. He'd had experience with French Intelligence operatives before. Accidents seemed to happen to people who'd crossed them. "What can you give me on the Japanese?"

The connection was so clear Bolan heard Kurtzman shift in his wheelchair. "Even less. There just isn't a whole lot known about Japanese Intelligence. They play their cards very close to the vest. But what bothers me is that I can't find the parent conglomerate for the Minato Oil Corporation. Minato Oil is the one bidding for the oil development rights to the islands. They're relatively new, and there's a series of groups on the echelon behind them. I can't pin down who is at the top. That's our major concern. For the most part the Japanese government likes to stay neutral in world affairs. Their corporations can be very ruthless, however, and their government often turns a blind eye to the activities as long as they are quiet and successful. Japan is oil poor, and they must be drooling over the potential of the Pacific Trust Islands. It might be the Japanese conglomerates rather than their government you have to watch out for."

"You think we might have some corporate raiders?"

"At this point I wouldn't rule out anything. Everyone and their brother is armed and has their finger on their trigger."

"Tell me something I don't know."

Kurtzman tapped his finger again. "We've got the whole team here crunching data on the Japanese corporate ladder, but it's one hell of a legal maze. It will take time, if we can get through at all. I'll give you more as soon as I have it. What do you plan to do at the moment?"

Bolan's lips tightened. "I'm going to police up security around the USO Oil compound as much as possible, and I'm going to the hospital in town and look at the coroner's reports on the murdered American civilians. I want to talk to the doctor in charge and see if I can find anything unusual. I'll send you anything I find."

"All right, Striker. Check back in twenty-four hours, regardless. Oh, and just a reminder. You'll be getting a package at 0200 hours.''

"What kind of delivery?"

"Wet."

"Coordinates?"

"Just about where you're squatting."

Bolan looked out at the tiny lagoon. "I'll be ready."

"All right then, Striker, Stony Man out."

Bolan clicked of the comm link and stowed it back into the case. It was time to go into town.

MACK BOLAN DROVE the remaining USO Oil jeep into town. Howard Redland and Chris Racine rode along. Both men were armed and nervous. "What's that?" Bolan asked, nodding toward a long, low building.

Chris Racine leaned forward between the front seats. "That's the Big House, or the community hall as it's known now. It was here before any of this modern stuff you see around you. They have to rethatch the roof semiannually and weave new mats, but I hear the floor beams and the carved pillars are centuries old."

Redland grinned. "You have to watch out for him. Like I told you, he went to college."

Bolan pulled up in front of the general store. Most of the USO Oil team's supplies came to them by boat from the United States, but water was always on the shopping list. The main island had only two sources of fresh water, and very little of it was available outside the town. With no running sources of water, the various international oil teams often had to come into town to acquire it, and the natives sold local bottled water or imported water at a premium. The beer and the local prostitutes available at the two bars in town were the other reasons to come into town, and it was these three necessities that brought foreigners into confrontation with one another and the natives.

The general store was a clapboard building with a porch and a small brass bell that rang as they opened the door. Rows of canned and dry goods filled the long narrow room. A tiny, wizened native woman stood behind a counter, wearing a floral-print sarong and little else.

"Hot day. You thirsty boys, no?" Her broken English had a heavy French accent.

Redland grinned back. "We're thirsty, all right. What have you got besides water?"

The old woman crossed her arms and leaned over the counter conspiratorially. "Got Budweiser, King of Beers. Red, white and blue can and everything. You American boys love it, no?"

Even the Executioner smiled. "We'll take a case."

The old woman eyed Bolan up and down appreciatively. "You big boy, better buy two cases. The French be in tomorrow, maybe drink up all your beer."

Bolan nodded. "All right. Two cases. And we need four, forty-gallon water bottles. Six if you have them."

The woman's eyes narrowed like a hawk at the mention of water. "You got money? Japanese come in yesterday and try to buy on credit. No deal. This a cash establishment."

Redland laughed. "You know us Americans. We always carry money."

The woman's smile returned. "Good. I like dollars. Nice and green." She waved an arm behind her expansively. "Water in the back. Beer behind counter. You help yourselves."

Redland pulled out his wallet as Racine went behind the counter and began hoisting cases. The bell over the door rang, and Bolan turned as Redland's jaw went slack in open admiration.

A striking woman stood in the doorway and inspected the three of them coolly. She was deeply tanned, and a native sarong and a black bikini top clung to her athletic-looking curves. Her thick black hair was cut short, with her bangs just starting to fall in her face, and her huge, widely spaced blue eyes were fixed on Bolan in frank appraisal. A hint of a smile began as the Executioner regarded her with equal frankness.

Redland shook his head wonderingly. "Christ, who smuggled her onto the island?"

The woman ignored him and continued to look at Bolan. Her English was smooth but heavily accented. "You are an American, too, no?"

Bolan smiled at her.

She frowned at Redland and Racine as they stood and watched. "Should you not be loading your car or something?"

Redland gave Bolan a knowing wink and slapped Racine on the shoulder. "Let's go roll out those water jugs."

The woman watched them go into the back, then looked at Bolan reproachfully. "You are not in my file."

Bolan raised an eyebrow. "Am I supposed to be?"

She nodded gravely. "Oh, yes. I have files on all the Americans stationed here. They were not difficult to obtain. I have files on all French as well. The Japanese, however, they are very difficult."

"So I understand. What is it that I can do for you?"

The woman extended a hand and Bolan shook it. She had a surprisingly firm handshake. She took a small leather ID badge out of her purse and handed it to him. "My name is Jeanine Maitland. I am a journalist covering this crisis here in the islands for *La Voix.*"

The Voice was a respected French newspaper, and Bolan had seen it a number of times when he'd been in France. He accepted her story and her ID at face value and smiled at her noncommittally. "What is it that I can do for you, Miss Maitland?"

She blew a stray strand of hair away from her eyebrow and sighed heavily. "Well, to be truthful, I'm not doing very well. The Japanese won't talk to me, and my countrymen, well…" She smiled ruefully. "They seem more intent on bending me over a barstool than talking about the current situation."

Bolan smiled and shrugged. "Overseas oil workers generally aren't known for their etiquette, regardless of their country of origin."

She nodded knowingly. "This is true." She suddenly broke

into a startling white smile. "You seem rather civilized, however. Particularly for an American."

Bolan folded his arms. She was a very attractive woman, and she was certainly pouring on the charm. "What is it I can do for you?"

She looked into his eyes challengingly. "Well, you are big, you are new here on the island and you are reasonably attractive. Why don't you buy me lunch tomorrow and let me ask you your opinion on what's going on here?"

"Where and when?"

She turned her head and looked out the store window. "There is a bar across the street. Its food is not so terrible. They have hamburgers and beer. Why not around four o'clock? It will have cooled off a little, and with luck, perhaps there will be a breeze."

"You're on."

She smiled ferociously. "I'm looking forward to it."

Redland came back in with Racine. Both men's heads turned to watch the Frenchwoman as she left. Redland shook his head again. "Good Lord, she's a racy looking one."

Racine kept watching until she was out of sight down the street, then turned to Bolan. "Who was she?"

The soldier picked up one of the cases of beer from the counter. "She says her name is Jeanine."

Racine waited a moment for Bolan to continue, then blinked. "Well, what did she want?"

Bolan handed the college boy the case of beer and hefted the second one with a shrug. "She wants to go out with me."

The young man's jaw dropped.

The Executioner stopped abruptly and cocked his head. He wasn't quite sure what he'd heard. After a moment he picked it up. It was a low steady thumping. Redland looked at Bolan questioningly. "What is it?"

The old woman appeared behind the counter, and she scowled so fiercely it almost threatened to collapse her seamed face. "Trouble."

Bolan slung the case onto his hip with one arm and walked

onto the store's little porch. Racine and Redland followed. A small mob had formed up the street in front of the Big House. Native men in sarongs were pounding on drums while others leaped into the air acrobatically with war clubs and long hardwood staves. The men shouted and let out piercing cries as they brandished their weapons. A number of native women cried out encouragement while they swayed to the music of the drums. Two native constables in white uniform jackets and sarongs stood by with submachine guns slung over their shoulders, and watched the proceedings with mild interest.

Bolan folded his arms across his chest. As he did, the fingers of his right hand deftly unbuttoned his middle shirt buttons. Beneath his left arm his hand rested on the grips of the snubnosed 9 mm Centennial revolver. "What's going on?"

The old woman stood in the doorway and continued to scowl. "War dance."

One of the dancers suddenly leaped forward and stared directly down the street at Bolan and his companions. He was a large man with a powerful physique and traditional tattooing over his body. He let out a horrendous roar and stabbed his long staff toward Bolan. The man's eyes rolled in his head, and he stuck his tongue out to demonstrate his ferocity.

The old woman turned and went back inside muttering in a mixture of French and her native language. "Going to be trouble. Big trouble."

The big man gave Bolan a final glare, then spun into the circle of dancers.

Bolan grimaced. "The beer is getting warm out here. Let's get back." He climbed behind the jeep's wheel and gunned the engine to life. His eyes narrowed. What the little stunt was all about was clear. The Isolationists knew exactly who had broken their ambush and killed four of their own.

They were letting him know they intended to do something about it.

THE SWIMMER ROSE out of the darkness.

The night was still and clear, and the starlight of the late evening was uncomfortingly bright for such a clandestine operation. Nevertheless, he had a mission to fulfill, and he had worked in much worse conditions before. Only the top of his head broke the water as he scanned the beach with his night-vision goggles. He turned his gaze to his objective.

Nothing moved.

The swimmer slipped back under the surface and started the engine of his underwater vehicle. It was little more than a powered skim board, and its tiny motor was designed for minimum disturbance from its small propeller. Under water it was nearly soundless, and his closed-circuit breathing apparatus allowed no bubbles to escape from his breathing as he moved along at a snail's pace. The swimmer was little more than a silent shadow, underwater in the middle of the night.

As he reached the wooden pier, he broke the surface again. The water was shallow enough to stand, and he pulled in the tethered equipment package that trailed him. The hulls of the USO exploration boats on both sides shielded his approach onto the sand. He scanned the darkness under the pier and nodded to himself in satisfaction.

Another perfect insertion.

"Baseball, hot dogs and apple pie!"

"Jesus Christ!"

The swimmer whirled with his 9 mm Heckler & Koch submachine gun leveled. A tall, powerful man stood in the water behind him stripped to the waist, regarding him with mild interest.

He had been in over seventeen combat operations, and he was used to being the one doing the lurking. He grinned sheepishly.

"You're Striker, I assume."

The big man nodded.

The swimmer lowered the submachine gun and shook his head ruefully. "You scared the hell out of me." He stuck out his free hand. "Chief Petty Officer Russell Wendt, U.S. Navy SEALs. I have a package here for you."

Bolan shook the SEAL's hand. "Thanks. I appreciate it."

The two men hauled the waterproof equipment container onto the sand at the end of the pier. The SEAL stood. "The U.S.S. *Sam Houston* is standing off the islands. Your next communication with…" Wendt gave Bolan a look and rolled his eyes. "Well, with whoever it is exactly you are in communication with, they'll give you our frequency. We'll be running up an antenna and listening for you. We're your extraction in case of an emergency. If things hit the fan, you give us the signal. Then you just start swimming like hell. We'll pick you up. No problem."

Bolan nodded. "That's good to know."

The SEAL unclipped the equipment package from his swimmer. "One other thing you ought to know, Striker. Yesterday, we detected a Japanese Yuushio class submarine moseying along quietly between two of the outer islands. Then, today, a French Rubis Class nuclear attack sub came motoring in like they owned the place and then dropped out of sight beneath the marine plateau." Wendt grinned. "It's starting to get crowded out there, friend. You be careful. If we can insert people, so can they."

"I'll keep that in mind."

"Be seeing you."

Bolan watched the SEAL submerge under the water and disappear. He turned to his package and opened the gasket locks. The container was six feet long and teardrop shaped, and it was nearly full. Bolan surveyed the small armory of weapons and gear the Stony Man team had sent him. Sterile weapons had been sent for the USO Oil team as well.

The Executioner smiled. Next on the agenda was a free lunch that promised to be interesting.

4

"Fire!"

Flame shot from the muzzles of the carbines in massed semiautomatic fire. Round after round poured out in a continuous stream of lead as brass shell casings fell to the sand as the weapons ejected them one after another. The sound of sustained gunfire was deafening. In seconds, the torrent was over. Six weapons clicked onto smoking, empty chambers. The little island was suddenly silent. The men stood grim-faced with their emptied weapons in their hands, surveying the carnage they had wrought.

Twenty-five yards downrange, a fallen palm trunk lay across the sand. Of the twenty-four beer cans that had been lined up on top of it, all but five sat unscathed.

The Executioner sighed. It wasn't a promising start. Except for Howard Redland, who was an avid hunter back in Texas, the men of the USO Oil team weren't exactly marksmen. Bolan had allowed each man to put five shells into his weapon's 30-round magazines to keep them from getting bullet-happy and hopefully to make them concentrate on each of their shots. Bolan didn't want to think about what would happen if they were allowed to put their weapons on full-auto. Surprisingly, Chris Racine had managed to hit three cans, and he had never fired a gun in his life. Two of the other men, Baxter and Smitts, had managed to account for a beer can each.

The other two men looked about sheepishly.

The Executioner put his hands on his hips. "All right. Load five more. Keep your muzzles pointed at the ground, and your fingers off the trigger." He jerked his head downrange. "Baxter, go reset the fallen targets."

The men held their weapons awkwardly as they ejected their spent magazines and began pushing fresh cartridges into them. Baxter jogged down to the target line and began resetting the fallen cans.

Redland stood next to Bolan and gave him an embarrassed grin. "Well, Chris shows some promise anyway."

Bolan nodded. "Mmm."

Along with delivering Bolan's personal equipment, Chief Petty Officer Wendt had also brought six folding stock, M-2 carbines of Korean War vintage, plus ammunition. Bolan suspected the weapons had traded hands many times and couldn't be clearly linked to anybody. The Executioner eyed the weapons critically as the men reloaded. The M-2s were obsolete by modern standards, and they lacked power and range. However, Bolan had to admit they were a user-friendly choice for men with little or no experience with weapons. The little .30-caliber carbines were handy and accurate at short range and had very little recoil or muzzle-blast. A small group of determined men could probably hold off an angry mob if they kept their heads. The Executioner acknowledged it might just come to that.

Bolan had no illusions. He couldn't turn these men into soldiers overnight. But, with luck, he might just teach them enough to keep them alive. He glanced at his watch. It was 2:45 p.m. Their impromptu shooting session was taking place on a strip of a coral about fifty yards long and about as wide. The little island was a couple of miles off the main island and far enough away so that no one would hear the gunshots.

Baxter jogged back to the firing line and took his reloaded carbine from Racine. Bolan noticed he kept the muzzle pointed downrange. Racine looked over at the soldier expectantly. "Clear?"

Bolan nodded. At least the men were picking up the rudiments of gun safety. Now, if he could only get them to hit the broad side of a barn, he might have something. The Executioner turned to Redland. "Keep them at it for another forty-five minutes. Make sure they keep their folding stocks extended, and keep their selector switches on semiauto. We don't have enough spare ammo for them to be hosing down the landscape, and I don't have time to teach them burst control. What I want them to learn is premeditated, aimed shots. Five rounds per loading. If we can get them hitting beer cans reliably at twenty-five yards, they'll probably be able to hit man-sized targets at fifty or a hundred yards.''

Redland nodded. The big man commanded authority, but Bolan treated him as an equal, and the Texan couldn't help feeling a little proud. The chief of operations considered himself a pretty good shot. But he had watched as the big man had taken up one of the carbines and demonstrated it for the men. He had fired with the stock folded, extended, from the hip, and on both semiautomatic and full. The man was so good it was frightening. He hit everything he aimed at.

''There won't be a can worth recycling by sunset. You got my word on it. But where are you headed?''

The men turned from the line and looked at him.

Bolan shrugged. ''I'm going to lunch.''

THE LITTLE BAR was only slightly cooler than the humid late-afternoon air outside, and the ceiling fan was struggling to make itself felt. Bolan bit into his hamburger and was surprised. Jeanine Maitland grinned at him winningly. She wore a little floral cotton sundress and very little underneath it. ''It's good, no? It's octopus.''

Bolan chewed and swallowed. He should've known. The Pacific Trust Islands were much too small to raise beef. They didn't raise potatoes either, and though the french fries looked normal, he had found out a moment ago that they were actually strips of deep-fried breadfruit. It tasted strange, but it actually wasn't half-bad. Bolan took another bite and smiled. ''It's good.''

Maitland's grin grew triumphant. ''I knew that you'd like it!'' Bolan scanned the bar again as she bit into her own burger. Two natives in Western clothes sat at a table to one side and pored over some papers spread across the tabletop. An immense native man in a Hawaiian shirt stood behind the bar. Bolan's real interest was the Japanese. Four of them in coveralls sat at a table in the back. They had turned and regarded Bolan with intense interest when he had walked in, then turned back as a unit and had ignored him ever since. They huddled over their food and talked in low voices.

The woman locked eyes with Bolan as he turned back to the table. "So, tell me, what is it that you do for USO Oil?"

Bolan took a sip of his beer. The bottle was already sweating from the humidity. "I'm a hydrologist."

The Frenchwoman's eyes narrowed as she looked him up and down. She smiled derisively. "You know, you don't look like a hydrologist, Monsieur Belasko."

He shrugged indifferently. "Your countrymen sent our last hydrologist home on a stretcher, Miss Maitland. The natives sent our last chief of operations home in a box. The new USO Oil company policy is for all overseas employees to be over six feet tall and look mean. What about you? You don't exactly look like a war correspondent."

Maitland blushed. "Well, I'm not. At least, this is my first time, anyway. Normally, I am a foreign correspondent in French Polynesia. I was based at the newspaper in Tahiti. It was cheaper for the paper to send me island hopping rather than fly in a correspondent from France. Also, they thought my experience living in the Pacific Islands might be useful with the natives."

"What kind of stories did you cover in Tahiti?"

"To be truthful, I mostly chased French movie stars and athletes for interviews when they were vacationing in the islands. I also covered fashion. I used to be a model." Her face became serious. "However, the crisis here in the Pacific Trust Islands is very real, as you well know. This could be a big break for me as a journalist."

"I don't doubt it."

She leaned forward. "So what can you tell me?"

Bolan leaned back in his chair. "What would you like to know?"

"Well, do you know anything about the native men killed the other day outside of the airport? It happened right after you arrived, I believe."

Bolan sighed and shook his head. "I heard some shots. But I didn't go back to find out what was going on, and I didn't feel like getting my name involved by talking to the authorities on my first day."

Her eyes narrowed slightly. "Mmm. Tell me…" Her voice trailed off as she followed Bolan's gaze onto the street. Seven men came up the steps and entered the bar. They wore heavily stained T-shirts and khaki work shorts. Each man had a matching khaki fatigue cap with a company logo and the French flag emblazoned on it. Most of the men were large, and even the two smaller men were wiry and powerful looking. One man in particular caught Bolan's eye. He was significantly larger than the rest of the men, and heavily muscled, but what the Executioner noticed most was his tattoo. On his right biceps was a large rendition of the African continent, and wreathed across it was the French flag with a scrolled ribbon banner beneath. As the man walked to the bar, Bolan could read the words.

The banner read, MARCHER OU MOURIR. March or die. Bolan had heard the saying before. It was an unofficial motto of the French foreign legion.

The men stared openly at Jeanine Maitland as they walked to the bar, and their eyes narrowed with frank hostility as they looked at Bolan. Two of the men stayed behind and leaned against either side of the door to the street. The Executioner took a final sip of his beer and put the bottle on the table.

There was going to be trouble.

Maitland looked at Bolan and whispered urgently under her breath. "Let us go. Now!"

The Executioner glanced at the two men by the door as they gave him the hard stare, then turned to his companion. "I don't think they're going to let us."

The French oil workers spread themselves across the bar and ordered beer. Once they had been served, they turned and looked at Bolan and Maitland's table. The big man took off his cap and ran a hand through his close-cropped brown hair as he casually leaned against the bar. He tilted his head and looked at Jeanine until he caught her eye. He leered in a jovial fashion. *"Bonjour, mademoiselle."*

The woman stared at her food unhappily and tried to ignore him. The big man grinned and spoke to her again. His voice sounded almost friendly, but Bolan was fluent enough in French to understand that the big man was calling Maitland a little whore who liked sleeping with Americans. He went on to make a few pointed references about the unusual ways Bolan was probably violating her.

Maitland's head snapped around and she hissed at the big man. It was too fast for Bolan to catch, but it sizzled. The men at the bar laughed out loud and clapped the big man on the shoulder. The big man smiled back at the woman, then looked at Bolan with mild interest. On cue, the shortest of the Frenchmen lazily pushed away from the bar. He was thin, but his physique was that of a bantam-weight boxer's. His nose had been broken, and when he smiled at Bolan he showed missing front teeth.

The man jerked his head at Bolan and spoke in thick English. "Eh, you, big boy. Yankee. You like screwing little French girls, huh?"

Bolan smiled at the man pleasantly. "Someone around here has to."

The Frenchman's eyes flared. Maitland gasped at Bolan in shock. At the bar the big man's eyebrows raised, and he grinned at the Executioner delightedly.

The soldier scanned the bar a final time. The Japanese sat at their table and looked back and forth between Bolan and the big man with silent intensity. Two of the Japanese kept their hands conspicuously under the table. The two native men watched the proceedings with avid interest. They were probably betting on the outcome. The Frenchmen by the door hadn't moved, except to pull on their work gloves. Maitland seemed to be extremely uncomfortable. Bolan decided to make one show of goodwill for the benefit of witnesses. He spread his hands. "Look, we're not looking for any trouble. Why don't you let me buy you and your friends a round?"

The big man made a show of rolling his eyes toward heaven. He seemed to have appreciated Bolan's defiance but apparently found his intended victim's sudden submission something of a disappointment. He jerked his head at the short man confronting Bolan and spoke in fairly good English.

"ZeeZee, feed him his balls."

ZeeZee gave Bolan his ugly, gap-toothed smile and advanced. The Executioner had no illusions. The French roughnecks probably didn't intend to deliberately kill him, but they would have no qualms about sending him home a cripple. The soldier rose smoothly from his chair. He stood well over a head taller than ZeeZee, but the ugly little Frenchman didn't seem to mind. He walked straight toward Bolan to close the distance. As he came into range, he started his attack.

As the blow came, Bolan realized he had been right. The man was adept at savate, the French form of boxing. Bolan recognized the technique. It was the purring kick, a savate specialty. The attacking leg rose up to maximum extension with no bending of the knee or preparatory shifting of the body. The kick was instantaneous and untelegraphed. Those who had never experienced the technique never saw it coming, much less were able to counter it. Jack Grimaldi was an avid savateur, and when he and Bolan sparred at Stony Man Farm, the pilot had repeatedly clocked Bolan with the purring kick until he was satisfied the Executioner could counter the blow instinctively.

Now, the Executioner countered.

As Frenchman's right foot blurred toward Bolan's jaw, the soldier rammed both of his forearms down in an X formation and intercepted the blow. He seized ZeeZee's ankle and stepped forward. The Frenchman tottered backward on one leg as Bolan raised his captured foot overhead. The Executioner

swung the man's leg down and around as if it were a golf
club.

The little man's supporting leg was brutally whipped out
from under him, and he twisted out of control through the air.
He lost more of his teeth as he landed facefirst into a table.

The Frenchman had a fighter's instincts, and he bravely
struggled to rise again, but his eyes rolled back and he swayed
drunkenly as he grabbed the tabletop for support. The Executioner stepped forward and jammed the sole of his boot into
ZeeZee's face. The blow nearly lifted the man to his feet. The
rest of the French crew at the bar stared wide-eyed as their
countryman fell before them bloody and unconscious to the
floor. For a moment the bar was silent.

The big man glared at Bolan.

The Executioner swept up his chair and took a step toward
the bar. The Frenchmen recoiled, and Bolan suddenly twisted
and swung the chair low.

The man behind Bolan howled in agony as the chair struck
his knees, sending him to the floor. Bolan raised the chair
overhead and brought it down heavily on top of the fallen man,
who raised his arms, desperate to defend himself. The chair
and his arms both broke as they met. The Executioner flung
the remains of the chair into the face of the other Frenchman
by the door as he charged.

The man stuck out his hands to deflect the broken wood
flying at his head. The Executioner stepped forward and seized
his adversary's outstretched wrist. Bolan yanked on his arm
and the man lurched off balance. Bolan swung his own
straightened arm, hitting the doorman's with all the strength
in his body. The clothesline hit the man across the throat,
knocking him to the floor and causing his head to bounce on
the wood with brutal intensity.

The Executioner spun as two men charged him from the
bar. He dropped into a low squat sweeping his outstretched
leg in a scything arc and cutting down one of the men at the
ankles. The man landed on his back, and the soldier rose as
the man's partner tried to step over his fallen comrade. Bolan

batted aside a punch to his face and whipped his open palm in a hooking blow directly below the man's ear. The Frenchman's jawbone snapped, and he screamed in pain. The Executioner shoved the man into an empty table.

The Executioner stood and faced the remaining two men at the bar.

The big man regarded Bolan with narrowed eyes. His partner was nearly as tall as he was but lanky, and he pulled a short, saw-toothed diving knife from the back of his belt. He looked at Bolan, and he had murder in his eyes as he stepped forward.

The big man grabbed his arm and shook his head. The man with the knife glared but put the weapon away. The big man turned and spread his arms out with a shrug. "Eh, you know what, big boy? You win." He smiled at Bolan. "I have men I must get to hospital. You have a nice day, huh?"

Bolan walked over to Maitland and took her hand. "Let's get out of here. I'll walk you to the hotel."

The Executioner and the big man kept their eyes on each other until Bolan and Maitland got outside. Bolan heard the big man speak in French to his partner, telling him to see how many of the men could still walk. The hotel, a small two story building, was just down the street. Bolan looked down and found his companion staring at him with huge eyes. She squeezed his hand. "Thank you for defending me."

"I was defending both of us, but you're welcome."

She smiled. "You are very good."

"I was lucky."

She frowned at him but didn't argue. "Why didn't you beat up the big man and his friend?"

Bolan shook his head. "His friend had a knife. I think the big man had a gun."

"Why didn't they use them?"

"I don't know."

Maitland stood on tiptoes and kissed Bolan's cheek. "I think maybe you are lucky. Maybe some of your luck will rub off on me." She kissed Bolan again, on the lips. She didn't open her mouth but she put a great deal of feeling into it. "We'll see each other again soon, okay?"

Bolan shrugged. "It's a small island."

She looked up at him in mock disapproval. "You'll see me again, don't worry. I'm something of a pest." She grinned at him as she turned, and Bolan watched her until she was safely in the hotel.

Bolan frowned. He knew why the big man hadn't attacked. The man was more than just an oil derrick roughneck, and he had kept his men lurking around to do more than just beat up the new American. The big man had wanted to see if Bolan was just another USO Oil worker, and he hadn't minded getting his men busted up finding out. Bolan had been tested, and he had failed with flying colors. The big man now knew he was a professional, and so would French Intelligence. The Japanese at the bar wouldn't have a hard time figuring that out either. The only consolation was that the French roughnecks wouldn't be dealing out any beatings in the near future. Bolan was now positive that French operatives were active in the islands as well.

The stakes were getting higher.

5

"Seven of them?" Chris Racine just stared at Bolan. News of the bar fight had spread across the island like wildfire and preceded Bolan back to the USO Oil compound. Racine and the rest of the crew sat around the conference table and stared at Bolan in awe. The Executioner's description was much less dramatic than the rumors they had heard, but it was still astounding. Within two days of his arrival, the new man had beaten the native Isolationists in a gunfight and whipped the French roughnecks in hand-to-hand combat. On top of that, he was dating the only good-looking single white woman on the island. If Bolan had suddenly stood up and ripped open his shirt and revealed a big letter *S* painted on his chest, none of the USO Oil crew would have been surprised at all.

Bolan shook his head. "There were seven of them in the bar. I only tangled with five."

Redland shook his head in wonderment. "What about that big bastard with the tattoo? Did you whip him?"

"No, he declined to join the party."

The Texan grinned. "I'd have paid good money to see you bring that smiling son of a bitch down a peg."

Bolan's eyes narrowed as he thought of the large legionnaire and how cool he had been about expending his own men's bodies to test him in combat. Bolan had no doubt the two of them would meet again. "You may get your chance yet, Red, but make no mistake. The stakes are going up. There are going to be reprisals."

The jubilation around the table sobered at Bolan's words. Redland scratched his chin. "So what do we do now?"

"What we're being paid to do. USO Oil still has a stake in these islands, and we need to run our operation like we intend to win it. As for our friends, we'll have to stay alert and be even more careful. No one goes anywhere alone. Not even for a swim off our own pier. We're going to maintain rotating watches at night. Keep your carbines out of sight but within arm's reach at all times. That's about all we can do at the moment without suspending operations completely."

The men nodded. Chris Racine suddenly grinned.

"So tell us about the French babe."

The men laughed and looked at Bolan expectantly. Most of them had been in the islands for months without a break, and since the troubles had begun, looking for any kind of action was asking to get ambushed.

Bolan shrugged nonchalantly. "She's a good kisser."

Racine's jaw dropped. Redland slapped the tabletop with glee. "Whip the bastards and steal their women. I like the way you do business, Belasko!"

INSIDE THE JAPANESE compound, the evening air resounded with rhythmic pounding. Blow after blow slammed into the straw matting wrapped around the top of the striking post. Hayata Yoritomo stood stripped to the waist in a deep straddle stance in front of the striking post. He drove his fists into the pad mercilessly. His thighs ached from squatting nearly parallel to the ground for over fifteen minutes, and sweat ran down his back as his chest heaved. The pain in his legs and the burning of his lungs were distant abstractions as Hayata stayed utterly focused on the post before him. With the thousandth punch, he let out a piercing roar, then brought his fists back to his hips.

Hayata stayed in position a moment more to center himself, then stood up stiffly. He walked to a small bench and dipped his hands into a bowl of Chinese medicated rice wine. The herbal liniment prevented the formation of calluses as well as bone and joint deformities of the hands. Many karate experts actively sought the brutal calluses and knuckle enlargement as badges of their dedication and training. Hayata didn't require such obvious signs of his training. As a matter of fact, he considered them detrimental to his work.

It wouldn't do to be recognized as a trained killer.

The ninja spent several minutes massaging the liniment into his hands, then toweled off while the day's events replayed themselves in his mind. He'd been planning to kill the big Frenchman when he and his coworkers had entered the bar earlier in the afternoon. Hayata was well aware that the man was responsible for putting two of the Japanese workers in the hospital. It was an affront that he wouldn't let go unanswered. The ninja looked forward to beating the big man to death with his hands. It would have been a perfect opportunity. People often died in barroom brawls. It would have been an unfortunate accident, and it would have given the French something to think about. Hayata and three of his coworkers had been hanging around town all day to attract them.

But the French hadn't been looking to fight the Japanese. Their target had been the new American. The American had swept through the French like a typhoon and left them lying broken and bleeding all over the floor, and, though outnumbered seven to one, he had deliberately refrained from killing any of them.

Clearly the man was much more than a security consultant.

Hayata heard footsteps in the sand behind him. He spoke without turning. "Report."

Hayata saw his subordinate's shadow as he bowed.

"Yes, Hayata-*san*. I have the photographs you asked for. Most were blurred. However, I'm sure many of them can be enhanced by the Tokyo office. Several, however, are excellent." Hayata turned as Minato Gosuke handed him the photos. Minato was the Japanese team surveyor and aerial photographer. He was very talented, and Hayata had made sure that he carried a concealed camera anywhere he went on the island for intelligence purposes. Photography was Minato's passion, and he had taken to his new responsibilities with zeal. He had taken many photos during the fight in the bar. The ninja examined the photographs Minato had developed.

Most of them were rather blurry and confused. That was to be expected. The subjects were in motion, and Minato had been aiming and operating the concealed camera by hand rather than by eye. Hayata stopped. One picture caught his eye. The big American's face was fuzzy, and most of his body was out of the picture. However, the palm-heel strike that was unhinging the Frenchmen's jaw was brutally clear. Hayata raised an appreciative eyebrow and leafed on. He stopped on another photo, and a hint of a smile moved across his face.

The picture showed the big American standing calmly in the middle of the bar. Injured men lay on the floor all around him. The American's impassive face was almost clear as he faced the remaining two Frenchmen at the bar. Hayata nodded his approval as he handed the photographs to Minato.

"Excellent. You have done very well. See that all of the photographs are sent to the head office in Tokyo immediately."

Minato bowed deeply as he took the photographs. "Thank you, Hayata-*san*, immediately." The young man hurried back to the main shack. Hayata ran a critical eye over his hands. They had absorbed the liniment and showed no sign whatsoever that he'd just struck a wooden post a thousand times. He thought about the way the American had single-handedly devastated the French. The man's skills would make him a formidable opponent in any kind of confrontation.

Hayata's mind wandered for a moment, and he spent several enjoyable moments considering counters to the tactics the American had displayed in his battle with the French and techniques he would use to kill him.

The Japanese man smiled as he suddenly clenched his fists. He doubted he would get the chance to engage the American in open combat. Subtlety would be required. He had observed the American's arrival as well, and followed at a discreet distance. He had seen the carnage he had left, and he had found an interesting souvenir before the local constables had arrived.

Hayata smiled again. If his plan succeeded, the natives would probably do his work for him.

He would begin implementing it tonight.

"WHAT HAVE YOU GOT for me, Bear?" Bolan sat on his heels in the sand and watched the sunset paint the sky in spectacular swathes of red and gold over the Pacific. Aaron Kurtzman's voice came crystal clear over the satellite link.

"Nothing I could prove in a court of law, Striker, but I have a lurking suspicion."

Bolan nodded to himself. If Kurtzman ever turned his energies to gambling, he could take his lurking suspicions to Vegas and become a millionaire. "Go ahead."

The computer expert's voice went cold over the receiver. "The Kanabo Corporation."

The Executioner's eyes flared. The Kanabo Corporation had attempted to steal American space warfare technology, and the men from Stony Man Farm had gone and stopped them in a bloody confrontation in New Guinea. The Kanabo Corporation was utterly ruthless, and its leaders ran their consortium almost as if it were a feudal Japanese clan. Their goal was the expansion of Japanese power, economic and otherwise, around the world. The word *Kanabo* was the name of the giant studded iron war club. The largest and strongest of the ancient samurai wielded it in the front ranks to break enemy formations, and its depiction on a red field was the Kanabo Corporation's company flag. They considered the world in feudal terms, and they considered themselves the iron war club that would break the ranks of Japan's opponents. In New Guinea, their tactics had been swift and savage.

Nothing short of open warfare would stop them.

"Are you sure?"

"No way to be completely sure, Striker. Japanese international consortiums are a maze of links, mergers and cutouts. But the Kanabo Corporation has distinct ties to Japanese oil interests, and people in your neck of the woods are turning up dead. It sure smells like them, but like I said, I doubt this is anything that we could prove. At least, not yet.'' Kurtzman paused a moment. ''What's your situation at the moment?''

''I have the USO Oil crew armed and on alert. Tell the SEALs thanks. I also had a confrontation with some French gentlemen earlier in the day.''

Bolan could hear Kurtzman straighten in his wheelchair. ''What kind of confrontation?''

''The physical kind. I believe they were feeling me out.''

''How so?''

''About five of them tried to clean my clock in a bar.''

Kurtzman considered that before continuing. ''Do you think they are operatives?''

''I believe their leader is an ex-foreign legionnaire.''

''They're a tough bunch.''

''That's the interesting part. He stayed out of it and observed while he sent his men in to bust me up.''

Kurtzman sighed. ''Your cover as a straight USO Oil employee may be blown. Couldn't you have taken a few punches and gone down?''

Bolan had considered that option, and decided against it. He shook his head as he looked out over the water. ''I would have gone home on a gurney, Bear. They weren't playing around.''

Kurtzman's tone grew concerned. ''Are you all right?''

''Couple of bruised knuckles.''

''How about the French?''

The soldier shrugged. ''Well, they'll live.''

''Anything else to report?''

''Yeah. Get me anything you can on a French national named Jeanine Maitland. She claims to be a foreign correspondent working for *La Voix* and who flew in from Tahiti to cover the troubles in the islands. She made contact with me a day ago in the general store.''

''I'll get on it immediately. Anything else?''

''I'm going to go talk to the local doctor and see if I can

learn anything on the native front and check the coroner's reports. By reputation, he seems to know what's going on in the islands, and he stitches up most of the casualties around here regardless of their nationality.''

"Tell me, have you had any more contact with the natives?''

"A little, at the same time I met Miss Maitland.''

"What kind of contact?''

"Eye contact.''

Kurtzman paused. "What do you think?''

"I think they don't like me.''

"Lots of people don't like you, Striker. What were the natives doing when they gave you the hard stare?''

"A war dance.''

6

René Sauvin folded his massive arms across his chest, lost in thought. The French test derrick was a little more than a mile offshore, and the little platform creaked with the evening tide. On the beach, the lights of the French shore facility were beginning to come on. Sauvin stood in front of the window of the control shack and let the evening breeze play over him as he considered the problem.

The American.

ZeeZee sat glumly in a chair and cradled his bruised face in his hands. The rest of the derrick crew was in the hospital. Guy had both arms and legs in casts. Philippe had a hernia from when the American had stomped him into the floor, and Nico's jaw would have to be wired back in place. Paul had a broken collarbone and a concussion. Sauvin looked back at ZeeZee again. The little Belgian had been the lightweight savate champion of Europe and fought successfully in Asia in brutal Thai-rules kickboxing matches before joining the legion. Other than losing even more of his teeth and having been beaten senseless, he was all right.

Sauvin chewed his lip in meditation and unconsciously flexed his biceps. This big American was going to be trouble. The simple solution would be to just put a bullet through his head and be done with it, but, unfortunately, his current operational parameters included only intimidation, surveillance and personal protection of the French oil operation. His superiors hadn't cleared him to kill anyone yet except in self-defense.

The French leader scowled. Politics and diplomacy. They continued to be an itch he simply couldn't scratch. However, he suspected the American had killed the Isolationists on his arrival, but not the men in the bar. He, too, had to be under political constraints. Sauvin smiled. It was interesting music that they had to dance to.

Regardless, he needed to find out who this American was, what organization he represented, and, most importantly, everything he knew. Sauvin turned with a shrug. There were worse things you could do to a man than kill him. The question, however, was getting hold of the man. He was undoubtedly well-armed and alert.

Sauvin grinned. He had an idea about that. It was time to put that idea into action. He turned to his downtrodden companion.

"Hey, ZeeZee. Cheer up. How would you like another shot at our American friend?"

ZeeZee stared up at Sauvin dejectedly. "My apologies, sir, but I don't believe I can beat this American."

Sauvin smiled. "I tell you what. I'll break his arms. Then you'll break his legs. Then we will make him sing like a bird for us. How would that be for you?"

ZeeZee gave Sauvin a huge gap-toothed grin as he sat up. "I like it. When?"

"In two days, possibly three. It must be arranged."

ZeeZee leaned back in his chair and put his feet up on a folding table. "I await your pleasure, sir."

HAYATA YORITOMO MOVED through the dark canopy of the palm trees like a shadow. Dressed in black from top to bottom and running silently in bare feet, he looked every inch like one of the ninja assassins of old. His equipment, however, belied that image. Much of Hayata's personal training had been taken straight from the ancient ninja ways. But many of the ways had changed in the intervening centuries.

The spies and assassins of feudal Japan hadn't carried Heckler & Koch 9 mm MP-5 submachine guns with attached sound suppressors. Nor had they worn Kevlar soft body armor or form-fitting uniforms woven of artificial fibers that dispersed body heat against searching infrared devices.

Hayata consulted the tiny readout on the screen of his Global Positioning Satellite navigation system. His target was two hundred meters away in a fold of the ground. As the ninja advanced higher up the hillside, he began to see the glimmers of firelight between the trunks of the trees. Hayata slid the GPS into the pouch of his nightsuit and began preparing for his objective.

At one hundred meters, he saw the sentry.

The native was a large man, and heavily built. He wore only a sarong and paddle-shaped hardwood war club that hung from his shoulder. He sat motionless in the darkness, looking outward into the trees with a .308 caliber FN assault rifle resting across his knees. Squatting in the darkness on the trunk of the tree, he was little more than a shadow himself. Through the night-vision goggles Hayata wore, the man was as clear as day. The Japanese warrior had been told that some Isolationists were well trained in their traditional ways of fighting. While he maneuvered in a wide circle around the lookout's position, Hayata wondered if this man was as impressive as he looked.

The sentry wasn't the target. To kill him would weaken the evening's ruse. It was better to let him fail in his duty and fill him and his brethren with the need for vengeance. Hayata moved toward the glow of the fire. As he closed in, he could see a small group of men sitting in a circle. All of them were armed in an assortment of traditional native arms and automatic weapons. A stout old man with close-cropped gray hair sat in the middle, and the rest of the men paid him obvious deference. His name was Malua, and he was one of the most respected elders on the main island. He was also widely rumored to be one of the ring leaders of the Isolationist movement, though he rigorously denied it in public. Yoritomo could hear him speak in low tones over the campfire in his native tongue. The ninja knew only a few words of the Polynesian dialect, and the distance was too great to make out what he was saying.

Hayata crept within what he considered adequate range and drew Howard Redland's .38 Colt revolver. The Japanese had retrieved the weapon from the site of the ambush of the big American on his arrival, and the headquarters in Tokyo had scrambled to get him a box of American-made .38 Special ammunition. The revolver was loaded with six 125-grain jacketed hollowpoint bullets.

Hayata held the pistol in a firm two-handed firing stance and shot the old man between the eyes.

The sudden thunderclap of the revolver in the night was deafening, and the men around the fire froze for a brief instant in shock. Hayata took a deep breath and roared in English at the top of his lungs.

"That's for Skip Porter, you murdering sons of bitches!"

The ninja discharged the revolver three more times into the trees over the men's heads, then started running. Hayata grinned as he ran. He was rather pleased with his Texas accent. It had taken him several hours of practice until he had felt comfortable with it, much longer than with the gun. Rifles began to return fire, but he was already far enough away. As he ran, he made no effort to conceal his trail. He deliberately trampled the undergrowth and left his footprints in the sand. He fired twice more over his shoulder, then dropped the spent revolver behind him. He could hear the natives yelling behind him as they fired their weapons and pursued him blindly. With his night-vision goggles, he quickly distanced himself from his pursuers as they stumbled after him in the dark. Hayata glanced up at the sky through a break in the canopy. It would be dawn soon. The natives would find his trail and the gun sometime later in the morning. They wouldn't be pleased.

The Japanese doubted there would be an immediate response. The Isolationists would call upon all the warriors dedicated to the movement throughout the islands. They would gather together, have a council of war and they would probably whip themselves into a frenzy with a war dance.

Then the Americans would have a full-scale siege on their hands.

IT WASN'T EVEN 10:00 a.m., and the morning was already stiflingly hot.

Dr. Ezekiel Tutarotaro glanced at the Executioner's USO Oil identification badge and raised a bushy white eyebrow at him across the desk. Bolan examined the doctor in return. He was an old man, and his long shoulder-length hair was completely white. A lifetime spent in the tropical sun had turned his skin dark brown and wrinkled. He had smiled when Bolan entered his tiny office. The doctor was no longer smiling. He was dressed incongruously in a white, short sleeve button-down shirt, a black tie, and a brightly printed blue sarong and sandals. Tutarotaro handed Bolan the ID card, then peered at him speculatively.

"I know of you, Mr. Belasko. You sent me quite a bit of business the other day." The doctor's English was perfect, but there was still a trace of an accent.

Bolan shrugged. "It was an unfortunate misunderstanding."

The old man almost smiled. "Yes, quite unfortunate for those five Frenchmen. All but one of them had to be flown to the larger hospitals in New Caledonia for more extensive treatment than I can provide here. None of them will be working on the derrick for months." He looked at Bolan again in appraisal. "You seem to have escaped the misunderstanding remarkably unscathed."

"I got lucky."

Tutarotaro's smile vanished. "You said you wished to see the bodies of the murder victims?"

Bolan nodded. "If that's possible."

The heavy lines in Dr. Tutarotaro's face drew into a deep frown. "Mr. Belasko, most of the bodies have been shipped back to their countries of origin, and, as a matter of professional ethics, I couldn't allow you, as an American representative, to exam the bodies of dead French or Japanese nationals."

"I understand. I would only ask to see remains of American civilians or coroner photographs if they are available."

Dr. Tutarotaro looked at Bolan dryly. "And?"

"And, as a doctor, your professional opinion on the murders would be appreciated."

The doctor nodded and sighed. "Very well, I will show you what I can. Follow me."

The doctor rose, and Bolan was surprised to find the man staring him in the eye. Despite his age, the doctor was a very physically impressive individual. He led Bolan to a staircase, and they descended into a noticeably cooler environment. The doctor took out a set of keys and unlocked a heavy door. He jerked his head at Bolan and led him inside.

The room was genuinely cool, and Dr. Tutarotaro spread his arms and pointed at the wall. "Behold!"

Bolan glanced at a gleaming silver, six-chambered cold storage unit along the wall. French writing and model numbers were written on the side. Bolan nodded. "Very impressive."

Dr. Tutarotaro smiled hugely. "Before the troubles, we just took a body and buried it. We didn't keep them around. Except the skull, of course, but that was in the old days, for religious purposes." The doctor made a show of scowling. "Before the missionaries came."

Tutarotaro walked toward the storage unit. "Corpses don't last long in tropical climates, as I'm sure you are aware. When the troubles started, all we could do was put the bodies on ice, which, at best, is a very temporary solution. Between the gruesome nature of the murders and the climate, the French, in particular, were appalled at the state of their cadavers when they saw them. They graciously donated this splendid medical refrigeration unit and air-conditioning system to the hospital."

"Very kind of them."

"Indeed. I'm thinking of moving my office down here. It's delightfully cool."

"May I see the files on the deceased Americans?"

"Surely." Tutarotaro opened the top drawer of a filing cabinet and pulled out a thick sheaf of files and set them on an empty gurney. "I don't have photos of the first two Americans who were killed. It was never procedure before, and for that matter, I never really filled out detailed reports until very recently. However, like many things, that has changed. These photographs were taken by the boy who works for the island newspaper. Here."

Bolan's face was expressionless as he took the files and looked at the photograph on top. It was a picture of a human body, but even decades of battle didn't completely prepare the Executioner for the state of the cadaver. It was one of the most horrendous corpses Bolan had ever seen. His eyes narrowed. "What kind of weapon produces wounds like this?"

The doctor turned and pulled a long object from a cabinet and handed it to Bolan gingerly.

"The shark-toothed sword."

Bolan hefted the weapon in his hand. It was heavy, a tapered baton of polished hardwood slightly over three feet long. Four long rows of large, triangular shark's teeth were set in the wood and bound by split cording down its length. It was exquisitely carved along its length with looping native symbols, and its hand polishing and intricate lacing almost elevated the object into a work of art. Bolan glanced at the photo of the corpse again and had no illusions. What he held was a beautiful piece of work, and quite possibly the ugliest weapon he had ever seen.

Tutarotaro shrugged as Bolan handed it back. "As you might probably surmise, it's really an impact weapon, more of a club than an actual sword. However, the shark's teeth have their own unmistakable secondary effect on the victim. Anyone beaten to death with one of these isn't going to leave a very pleasant corpse. I would guess that our friend here in the photograph was killed by several similarly armed individuals, and that the beating continued for some time after he was dead."

"What other methods of killing have you encountered?"

The doctor cleared his throat. "Well, I've gotten a number of people who have been shot. The level of violence is increasing, and everyone is arming themselves. Two weeks ago I had a Frenchman hacked to death by machetes. He had apparently gone down to the beach at night to meet a native girl, and it seems she had some friends waiting for him. Machetes have always been very popular in the islands. They aren't strictly a native implement though. They have to be imported. But nearly every islander owns one, like Americans own lawnmowers. I suspect for many they are cheaper and easier to get hold of than shark-toothed swords and war clubs, and they are just as effective.''

Bolan grimaced. Tutarotaro looked at him closely. "You think we are savages? Some people might call our Isolationists patriots.''

The Executioner's eyes narrowed, and the two men held each other's gaze. The doctor didn't flinch as he continued.

"Have you been to Hawaii, Mr. Belasko? I have. The native Hawaiians are a minority in their own islands. They form the poorest level of society. Many of them live in slums while Europeans and Asians run the government and control the islands' wealth and commerce. Many of their native plants and animals are now extinct because of overdevelopment and the overrunning of their habitats by imported species. It's much the same on many islands in the Pacific. The Pacific Trust Islands are a small chain, and it would take very little to desolate them, ecologically, economically and culturally. Many of my people don't want that. They want the old ways. There have been many councils on this subject. Many believe that the only real solution is to kill any nonnatives who wash up on our shores. Sometimes I find it hard to fault their logic.''

The Executioner's face was expressionless as his hand rested on the stack of coroner's reports. "The men in these files were just doing their jobs at the invitation of your government. That same government left them defenseless and stood by and watched while they were butchered.''

Tutarotaro slowly lowered his gaze to the photographs. "No, you're right. They didn't deserve to be butchered.'' He turned and went over to the refrigeration unit and opened one of its doors. "The last murder victim I had was at the start of last week, an American." He pulled out the long gurney and opened the body bag. "This is Mr. Anthony 'Skip' Porter. He was the chief of operations in the islands for USO Oil, until his demise." Tutarotaro frowned heavily. "I had met him on several occasions. He seemed to be a good man."

Bolan examined the body. Skip Porter had been brutally killed with one or more edged weapons. His death certificate said multiple assailants armed with machetes. Porter's killers had hacked his body almost beyond recognition. Bolan's eyes flared slightly as he looked closer. Beneath the brutal cross-hatching of the chopping wounds on the corpse's torso, a long very deep cut was detectable that ran from his collarbone down past his sternum. The Executioner looked closer. The right hand had been severed at the wrist, and while his throat had been cut several times, one particular cut ran cleanly through to the neck vertebrae and had nearly decapitated him.

Bolan turned to Tutarotaro. "How closely have you examined this body?"

The doctor raised himself to full height and looked at Bolan coldly. "In the last month and a half I have seen more bodies than I did during World War II. Frankly, Mr. Belasko, Mr. Porter's cause of death seems to be rather obvious to me. I didn't particularly feel like performing a postmortem. I'm a general practitioner. I was drafted into becoming a coroner because I'm one of the few medical doctors in the islands. As a rule, I prefer working with living people."

Bolan softened his tone. "I mean no insult, Doctor, and I understand how unpleasant your position is. However, I would appreciate your medical opinion on something."

Tutarotaro was intrigued in spite of himself. "Oh?"

"Beneath the more obvious wounding to the torso we have a single long, deep cut, starting here." Bolan pointed to the shoulder and traced a line with his finger. "The blow severed the collarbone and traveled uninterrupted in a downward motion, slicing cleanly through the ribs and the sternum."

Tutarotaro removed a pair of wire-rimmed glasses from his

shirt pocket, put them on and bent over the corpse. His eyes widened noticeably. "I believe you're right."

The Executioner pointed to Porter's arm. "And here, the right hand was severed from the wrist, cleanly, with one blow."

The lines in Tutarotaro's face deepened.

Bolan continued. "And, at the neck. There are several wounds, but look at this one, here." He drew another line with his finger. "Unlike the others, it entered cleanly and nearly severed the spine. It was done by a cutting motion, not hacking like most of the other wounds to the body."

Tutarotaro's face was unreadable. "You're very observant, Mr. Belasko. As observant as I should've been."

Bolan held his gaze. "In your medical opinion, Doctor, could any of these three wounds been caused by a blow from a machete?"

The old man's shoulders sagged, and he let out a long slow breath. "No. A machete couldn't have produced wounds of this nature."

The Executioner's gaze was unrelenting. "Do you have any speculations on what could have?"

Tutarotaro's eyes seemed far away as he spoke. "Many years ago, when I was a young man, before I went abroad for my medical training, the Japanese came to our islands. This was during World War II, at the outbreak of the war in the Pacific. The Japanese came here to set up an observation post to monitor Allied naval movements. Their occupation of the islands was ruthless, and the troops committed many atrocities. Anyone who disobeyed or resisted was executed." The doctor locked eyes with Bolan. "Yes, Mr. Belasko, I have seen many wounds like these before. It was long ago, during that war. They were inflicted on my people, by Japanese officers with their samurai swords."

7

Tokyo sweltered in the morning heat of midsummer.

On the thirtieth floor of the Kanabo building, Raizo Tanaka's blood went cold.

He had just been given an enlarged photograph by a special messenger. The picture depicted, a tall, powerful-looking Westerner. He appeared to be standing in the middle of a small bar or a restaurant. Bloodied and beaten men lay at his feet, and he calmly stood and faced two more men. The big *gaijin*'s face was slightly turned in profile, but his features were mostly visible, and to Tanaka, unmistakable.

Tanaka was sure, but as he sat down at his desk he pressed the button of his intercom and spoke icily to his secretary.

"Miss Nishiki, bring up the Skylance files. Specifically the security camera photos of the New Guinea complex."

His secretary's voice answered immediately. "Yes, sir, at once."

Tanaka seethed as he waited. In a moment the file came up, and he rapidly punched commands into the computer. His color monitor blinked, and a photograph filled the screen. The photo was an enhanced enlargement of the security camera that had monitored Mr. Ito's office in New Guinea. Mr. Ito had been in command of the New Guinea complex and had spearheaded the attempt to take the American Skylance technology. Mr. Ito was dead. The man caught in the lens of the hidden security camera had killed him. He was a large man and clad nearly head to toe in a dark, close fitting raid suit. He was heavily armed. Kanabo Corporation armorers had identified the weapons he held in either hand as a .44 Magnum Desert Eagle and a 9 mm Beretta 93-R pistol. In New Guinea, the man had wreaked utter havoc with them.

He and a handful of Western commandos had destroyed half of the New Guinea complex, killed Mr. Ito, and recovered the Skylance technology without taking a single casualty. Tanaka was there in the burning complex and helplessly watched them escape. The review of his actions in the affair had gone all the way up to the old man himself. The situation had been fairly clear. Tanaka had obeyed orders. He had done everything to stop the Americans. He had been absolved of blame. Still, the fact remained—he had been defeated. It followed him like a shadow. It was more than Tanaka could bear.

Only the direct order of the old man had prevented Tanaka from committing suicide.

Tanaka looked again at the computer screen and the image of the heavily armed man from the New Guinea Skylance file. He slowly turned his head and looked down at the photograph that had been sent from the Pacific Trust Islands. Tanaka had to keep from trembling. There could be no doubt.

The two men were one and the same.

Tanaka stabbed the button of his intercom. "Miss Nishiki, contact Mr. Yabe's secretary and tell him that I need to speak with Mr. Yabe immediately."

Tanaka's secretary paused for a split second. Mr. Yabe was the founder and head of the Kanabo Corporation. In many ways, the old man was the Kanabo Corporation. After World War II he had built up the corporation from nothing. He was a figure of nearly mythic proportions. One simply didn't demand to talk to him. However, one didn't lightly question Raizo Tanaka's orders either.

"I will contact Mr. Yabe's secretary immediately."

Tanaka sat back in his chair and waited. He knew that the old man had felt the sting of defeat just as much as he had in the New Guinea affair. The loss of the captured American Skylance technology was a stain on the Kanabo Corporation's honor, and one that demanded to be washed away in blood.

Tanaka once again looked at the photograph of the warrior filling the screen before hitting the print command on the computer.

The old man would be very interested in what he had found.

THE EXECUTIONER RODE SHOTGUN as Chris Racine drove the jeep into town. Racine's carbine lay with its stock folded under a tarp just behind the seats. In his last two practice sessions the young man had started to become very accurate with it. Bolan's 93-R pistol and four spare magazines rode in a shoulder holster beneath the oversized Hawaiian shirt that had been specifically tailored to conceal them. The .44 Desert Eagle and a small assortment of grenades were concealed under his seat. Bolan didn't expect an attack in full daylight. The next attack would be more subtle. Still, a single man going into town alone was too much of a target of opportunity. The rules remained the same. No one left the compound alone.

The main street was very quiet as they headed inland. Other than a cat sunning itself and a few dogs lying in the shade, no one was about. The street was as still as the morning air. As Racine pulled the jeep in front of the general store, Bolan was surprised to see Jeanine Maitland sitting on the wooden steps. She smiled as the vehicle ground to a halt and gave Bolan a friendly leer. "Hey, sailor, you want a date?"

"Always. You want a beer?"

Jeanine grinned. "Always."

"I'll be right back. Don't go anywhere."

"I'm not moving."

The little bell over the door rang as Bolan and Racine entered. The old woman nodded at them stiffly, then ignored them as she began scrutinizing her countertop with extreme seriousness. Bolan nodded back, then went down an aisle. As Racine followed, Bolan spoke quietly. "Something is wrong."

"You mean the old woman?"

"Exactly."

The young man shrugged. "So, she has a bug up her butt today. So what?"

Bolan frowned. "She's a sharp trader. If she had a bug up her butt, she'd keep it to herself until after business hours. Look around. There's no one on the street, either. I believe you are the one who told me most people on the island do their business in the morning before it gets hot."

Racine glanced out the store window. "Yeah. That's true. It's kind of quiet, isn't it?"

"Dead quiet."

"What do we do?"

"We do our shopping and get out of here. Quick and quiet."

Racine picked a bottle of sunscreen from the shelf. Bolan turned at a small noise behind him and found the old woman at his elbow, leaning on a broom. She gave Bolan a halfhearted smile. "You find everything okay?"

Bolan nodded. The old woman looked at the door and leaned closer. For a moment her jovial nature reasserted itself. "French girl sitting on steps all morning, big boy, ever since I open up. I think she a horny girl." She grinned up at him. "I think maybe she waiting for you."

"Thanks for the tip."

The old woman folded her arms across her bare chest and looked out the window. She scanned the street for a moment and the lines in her face drew down into deadly seriousness. "I like you, big boy. I give you another tip for free. You and your friend, get out of town. Take your little French girl with you. If you smart, maybe you get off the island."

The Executioner locked eyes with the old woman. "What's going to happen?"

The old woman stared at Bolan for a long moment but didn't flinch. "Trouble. Bad trouble." She looked the soldier up and down gravely. "Too much trouble, even for big boy like you."

Bolan knew she wasn't going to say any more. She was risking her neck just talking to him on this particular morning. He turned to Racine. "How much money did Red give you?"

The young man pulled a roll out of his shirt pocket. "About five hundred bucks."

"Give it to her."

Racine looked at Bolan, then handed the old woman the money. She looked at it for a moment, then quickly riffled through the bills and counted it. She nodded as she tucked it into her sarong. She glanced out the window again cautiously and began sweeping her already clean floor. The Executioner followed her gaze for a moment, then turned to Racine. "Let's get out of here."

The street was still empty as they went outside. Maitland gave Bolan a false frown as she looked pointedly at his empty hands. "I thought you were treating me to a beer?"

"I am. How would you like a guided tour of the USO Oil compound and a free lunch?"

Maitland's eyes widened. "Very much so." Her eyes suddenly narrowed again. "It will be unseemly, though, if people see me drive off with two American men. People will talk."

Bolan looked up and down the empty street. Almost all of the shops were closed. Nothing moved. Even the cats and dogs had disappeared. Every hard-won instinct the Executioner had earned in battle was tingling. He took the woman's hand.

"If we don't leave soon, there's going to be a lot more than talk."

Maitland jumped into the jeep without saying a word.

MINORU YABE SAT on a simple camp stool.

The stool was loosely draped with the skin of a tiger he had personally hunted. The room where he waited was at the top of the Kanabo Corporation's headquarters building, one of the tallest skyscrapers in Tokyo. A large banner of the Kanabo Corporation's flag, with its red field and stylized iron war club, was mounted on one wall. Directly behind Mr. Yabe was a wooden rack on a raised dais. In its cross beams was a genuine kanabo. The iron war club was the weapon from which the Kanabo Corporation took its name. The weapon was centuries old. It was over five feet long and made of solid iron, and looked for all the world like a giant octagonal baseball bat, with rows of raised iron studs running its length from the handle on all sides. Only the strongest men could handle such a weapon in battle. One of Yabe's ancestors had wielded that club in the battle of Sekigahara for the shogun in 1600.

The Yabe family name had been synonymous with honor and heroism throughout Japan's tumultuous history.

Minoru Yabe was no exception. He had served with distinction as a decorated fighter pilot during World War II. When his left eye had been injured in a dogfight, he had begged his squadron commander to allow him to fly a final kamikaze mission against the Allied warships. His commander had considered him too valuable. They were losing the war, and the Imperial Japanese air force was drastically short of pilots. Yabe's considerable skill was desperately needed to train the pilots. The Japanese soldier had watched as he trained and sent out scores of new pilots, and fewer and fewer returned with each mission. The emperor's final surrender to the Allies in the face of Hiroshima and Nagasaki had been a humiliation beyond endurance. Only the emperor's assumption of full responsibility for the surrender and his direct order forbidding suicide had prevented Yabe from ripping open his belly with his officer's sword.

Most of his family and its holdings had been destroyed in the massive Allied bombings. Yabe had built the Kanabo Corporation from a shoe repair shop in a Tokyo back street. It was now one of the most powerful consortiums in Japan, if not the world.

Minoru Yabe was its undisputed ruler.

The Japanese soldier had spent a great deal of time studying Japan's military history. He firmly believed that history repeated itself. Several times before, men of great vision had unified Japan. Yabe believed it was time to unify Japan again. It needed someone to unite its military, economy and political system into one power. In olden times this man was called shogun. Yabe believed it was time for such a man to rise again. He believed he was eminently qualified for the job. It was simply a matter of acquiring power at home and overseas or crushing his opponents—whatever was necessary. It was simply a matter of time.

Unified under the Kanabo banner, he would make Japan the most powerful nation on earth.

Yabe returned from his reverie and looked at the low wooden table before him. Two photographs lay on it. One was a color enlargement. The other was a printout from a computer. He looked at them again carefully. Tanaka was right.

It was the same man.

Yabe appeared to speak to the room around him. "Send in Tanaka."

The massive door opened, and Raizo Tanaka entered and swiftly bowed. Yabe nodded back and gestured for him to take a seat. Tanaka knelt on a circular cushion to Yabe's right at rigid attention. The old man gave him a small smile.

"It is good to see you, Tanaka-*san*."

Tanaka bowed again. "Thank you, Yabe-*sama*."

Both men knew that Yabe hadn't wished to see him. The Skylance affair had left Tanaka in an uncomfortable position. He had acted according to orders, and yet the Skylance technology had been stolen away, Mr. Ito had been killed and much of the New Guinea complex damaged. Mr. Ito had been a close friend of Yabe's since the war. Tanaka couldn't be blamed, yet he was nonetheless associated with the immense dishonor the Skylance affair had brought upon the corporation. The old man considered Tanaka much too valuable to be allowed to commit suicide, and had brought him back to the Tokyo office. His work in Tokyo had been exemplary, but Yabe knew that Tanaka found it unbearable to be working behind a desk.

In a way, Yabe felt he owed Tanaka, and he was very pleased that the younger man had found such an excellent way to redeem himself. It further proved his worth. Yabe let his face grow serious.

"Tanaka-*san*. Your talents are wasted working in the office."

Tanaka bowed and then looked straight ahead without blinking. "Thank you, Yabe-*sama*, I agree with you completely."

Yabe snorted. Tanaka was bordering on being disrespectful. However, the old man was fond of the young businessman. He was the perfect blend of the old ways and the new world. Yabe believed Tanaka was exactly the kind of warrior Japan needed. The old man would utilize his talents.

"Tanaka-*san*. I want you to go to the Pacific Trust Islands. You will assume operational command. You'll do whatever is required to attain the offshore oil development rights."

Tanaka bowed again. *"Hai."*

Yabe paused a moment. "You will kill the American commando—and bring me his head."

8

Aaron Kurtzman sounded surprised over the satellite communication link. "You know, I was just about to call you, Striker."

Bolan spoke quietly into the microphone of his headset. "Aaron, I need a full satellite recon of the islands. I need to know about any kind of unusual activity, any kind at all, and I need it ASAP."

"I'm way ahead of you."

"What have you got for me?"

Kurtzman's voice turned tense. "We've got fires."

"How many, what kind and where?"

"Stony Man has access to a Pentagon satellite that has been observing the Pacific Trust Islands since the trouble began. The satellite's infrared camera shows dozens of fires, bonfire size, burning all over the island chain. Does this have any meaning for you?"

Bolan's eyes narrowed. It meant a lot. "I think the natives are restless."

"What did you do to them this time?"

The Executioner frowned. "Nothing new, at least, not that I know of. But something was wrong when I went into town this morning. Everything was quiet—dead quiet. There was nothing moving. An old native woman the oil team does business with tipped me off."

"What did she say?"

"She told me to get the hell out of Dodge while I still could. And I don't think she was kidding."

"What do you think is happening?"

"I think the Isolationists are massing. If they're lighting bonfires, I'd bet they're working themselves up to do something. I think someone is going to get hit and hit hard."

"You, the French, or the Japanese?"

"I don't know. I also don't know what has gotten them riled up. But the town is almost completely closed down, and everyone is keeping out of sight. I'd say whatever is going to happen will only be on the main island."

Kurtzman considered this before responding. "The Japanese are based on a small atoll they've leased between the main island and its sister. I'd say that makes the native's target either you or the French, if not both."

"I don't think they'd split their forces, at least, not initially. If it breaks into a riot, there may be some spillover. But I get the feeling something has happened, and there's going to be a reckoning."

"You want to extract, Striker? If you pack up the crew into one of the boats and get offshore right now, we can have you on the *Sam Houston* steaming for Hawaii in half an hour."

The Executioner thought long and hard. "No. If we extract now, USO Oil is probably finished here in the islands. It will be like admitting guilt for something we haven't done. If we leave the complex undefended, the Isolationists will probably burn it to the ground. France or Japan will get the oil development rights."

"That would be too bad, Striker, but it would be preferable to having you and the rest of the crew strung up and torn to pieces by a howling mob."

"I don't like it either, but there's another factor to consider. I think I might have a lead on the murdered Americans. If we extract now, that part of the mission is a wash as well."

Kurtzman's voice turned grim. "I still don't like it. I've seen pictures of your little encampment on the beach, Striker. It isn't exactly Fort Knox. You've got a chain-link fence and some prefab sheds to protect against possibly hundreds of armed opponents. I don't want to sound skeptical, but you and ten oil workers with M-2 carbines aren't going to stop them. If they're motivated, they'll take you down.''

"I know."

Kurtzman attempted to sound cheerful. "How about we send you a platoon of Marines? They love fighting in the sand.''

"I'd like nothing better. But if we land the Marines, we're forcing them to react."

"Well, then, how about a team of Navy SEALs? They're sneaky.''

The Executioner shook his head. He would personally prefer a full U.S. Navy Carrier Battle group, but he had to act within the political parameters of the situation. It wasn't making his job any easier. A deep line formed between the Executioner's eyebrows. "Aaron, if we use lethal force, we're finished here. Even if it's just me and the rest of the USO Oil crew. If we start openly killing natives, the United States is history in these islands. Neither one of our objectives get accomplished. The mission is over, and we lose."

Kurtzman took a deep breath. "Let me get this straight, Striker. You want a nonlethal deterrent and deniable reinforcements?''

"Exactly. I'm glad we're thinking along the same lines on this one. This is what I want you to do.''

JEANINE MAITLAND LOOKED UP as Bolan entered the compound. She was munching on a thick ham-and-cheese sandwich and was apparently working on her third can of beer. Howard Redland, Chris Racine and three others were watching her eat with great seriousness. The Texan looked up at Bolan and smiled. His smile died as he saw the Executioner's face. "So, what's the good word?"

"I need all the men in here, now. We have to have a meeting. It's an emergency."

Racine jumped to his feet. "I'll go round up the men."

Bolan nodded, and Racine raced from the room. The soldier

looked at Maitland. "I'm sorry. This has to be company personnel only."

The journalist's eyes narrowed. "Just what is this meeting to be about?"

"Survival, and if we survive, you'll get the full scoop."

Maitland didn't appear pleased, but she wrapped her sandwich in her napkin and started to get up. "Will this take long?"

"All I really need is a simple vote by all the men. Yes or no." Bolan pulled a cold can of beer from out of the fridge and tossed it to her. "It should take less than a beer."

The woman caught the can with one hand and shrugged indifferently. "I'll be down by the pier."

Racine came into the conference room with the rest of the team in tow. They all had their carbines with them, and Bolan was pleased to note that most of them had their folding stocks extended and their safeties on. They crowded around the table and looked at the Executioner expectantly. Redland made a quick head count, then folded his arms as he nodded at Bolan. "So what's happening."

The soldier saw no reason to sugarcoat the situation. "I believe we're going to be attacked."

The room was silent for a moment. Racine cleared his throat. "Attacked by who?"

Bolan looked at him grimly. "By the Isolationists. Something has happened. I don't know what. But they are massing, and I think they are going to attack our compound. Probably tonight."

Nelson looked at Bolan uncertainly. "Well, attacked by how many? Do you know?"

The Executioner took a deep breath. The young man had every right to be nervous. "I don't know for sure, Nelson. If I had to guess, I'd say at least dozens, if not a hundred or more."

Redland's eyes flared. "Jesus Christ! A hundred or more? What the hell are we supposed to do?" The tall Texan shook his head. "No disrespect, Mr. Belasko, but goddamn it, I'm not John Wayne, and this isn't the Alamo. And I'm not so in love with USO Oil that I'm prepared to die for the company. You know I respect you, and God knows we all appreciate what you've done here, but if the Coconuts start coming out of the woods by the hundreds, we're going to get slaughtered.''

Most of the men around the table muttered and nodded in agreement. Bolan waited for them to settle down.

''Gentlemen, the situation is fairly clear. I don't believe we can defend this compound with the armament we have. But if we leave, the Isolationists will tear it to the ground. As you all know, we're in competition with the Japanese and the French. If we run out, we lose. I don't think any of us have any illusions about the local constables doing anything to help us, much less risking their necks against their own people.''

Redland sighed heavily. ''Swell. So we stay here, shoot a few of the Coconuts, piss them off even more, then let them rip us to pieces.''

The Executioner locked eyes with Redland and held his gaze. ''Red, do I seem like the martyr-type to you?''

The Texan cleared his throat and looked away guiltily. ''Well...no.''

Bolan nodded. ''Thank you.''

Racine suddenly perked up and looked at Bolan closely. ''You have a plan.''

''I do.'' The Executioner folded his arms across his chest. ''Red is right. I'm not about to order any of you to stand and die for USO Oil. I'm hoping you'll stay and help. If my plan works, none of you will even have to fire a shot. If the plan goes to hell, all of you will get in the boats and head out to sea while I cover you.''

Redland looked at Bolan curiously. ''What exactly do you want us to stick around for?''

''The ten of you and myself are the only Americans who are legally in the islands at the moment. When the constables do come, my story is going to sound very strange if all of you are gone.''

Racine smiled. "We're getting secret reinforcements, aren't we?"

Bolan raised a bemused eyebrow. "That would be illegal, Chris."

RAIZO TANAKA SAT in a first-class seat of a Japan Airlines 747 jumbo jet and sipped at a cup of warm sake as he flew across the South Pacific. He had been startled to find the sake had been brewed in California and had been even more surprised to find that it was excellent. Tanaka stretched his legs and smiled to himself.

He was going to enjoy killing the American. Tanaka savored the idea for a few moments until the flight attendant interrupted him.

"Mr. Tanaka, you have an urgent phone call. Do you wish to take it in private?"

Tanaka nodded. "Yes, thank you." He stood and took his carry-on from the overhead rack. He removed a thin aluminum case from his pack and the flight attendant led him to an alcove by the stairs. As the woman left, Tanaka opened the case, flipped the switches on one of the devices built into it and scanned for bugs. Once he was satisfied, he removed the mouthpiece of the white telephone on the wall and plugged it into his signal scrambler. He flicked another switch, then spoke.

"Tanaka-*san*."

The voice of Mr. Saburo, Mr. Yabe's personal secretary, came through the line. Secretary was actually a poor choice of words for Saburo's position. Retainer, in the true feudal sense of the word, was more applicable. Saburo was Yabe's personal adviser and spear carrier. In a very real way, Yabe was a modern warlord, and Saburo was his most trusted samurai.

"Tanaka-*san*. Events are occurring in the islands that you must be made aware of."

"Saburo-*san*, you have my complete attention."

"As you know, Hayata Yoritomo is in command of the operation in the Pacific Trust Islands."

Tanaka knew this all too well. Hayata was roughly Tanaka's equal in the Kanabo Corporation's field operations. The man had been a personal protégé of Mr. Ito, and his sneering attitudes had left no doubt of his opinion of Tanaka and his role in the Skylance affair. Tanaka had been looking forward to usurping command from him.

"Hayata has initiated an action against the Americans. In all likelihood, the natives will attack the American complex tonight in large numbers due to his actions. The main island will be unsafe for any nonnatives. There is a slim chance that the locals may attack the French compound and possibly our installation on the atoll. This is deemed an acceptable risk. Hayata is coordinating with our submarine in the area, and they are taking measures to counter any seaborne attack against our compound that may occur. Given the speed with which events are occurring, Hayata will remain in command until the present situation settles itself. Upon reaching the island, you will be met and taken to the atoll as swiftly as possible. You will obey Hayata's orders until further notice."

Tanaka went rigid with rage. His only thoughts for the past eight hours had been of killing the American and restoring his honor. The idea of being placed under Hayata's command and watching while his victory was snatched from him was intolerable. Tanaka's teeth ground in frustration, then with an immense effort of will he swallowed his anger.

"Yes, Saburo-*san*, I understand. What actions, if any, are the Americans taking?"

Saburo's voice warmed to the subject. "None that we can discern. The American Navy has kept warships within a hundred miles of the islands, ostensibly on maneuvers to intimidate us and the French. However, none of them have made any move toward the islands, and there is no way any of them can reach the area in time, even if they went to full speed immediately. Their aircraft carrier is still nearly a thousand miles away and appears to be on stand-down status. Satellite photos taken within the last fifteen minutes show no evidence of any attempts by the USO Oil employees to fortify their compound, and both of their boats are anchored.''

Tanaka despaired. He had seen photographs of the Oil compound. If the Isolationists rose against it en masse, there could be little doubt of the outcome. A few Oil employees with small arms, even if they were led by the American commando, would be quickly overwhelmed. Tanaka's mission appeared to be over before it had even started.

''So the Americans will be slaughtered.'' It was a statement, not a question.

''Their position is bad and hard to defend. Their compound, itself, is weak, and they are armed with only small arms and possibly some grenades. Their situation does seem desperate. Even if they miraculously kill enough of the natives to drive them away, it will be a stain against them with the native population that no amount of dollars will be able to erase.'' Saburo sounded as close to being happy as Tanaka had ever heard him. ''Barring a miracle, the Americans are finished.''

9

Gary Manning squatted uncomfortably in the bomb bay of the B-2 and breathed oxygen out of a bottle. It was dark and cold inside the belly of the bat-winged strategic bomber. It seemed no one on the Northrop Aerospace design team had given much thought to comfort when they had designed the high-tech bomber's weapons bay. All Manning knew was that he and the rest of the men from Stony Man Farm were somewhere over the Pacific Ocean.

According to Kurtzman, Mack Bolan needed the kind of backup only the Farm could provide, and he needed it before nightfall, his time. Manning, David McCarter, Gadgets Schwarz, Carl Lyons, Calvin James, Rafael Encizo and T. J. Hawkins had been at the Farm that morning, and they had been turned out with Manning nominally in charge until they reached the islands. The Pacific Trust Islands were roughly nine thousand miles from Virginia. Getting there before nightfall was the trick.

Six General Dynamics F-111 fighter-bombers had scrambled from the Alexandria Air Force base. Each plane had taken a team member in the bombardier's seat to the West Coast of the United States with afterburners on at Mach 2.2. At the same time, a B-2 stealth bomber had been flown out of Nellis, Nevada, to rendezvous with them in Hawaii. Six F-14 Tomcats from the U.S.S. *Nimitz* had been fueled and waiting for the team in San Diego. Manning and the rest had flown nonstop to Hawaii at twice the speed of sound, slowing only long enough to refuel in flight from a tanker aircraft.

The men from Stony Man had only fifteen minutes to stretch their legs and suit up when the immense, boomerang-like B-2 bomber had taxied onto the tarmac at Hickam Field, and they and their equipment had been loaded into the black aircraft's weapons bay.

Manning glanced around in the gloom. He had to give the bomber's designers credit. It might not be particularly comfortable, but the ride itself was remarkably smooth and quiet. The B-2 was a technological marvel. The team's final leg to the jump point would be invisible to any radars searching for them from below or from satellites scanning from above.

The big Canadian considered the actual jump. The B-2's engine intakes were mounted on top of the flying wing's fuselage, and the plane had no tail surfaces to get snagged on. From a skydiving point of view, the B-2 ought to be a remarkably easy aircraft to fall out of. Manning knew "ought to be" were the operative words in this situation. To his knowledge, he and the rest of the Stony Man team would be the first humans stupid enough to pull this stunt.

The jump would be a daylight, high-altitude low-opener to minimize the team's exposure. The U.S.S. *Sam Houston* would be at antenna depth and would send them a signal to home in on. With luck, the team would touch down nearby, and the submarine would fish them out of the water. After that, the team would enter the USO Oil compound under the pier using Navy SEAL swimmer delivery vehicles.

The B-2's pilot spoke to Manning through his radio headset. "Five minutes, jump leader."

"Acknowledged." Manning's head just touched the bombbay roof as he stood and stretched. "Five minutes, gentlemen. Let's run a final check."

The men paired off and checked one another's packs and straps a final time, making sure no gear was loose or flapping. They took the hoses from the oxygen tanks they had been breathing out of and began to breathe out of their bailout bottles.

The pilot spoke again in Manning's earpiece. "Two minutes."

"Acknowledged."

Manning checked his gear bags again out of habit. The team's armament for this mission was unusual, to say the least. He intended to talk to the big guy about that if there was time.

"One minute. Opening weapons bay."

The team stepped back in pairs as the bomb-bay doors suddenly opened and sunlight began to filter in. As the doors slid open, the Pacific Ocean gleamed thirty thousand feet beneath them. The sun was just beginning to set. The view below them was nothing short of spectacular.

"Brilliant jump conditions," McCarter commented as he gazed at the blue-gold waters below them. "Bloody marvelous."

Manning grinned. The job did have its perks.

The pilot spoke. "We have *Sam Houston*'s signal. We're over the target area."

Manning consulted the directional receiver strapped to his forearm and nodded with satisfaction as it received the submarine's homing signal. "Confirmed. Jumpers ready."

"Confirmed, we are directly over target, jump leader. You're clear to go!"

Manning looked through the bomb-bay doors at the ocean below. There was no time like the present. He sliced his hand down decisively.

"Go! Go! Go!"

James leaped through the open doors, followed by Hawkins. Lyons, Gadgets Schwarz and Encizo jumped in rapid succession. McCarter gave Manning the thumbs-up as he leaped, then Manning stepped out after him.

Seven of the most dangerous men in the world fell toward the staggering blue of the Pacific Ocean.

MACK BOLAN WATCHED the sun as it began to set out across the water. Jeanine Maitland glanced at him with just a hint of sarcasm. "Well, it was very peaceful today, Mr. Belasko."

Bolan nodded without looking at her as he scanned the horizon. "Very peaceful."

The woman eyed him critically. "The calm before the storm, no?"

The soldier watched the water.

"The drums have stopped."

That was an obvious statement. An hour ago, they had heard the distant reverberation of drums inland, probably in or around town. It had gone on for about half an hour, then stopped. The island had been silent since. Bolan looked at Maitland for a moment. She was actually very nervous, but she was being cool about it. He had wanted to put her in one of the boats, but she had insisted on staying. She was a journalist, and she wanted action. Bolan had no legal authority over her.

Maitland looked around the USO Oil compound and blew a stray lock of hair out of her eyes. "You don't seem to have done much to, how would you say, fortify, the encampment."

Bolan nodded. There wasn't too much that really could be done. He had locked the gate and parked the jeep in front of it, but the Executioner knew that given enough motivated bodies, the perimeter fence could be torn down in moments. He had made sure both of the boat engines were fueled and warmed up for a fast getaway. Every man had his carbine locked and loaded, and had six spare 30-round magazines, as well as whatever handguns they'd smuggled onto the island personally. Bolan glanced at the diver's watch on his wrist. Time was the critical factor. Hopefully the reinforcements would arrive.

"Do you think they went home?"

Bolan turned from the water and glanced inland casually. "They're over there. In the trees. Don't look."

Maitland's eyes widened, but she kept them on Bolan. "What are they waiting for?"

The Executioner turned to the ocean and watched as the sky slowly turned to a brilliant shade of gold. "For the sun to go down."

Her head snapped around, and she looked intently at the sun as it began to dip toward the horizon. "How soon is that?"

Bolan shrugged. "I'd say actual sunset will be in twenty minutes. They could come any time after that. Probably within the hour."

The woman locked her blue eyes with Bolan's. "You seem very calm."

"So do you."

She looked at him in surprise and suddenly smiled. "Well, I am French."

A small smile twisted a corner of Bolan's mouth. "Well, that explains everything."

The soldier turned his gaze to the pier.

"What are you looking at?"

"Don't be obvious about it, but look under the pier. Between the boats."

The woman moved only her eyes as she searched beneath the pier. Her eyes widened suddenly.

Things were moving in the shadows.

The things were dark and nearly shapeless. Slowly, they moved into the shallows and stayed in the dark surf underneath the pilings. Clothed in black wet suits and masks with respirators, they were hauling their gear bags behind them.

Maitland spoke quietly. "Who's that?"

Bolan casually looked away and stretched his arms as he whispered. "The cavalry."

The journalist cocked her head and looked at him blankly.

The Executioner smiled. "The hussars are coming over the hill."

The woman grinned from ear to ear. "Ah."

Bolan picked up a small shell from the sand and skimmed it into the water. "Would you like to help?"

"What is it that you wish me to do?"

He skimmed another shell. "The line of sight from the tree line to the pier is fairly awkward, but I still need to get six men from the pier to the main shed without being spotted. We don't have time to wait until dark. I need a diversion."

Her nose wrinkled as she looked up at him quizzically for a moment. "A...diversion?" She suddenly brightened. "Ah! A distraction!"

"Exactly. Do you think you can manage something?"

"Well, that should be easy enough to do." She lunged forward and planted her lips against Bolan's while she crushed herself against his body and writhed enthusiastically. His eyebrows rose in surprise as she jumped back and faced him with a calculating look in her eyes. With one smooth movement, she pulled her sundress over her head.

Jeanine Maitland wasn't wearing underwear.

She flung the dress at Bolan's head, and, with a giggling shriek, turned and scampered naked into the surf at a full run. She turned a spectacular cartwheel in the shallow water and landed with a tremendous splash. She rose out of the ocean and kicked water at Bolan. He waved a dismissing hand at her and walked back toward the main shed. A clod of wet sand narrowly missed his head as he walked away. Behind him there was another delighted shriek and an even bigger splash.

The soldier suspected the men in the tree line were no longer watching the compound.

RAIZO TANAKA JUMPED from the small, twin-engined plane's cockpit and glanced at the setting sun. The airstrip was abandoned. It seemed no one had wanted to work the runway, and even his pilot hadn't wanted to fly into the Pacific Trust Islands that evening. Only the promise of many yen had gotten Tanaka on the main island before dark.

Hayata Yoritomo and two men stood at the side of the tarmac beside an open-topped Land Rover. Tanaka grabbed his bags from behind his seat and walked over. He bowed with formal stiffness to Hayata. The other man bowed back. Not quite as low, and with a slight amount of casual contempt. "Welcome to the Pacific Trust Islands, Tanaka-*san*. I trust your journey was pleasant."

Tanaka nodded. "What is the situation?"

It was a slight bit of rudeness, but Hayata overlooked it.

"Our intelligence satellites show that over a hundred natives have massed in the forest just beyond the USO Oil compound." He glanced up at the descending sun. "I suspect they will attack quite soon."

"What are the Americans doing?"

The ninja smiled. "Apparently nothing. They either don't realize their situation, or they are cowering in their compound. They have no warships in the area, and satellite surveillance has shown no planes anywhere nearby. It appears they are helpless."

"I suspect the Americans have firearms."

Hayata shrugged. "Oh, undoubtedly. If they manage to kill some natives in the bargain, it will make the American position in the islands even worse."

Tanaka's spirit sank, but he didn't let it show. He almost hoped Hayata Yoritomo's plan would fail. However, he had to give the man credit. The current commander was nothing if not capable. Making it look like the Isolationists had murdered the French and the Americans had been a clever tactic, indeed. Arranging for the natives to actually kill the rest of the Americans and destroy their compound was a stroke of genius.

Tanaka nodded and bowed slightly. "Your plan is excellent."

Hayata gave Tanaka a bland smile and bowed almost imperceptibly in return. "Thank you, Tanaka-*san*. I'm glad you approve."

Tanaka went rigid. It required every ounce of will he had to keep from striking the man. He considered himself Hayata's superior, and both men knew it. However, on this mission, at this moment, Hayata Yoritomo was Tanaka's commander. He wasn't about to forget that. Striking a superior would be suicidal for his position in the corporation. For that matter, it would probably be physically suicidal as well. Tanaka was all too aware of Hayata's martial skill. The man would probably love to cripple Tanaka with his hands or a blade and send him back to the Tokyo headquarters for judgment.

Tanaka pushed his anger deep down within himself. Hayata was in command at the moment. There was nothing to be done about it. The ninja had best pray to the gods that his plan didn't fail. He wouldn't like it when Tanaka was in command. He shrugged inwardly. The two of them were destined to clash. It would be no duel. There would be no ritual combat between them.

When the time came, he would simply shoot Hayata like a dog.

10

Gary Manning looked at his armament, then over at Calvin James, who nodded in sympathy. At first glance, their weapons certainly looked impressive. The 40 mm South African Armscor grenade launcher looked like one of The Untouchables' drum-fed tommy guns on steroids. It wasn't the weapon that had Manning nervous. He had used South African kit before on several occasions, and it was nothing if not reliable.

It was the designated ammunition that was giving him second thoughts.

The Armscor grenade launchers fed semiautomatically through a rotating 8-round cylinder much like a giant revolver. The first three chambers of Manning's weapon, like the rest of the team's, were loaded with CS tear-gas grenades. The next six were loaded with 40 mm nonlethal, antiriot rounds. They were almost an exact copy of the U.S. personal defensive munition, which turned a grenade launcher into a 40 mm shotgun. At close range, the munition's massive buckshot load and wide dispersal pattern sent a lethal wall of lead at the opposition. Manning shook his head grimly. The difference between the U.S. round and the South African rounds he had in his weapon was that the buckshot was rubber rather than lead.

Manning cocked an eyebrow at the Executioner. "How much opposition are we looking at?"

Bolan considered the question as he checked over his own grenade launcher. "I suspect at least a hundred."

"What kind of armament?"

"Automatic rifles, pistols, submachine guns, shotguns,

spears and war clubs." Bolan paused for a moment in thought. "Possibly dynamite and offensive grenades."

Manning nodded as he pondered this information.

He looked over at Calvin James again, and the ex-SEAL shook his head in mock helplessness. It was going to be seven men armed with rubber bullets and irritant gas against more than a hundred fanatics armed to the teeth with stone-age weapons and automatic rifles. Manning looked at McCarter. The Englishman seemed perfectly at ease. He had fought in Ireland and seen many riot situations. Being forced by political constraints to use kid gloves on swarms of armed and dedicated opponents was nothing new to him. He had done it before and won. He would do it again.

Manning looked over the rest of the team. All seven of them wore khaki USO Oil workman's coveralls and caps, and a gas mask hung around each man's neck. They looked awfully militant for oil men, but at a distance and through tear gas they ought to pass at first glance. The real crew was crouched and waiting by the boat shed. If the compound fell, they were to get into the big boat and head for open water while the Stony Man team covered them. Manning looked around. Gadgets Schwarz was strapping extra grenades onto his belt. Lyons squatted in the sand by the corner of the shed and peered at the tree line from between a pair of fuel drums filled with sand. Manning looked over at Hawkins.

The ex-Ranger was squinting at the surf. He shook his head slowly in wonderment as a shriek of glee reached the main shed.

The woman had been out there for nearly half an hour. She was little more than a shadow now that the sun had fallen, but not one member of the team had missed her performance when she had flung herself at Bolan, then danced naked into the sea. Giggling and shrieking still reached the main shed. She seemed to have a great deal of energy. Hawkins looked over at Bolan. He had known for a long time that Mack Bolan was a master of improvisation in battle. Yet even he had taken it to new heights.

The Executioner finished inspecting his weapon and squatted on his heels in the sand. The men from Stony Man gathered around him. "I want to go over this one more time. I know that no one is pleased with this situation. It can't be helped. The rules of engagement stand. I want no lethal force used unless the compound has fallen. However, this isn't a suicide mission, no matter how much it seems like one. If the compound falls, the United States is finished in the islands, in which case we use any force necessary to cover the USO Oil team's escape. The same goes for ourselves—any force necessary to break contact and extract."

Lyons spoke without taking his eyes off of the tree line. "How do you want to run it?"

Bolan drew an arc in the sand with his finger. "By the numbers. The second they come out of the trees, I want a blanket of CS gas around the perimeter. The evening breeze is in our favor, and it should continue to carry the gas into the trees. The opposition shouldn't have any defense against CS other than determination." Bolan looked around the small circle of men. "Expect them to be stubborn. If they keep coming, then it's repel all boarders. I don't want any casualties that can be avoided. Remember, the submunitions in the riot rounds are hard rubber, but they're still leaving the muzzle at over a thousand feet per second. At point-blank range, head shots will be lethal. Keep that in mind. If the fence is down, we fall back to the boat shed, grab our guns and give the natives a dose of the real thing. Once the USO Oil boys are clear, we take the little boat and head out to sea. From there the *Sam Houston* picks us up."

Bolan turned to Gadgets Schwarz. "Your little surpass is ready?"

Schwarz nodded. "It's not quite the surprise it could be, but it's ready."

"Go over it with Redland one more time to make sure."

He rose to his feet. "You got it."

Bolan looked around at the men in his command. "Any questions?"

Hawkins jerked his head toward the beach and grinned. Jeanine Maitland could still be heard frolicking in the surf. "Yeah. How do I get involved in your next diversion?"

The men laughed. Bolan shook his head at the young soldier. "I'm sorry, T.J., but we've all seen you naked. It's not much of a distraction."

James slapped Hawkins on the back as the men continued to laugh. As usual, their situation was precarious, and, as usual, morale was high. The Executioner rose and pointed to a line of metal drums and barrels they had filled with sand to make bullet stops. "All right. Let's get those barrels into position."

James stood and stretched his lanky frame. "Where're you headed, Striker?"

Bolan turned toward the water. "I have to go retrieve our secret weapon."

JEANINE MAITLAND STOOD in the ankle-deep water and smiled coyly at Bolan as he approached. "Tell me, was I distracting enough?"

"The United States Marines could have landed, and no one would have noticed."

She grinned victoriously and scooped her dress off the beach and shook the sand out of it. Her smile faded slightly in the gloom. "It will come soon, no?"

Bolan looked up at the darkening sky and could begin to make out stars. "Any time now. You need to get undercover. I want you at the boat shed with the rest of the USO crew. If they bug out, you go with them."

Maitland pulled her dress over her head and grabbed her sandals. As she drew close, Bolan could see a deep frown line between her brows. "Do you think you can win?"

"I don't know. It will depend on how determined our friends out there really are. After the ambush at the airstrip, they know we have small arms. If they're still going to attack, then they'll be expecting some kind of resistance. But there's no way they're expecting what we have waiting for them. If we can break their will to fight, they just might disperse without any casualties. If not..." Bolan let the sentence trail away. "You just make sure you're on that boat when it launches."

She looked up at him for a long moment. "You make sure you're careful." She stood close and leaned up on her toes to reach Bolan's face. There was nothing flirting or coy about the way she kissed him. It was slow, and it lingered. She suddenly leaned back from him and turned on her grin again as she squeezed his arms.

"For luck."

Bolan squeezed her arms back. "We need to get back, now."

The Executioner's hand slipped under his arm to the Beretta 93-R's shoulder rig. A deafening roar rose out of the tree line as an army of men raised their voices as one in a blood curdling war cry. Bolan seized Jeanine Maitland's hand.

"Run!"

BULLETS KICKED UP the sand all around them as Bolan tackled Maitland behind one of the USO Oil jeeps for cover. Carl Lyons was a few yards away behind a makeshift barricade of sand-filled fuel barrels. He tossed Bolan his grenade launcher and a bandoleer of spare grenades. Lyons flicked the safety off his own launcher and watched the Executioner patiently for the signal.

Bullets flew everywhere. From under the jeep, Bolan could see the tree line lit up with orange strobing from the scores of firing weapons. The prefab sheds of the compound rattled on their frames as hundreds of bullets tore through the thin aluminum walls. The Stony Man warriors hunched in their positions as the storm of lead screamed all around them. The jeep Bolan and Maitland hid behind shuddered as bullet after bullet struck it. The Isolationists were emptying their weapons in a massive salvo of gunfire.

The lethal hailstorm stopped as suddenly as it had began, and for a moment a deafening silence fell over the beach. The only sound was the gentle rolling of the surf. In the trees, a weird harmony of clicking and metallic ratcheting noises began. The natives were reloading their weapons en masse. Bolan whispered in Maitland's ear. "When I give the signal, you stay low and run for the boat shed. Keep the jeep between you and the tree line. The boat shed has a concrete foundation. Stay underneath the steps with the USO crew. If Red says it's time to go, you go."

The woman swallowed and nodded.

Another war cry rose like thunder. Dozens of armed men erupted from the trees, and the war cry was extended to a charging roar. The Executioner's voice rang across the compound with the unmistakable thunder of command.

"Hit them!"

Seven 40 mm grenade launchers began their barrage, together in rapid semiautomatic fire. Bolan's weapon recoiled into his shoulder as he rose and fired over the hood of the jeep. He snarled at Maitland.

"Move!"

The journalist scrambled on all fours in a mad dash toward the boat shed. Yellow flame roared from the launcher's 40 mm maw as Bolan fired again. He shot his third round and lowered his sights. In less than two seconds, twenty-one 40 mm CS canisters hit the sand in front of the charging mob. The grenades were triple chasers, and as they hit they broke into three separate components that skittered and hissed across the sand, shooting out plumes of thick white gas. The natives came in a wave. They hit the gas cloud, firing their weapons as they moved in. For a moment, they disappeared in the smoke. The Executioner shouted over his shoulder.

"Red! Lights!"

The compound's floodlights snapped on and threw their harsh glare across the sand as Redland cranked the circuit breaker. The Isolationists charged through the smoke and into the light. Some of them staggered, and their war cry turned ragged as the burning gas seared their lungs and throats. But they kept coming, leading with bursts from their weapons.

The Stony Man warriors had arranged their positions in a

rough triangle. As they lowered the sights of their launchers, their positions formed interlocking fire lanes. Bolan roared as the natives moved in.

"Hit them!"

The Executioner tracked a group of men as they charged the fence. All of them were heavily armed. Most carried rifles or submachine guns and had machetes strapped to their backs. Others had a spear or a war club in one hand and a handgun in the other. Some even ran with burning torches. Bolan took aim. Most of the rubber buckshot would be deflected as he fired directly through the chain link, but each munition held twenty-seven beads of buckshot firing out of a 40 mm muzzle. Deflection would be minimal and the patterns wide. As the natives came into range Bolan fired.

The lead man jerked and fell as he took the brunt of the rubber buckshot in the chest. The three men behind him staggered as they were hit by the outer edge of the pattern, then fell as Carl Lyons hit them square on. More shapes emerged from the gas cloud, and Bolan fired. The shapes staggered but kept on. The Executioner grimaced. The rubber buckshot began to lose too much velocity and became ineffective past the fence.

They were going to have to let the Isolationists get closer.

The rest of the team had figured that out as well, and for a moment the hollow booming of their launchers fell silent. The ragged chattering of the natives' weapons continued as they charged. Bolan snapped the stock of his launcher up to his cheek as he sighted. As the natives approached, seven 40 mm grenade launchers suddenly exploded into a sustained roar of synchronized semiautomatic fire.

The natives rushed headfirst into a point-blank cross fire.

Men screamed and fell as the swarms of buckshot hit them. The natives who didn't fall beneath the onslaught staggered backward only to retreat into the clouds of thick, choking gas. Bolan's voice roared over the sound of battle.

"Cease-fire!"

Most of the team had fired their weapons dry already. Bolan

quickly scanned their positions. All six men gave him the thumbs-up. The Executioner broke open the launcher's cylinder breech and began rapidly reloading as he shouted commands. "Load six CS gas, three buck!"

The men from Stony Man Farm reloaded their weapons with smooth efficiency. The Executioner snapped his cylinder shut. "Red! You all right?"

Redland shouted from behind the raised concrete foundation of the boat shed. "We're all right, Belasko! What's happening?"

"Round one is over, Red, but sit tight! It isn't over yet!"

Bolan looked at Carl Lyons, who shrugged. "You think they'll hit us again?"

The soldier nodded. "I'd bet on it."

Lyons smiled with rare humor. "They do seem feisty."

The Executioner raised his weapon's muzzle higher as he calculated the distance. "I want to hit them in the tree line! Three rounds rapid! Now!"

Dull booms roared as the 40 mm weapons arced their payloads high into the air. The projectiles crashed through the treetops skirting the beach. Piercing hisses arose among startled and angry shouts as the skip-chaser tear gas grenades broke apart and began emitting white gas among the hidden natives. The angry shouts turned to war cries.

Bolan shouted over them. "Three more rounds into the perimeter cloud. Hit it!"

The team lowered its aim and fired rapidly into the widening cloud across the sand. The war cries turned into the roar of the charge. Bolan and the rest of the Stony Man team broke open their weapons and loaded the cylinders with buckshot rounds as the shapes of charging men surged through the gas cloud.

The Isolationists burst into the clearing in front of the fence. There were a lot more of them this time, and the Executioner didn't believe they were holding back any reserve. This charge was more massive, but slower. The native warriors had been forced to charge through fifty yards of CS gas. Some of them had already been exposed on the first advance, and many of them were reeling as they cleared the gas. Their eyes would be watering and their lungs and throats would be burning, but they continued on with grim determination. Those who could breathe raised a ragged roar of defiance as they came on.

The Executioner shouted over the howling horde. "Let them have it! Fire at will!"

The launchers boomed one after the other as the Stony Man team cut loose. The men leading the charge withered and fell, but the ones behind pressed on. Groups of natives charged, firing their weapons as they ran, but the gas had taken its toll and their aim was hindered by their burning eyes and choking lungs.

The Stony Man team was efficient.

Bolan grimaced as he methodically aimed and fired. Men reeled and fell beneath the swarms of rubber buckshot, but more kept pouring out of the gas cloud. Many of the team's launchers had fallen silent as the men rapidly fed fresh shells into the smoking breeches. Bolan's own weapon cycled dry and the natives closed. There were too many of them. They were going to reach the fence. Bolan crouched behind the jeep and stuffed fresh rounds into his launcher as bullets screamed all around. He roared to make himself heard over the barrage.

"Gadgets!"

Schwarz looked up as he reloaded without stopping what he was doing. Metal link suddenly rattled and shrieked with strain as a wave of bodies hit the fence. Bolan snapped his weapon shut and nodded at Gadgets the Able Team commando.

"Do it!"

Schwarz shouted at the top of his lungs. "Hit it, Redland!"

Sparks flew all along the fence, and the compound's floodlights pulsed and dimmed as the air filled with the sudden smell of burning ozone. It had taken Schwarz all of six minutes to rig a wire from the compound generator through a transformer to the perimeter fencing. The voltage was high enough to give a nasty shock, burn hands and rattle jaws, but the current level wasn't high enough to be lethal. Redland controlled the switch from the boat shed. Along the fence, men screamed and jerked as their hands locked convulsively in the links. The floodlights brightened as the Texan cut the pulse of electricity, and men fell away from the fence. The assault had ground to a halt as the natives began to pick up their comrades who had been beaten down by the buckshot or jerked and shivered with the aftereffects of the electricity. All of them were choking and gagging from the CS tear gas.

They had stopped them, but Bolan couldn't allow them to regroup and attack again. They had to be beaten. The Executioner rose with his launcher fully loaded with buckshot.

"Hit them!"

The team opened fire into the milling mob. Some of the natives tried to drag their fallen comrades away. Most broke and ran back into the choking gas. Others simply fell. The combination of the choking gas and the savage beating of riot ammunition was too much. The men from Stony Man shot anyone who was still standing or moving forward. In seconds, they had fired their weapons dry. The muzzles of their weapons radiated heat, and smoke poured from their chambers. The only sound was the moaning and the choking of the fallen. Bolan spoke clearly across the compound.

"Red! Cut the lights!"

A moment passed, and the floodlights dimmed and went out. The beach was suddenly plunged into darkness. Bolan gingerly reloaded his smoking weapon by touch in the dark. He could hear Lyons moving stealthily to his position. The Able Team leader spoke low in the dark beside him. "On your left, Striker."

Bolan reached out his hand, and Lyons handed him a pair of night-vision goggles. He strapped the goggles over his face and hit the power switch. The night suddenly lit up in flat tones of gray and green. Bolan stood and looked around. All six members of the team were up and had their night-vision equipment on and their weapons ready. The Executioner surveyed the battlefield.

11

It was nearly eleven o'clock in the morning when the local investigation came. By dawn, there hadn't been a single native left on the beach. Thousands of small, gray, hard rubber balls littered the sand, and the morning air still smelled sulfurous from the massive concentration of the CS gas. Spent brass shell casings lay glittering all the way to the tree line. Except for the Executioner, the men from Stony Man Farm were long gone and already back aboard the U.S.S. *Sam Houston.* Bolan had run a dawn recon of the forest edge and found that the natives were nowhere near the compound. He and the USO Oil crew had gathered nearly fifty fallen small arms from the beach and stored them in the hold of the small boat. By eight o'clock they had begun repairing the compound facility.

At 10:48 a.m., a Land Rover, whose hood mounted two small twin flags of the Pacific Trust Islands, pulled up in front of the compound gate. A large native man wearing a Western-style blue suit emerged, flanked by two native constables wearing sarongs and bright white jackets. The constables kept their French-made MAT-49 submachine guns slung and stared curiously at the ocean of hard rubber balls and spent shells they were standing in.

Mack Bolan walked up to the gate dressed in a USO Oil coverall and smiled politely at the big man in the suit. The man's bulk strained the seams of his suit, and he was already sweating in the heat. He took off his sunglasses with great ceremony and looked at Bolan sternly. "I am Solomon Fala-hola, deputy minister of security of the Pacific Trust Islands."

The Executioner inclined his head respectfully. "Thank God you're here."

The deputy minister's eyes widened momentarily. "Yes, I understand there has been a disturbance here, and the illegal use and possession of firearms has been reported."

Bolan nodded. "Yes, we were attacked by an armed mob last night. The compound has been extensively damaged."

The Executioner spread his arm expansively at the compound behind him. The prefabricated sheds were riddled and torn with bullet holes. Falahola grunted begrudgingly. "Yes, it appears you were attacked. I hope none of your people were killed or injured."

"No, luckily, myself and the men managed to escape harm."

The deputy minister's eyes slitted. "Remarkable. How did you manage to defend yourselves?"

Bolan looked at Falahola earnestly. "USO Oil is very aware of your government's policy about the use and ownership of firearms on the island."

Falahola's eyes threatened to disappear as they narrowed further. "I believe myself and my men will have to search your compound for illegal weapons. I must warn you, if any are found, the owners of the contraband will face stiff penalties and possible imprisonment. We won't have foreigners flouting our laws."

Bolan nodded. "I understand perfectly. However, I don't believe that will be necessary, Deputy Minister."

Falahola's eyes widened. Bolan continued before he could speak.

"I'll be happy to show you our armament."

"Very well. I'm noting your cooperation, but I won't be able to turn a blind eye if you have broken island law."

Bolan nodded as humbly as he was able. "Of course. Please, follow me."

Bolan led the man and his constables to the middle of the compound. Redland and the rest of the crew looked up from their repairs, smiled and nodded pleasantly at the constables and the deputy minister. In the middle of the compound, USO Oil's one remaining, functioning jeep was parked with a tarp across its hood. On the tarp were four single-barrel police tear-gas launchers that the Stony Man team had brought with them from San Diego. Two bandoleers of grenades lay coiled beside them. Deputy Minister Falahola stared down at them for a moment expressionlessly. "Exactly what kind of weapons are these?"

Bolan pointed at several of the loose CS canisters on the hood. "Gas guns."

The deputy minister blinked. "Gas guns?"

The soldier nodded. "Oh, yes. As I said, we at USO Oil know and respect your laws regarding firearms. However, as you know, there have been attacks on USO employees, and there has been anti-U.S. rioting in the islands. The company thought it best to equip their compound with a nonlethal response. The launchers can throw tear gas and rubber buckshot out to some distance."

Falahola's eyes slitted again. Bolan had expected whoever came wouldn't be pleased at the way the island laws had been circumvented. The Executioner spread his hands ingratiatingly.

"My men and I were attacked, sir, and, facing imminent injury or death. We felt compelled to defend ourselves. Luckily, no one was seriously injured or killed. However, I can understand your position. Clearly, we have stepped into a legal gray area." Bolan pointed at the bandoleer of grenades. "Perhaps it would be for the best if you confiscated the weapons and their ammunition."

The deputy minster looked where Bolan was pointing. Several of the bandoleer's cartridge loops were empty of grenades, and the corners of several thick wads of green American bills were subtly visible. Falahola nodded thoughtfully and picked up the bandoleer. His left eyebrow raised as he noted how thick the rolls of money were. The tops were slightly fanned out in one corner to allow the denominations to be easily visible as well, and the deputy minister's right eyebrow shot up to join the left one. Falahola smoothly coiled the bandoleer and motioned his constables to take the remaining weapons.

"Of course, I must confiscate these weapons, as they might be evidence in a possible crime. This will bear further investigation. However, as I have said, I have noted your cooperation. I'm pleased that none of your employees were injured in the unpleasantness, and, for now, I'm not going to detain or charge any of your employees until I have looked into the matter further."

Bolan nodded and smiled. "Thank you, Deputy Minister. Please rest assured that you will have USO Oil's complete cooperation in any investigation you deem required."

Falahola put his sunglasses back on as his men gathered the grenade launchers. He stared at Bolan for a moment and spoke in his most authoritative voice.

"Have a nice day."

RAIZO TANAKA LOOKED at Hayata Yoritomo blandly. The older man sat at his desk and looked into space with an expression of total incomprehension. The situation was unbelievable. Tokyo headquarters had relayed satellite reconnaissance data throughout the night, and the film showed signs of a major battle at the USO Oil site. There had been numerous heat flares, the satellite's cameras had shown waves of figures attacking the compound and the lights of the compound had pulsed and then gone off. The evidence appeared to show the American oil crew fending off the siege.

That was fairly incredible, yet Hayata had allowed for the fact that the Americans might repulse the attack. However, he'd engineered the situation so that even if they survived, they'd lose the war and be thrown out of the islands.

Hayata had sent men to the main island that morning, and they had reported back. He shook his head again. Their findings were beyond reason. No one seemed to be dead. The hospital wasn't flooded with corpses and wounded. The rest of the native population wasn't up in arms. In fact, the main island had been eerily quiet. His men had driven by the USO

Oil compound, and they had watched an official's car leaving. Inside were only the deputy minister and a pair of constables. They didn't seem to have arrested anyone. As Hayata's men had passed the compound, they had seen USO Oil employees effecting repairs. The compound appeared shot up, but none of the crew looked wounded.

According to his agents, most of them had been observed smiling while they worked.

Hayata stared into the distance. It defied comprehension. His plan had been perfect, but he had failed.

Tanaka modulated his voice to one of artificial politeness. "Is something wrong, Yoritomo-*san?* May I be of assistance?"

The man stared at him, and his eyebrows drew together in rage. Tanaka almost beamed. To make this self-styled samurai lose his composure was a victory beyond price.

Hayata's knuckles whitened, and he stared at Tanaka for several long moments as he visibly reined in his temper. When he spoke his voice was utterly cold. "The plan has failed." His cheek muscles clenched as he spit out the words. "I don't know how."

Tanaka nodded with immense sympathy. "Ah, Yoritomo-*san.* The fortunes of war. They can turn against anyone."

Hayata locked eyes with the younger man with renewed rage. Tanaka looked back unflinchingly. The facts were the facts. Hayata had failed. They both knew it. They regarded each other for a moment until a polite knocking came from the door. The ninja broke their gaze and grunted at the door. "Enter."

Toda Tatsuo entered the command, and the stout communications man looked nervous. He bowed quickly and handed Hayata a telex. He read the message and became as motionless as a statue. After a long moment, he held out the paper to Tanaka without meeting his eyes.

The younger man took it. He had to restrain himself from grinning. The message was short and simple. Tanaka was to take command of paramilitary operations in the Pacific Trust

Islands. Hayata Yoritomo was to be second in command. Tanaka's dual mission was to be the same as it was before he had been one-upped by Hayata. He had to secure the oil development rights of the Pacific Trust Islands for the Kanabo Corporation by whatever means necessary, and he was to kill the American commando and bring his head to Yabe.

Tanaka nodded and handed the telex back to Tatsuo. "Thank you, Tatsuo-*san*. Communicate to headquarters that their orders are confirmed."

Tatsuo bowed. "Yes, Tanaka-*san*, immediately."

The new commander turned to Hayata and eyed him critically. Hayata Yoritomo had failed. He had been demoted. Nevertheless, the man was an extremely useful tool. Tanaka would utilize his skills to their full potential to accomplish his mission. To Tanaka, the situation was very simple. Somehow, the American commando had saved the USO Oil crew. The man would continue being their shield until he was eliminated.

MACK BOLAN DROVE the surviving jeep into town as the sun dipped into late afternoon. Jeanine Maitland rode beside him, with Chris Racine in the back. The island was very quiet as they pulled up in front of her hotel. Bolan glanced up and down the street. A few people were out on their porches, and the sound of music came from the radio in the bar. A storm had been weathered. Bolan turned to Jeanine.

"Are you sure you'll be all right by yourself? You're welcome to stay at the compound."

The woman smiled. "No, but thank you. I don't think I'm in too much danger now. The Isolationists don't consider me an enemy. I have written several sympathetic pieces about their cause. Last night, during an attack, a white woman might have been a target. Today..." She shrugged. "I don't think so. Besides, if I take up residence at your compound, it might tarnish my journalistic credibility, no?"

"You're probably right, but be careful anyway."

She nodded. "Oh, I will, and you, too." She suddenly grabbed his arm. "When will I see you again?"

"I'm going to go talk to Dr. Tutarotaro this afternoon, and there's still a lot of work to be done on the compound."

"Yes, I have a great deal of writing to do as well. How about tomorrow evening?"

"I can't promise."

"Well, then, tomorrow evening or the next." She leaned over and kissed him quickly. "You let me know."

"I will."

The two men watched her walk into her hotel. Racine shook his head. "Man, you have a hell of a lot more self-control than I do. I'd be in there right now."

Bolan put the jeep in Park. "I'm not here to go on dates, Chris. I'm here on business."

"Yeah, but she's one hell of a perk."

"She is." The Executioner got out of the vehicle. "This is the plan. I'm going to go have a talk with the doctor. I want you to hang around outside as unobtrusively as possible. If an army of angry natives comes down the street, you let me know. For that matter, let me know about anything suspicious. All right?"

Racine tapped the tarp in back of the jeep that covered his M-2 carbine. "I've got your back covered."

Bolan handed Racine the keys. "You be careful."

DR. TUTAROTARO LOOKED UP, startled, as Bolan entered his office. He stared at the Executioner inscrutably, then slowly rose and extended his hand. "Good afternoon, Mr. Belasko."

Bolan shook the offered hand. "How are you today, Doctor?"

The doctor sighed and sank his large frame back into his chair. "I'm very tired."

"A long day?"

Tutarotaro looked at Bolan again for a long moment. "Yes. I have had a very long day. I've made many, many house calls. I have seen more massive contusions, blunt trauma bruising and minor respiratory complaints today than I have seen in my entire career in medicine."

Bolan nodded. "I can imagine."

The doctor's dark eyes watched Bolan like a hawk. "Frankly, I'm of two minds about you, Mr. Belasko."

The soldier met his gaze. "How so?"

"On one count, I must offer you my thanks."

Bolan's expression didn't change. "For what?"

"For not killing my people. Scores of them would've died if you had engaged them with gunfire when they had attacked."

Bolan shrugged. "Much of that was self-serving, Doctor. If I had slaughtered dozens of your countrymen, USO Oil would be history in these islands. However I'm glad it was done without a lot of bloodshed. I believe I can sympathize with the way some of your people feel."

Tutarotaro's face went cold. "If that is so, then why did you assassinate Komo Malua?"

Bolan's eyes widened slightly. He knew the name Komo Malua from the briefing files Barbara Price had given him. Malua was thought to be a leader of the Isolationist Movement, and he was highly respected among his people. Bolan looked at Tutarotaro flatly. "I didn't kill him."

The doctor looked at him without blinking. After a moment he spoke. "I'm tempted to believe you, Mr. Belasko. However, you seem to be a very talented man. I would be a fool to believe you are not talented at hiding the truth as well."

"When was he killed?"

Tutarotaro looked carefully at Bolan. "Two nights ago, during a meeting in the forest. He was killed with an American revolver. His attacker shouted his motive, saying it was revenge for your former chief of operations, Mr. Skip Porter. The attacker had an American accent."

Bolan raised an eyebrow. "That was the same day you and I had our discussion in the morgue. Based on what we discussed, it would seem foolish of me to go out the same night and assassinate one of your people."

Tutarotaro nodded slowly. "I've considered that. That is why I didn't shoot you when you came through the door."

Bolan looked at the doctor bluntly. "Thank you."

"Don't thank me yet." Tutarotaro locked gazes with Bolan again. "I don't know for sure what games you Americans might be playing in our islands. I'm an old man, and there is much I don't know. But I will tell you this. Komo Malua and I had our differences of opinions, but we were friends almost since birth. If I genuinely believed you had killed him, I would kill you."

Bolan saw the stern resolve in the old man's eyes and felt the calm power of his manner. It wasn't an idle threat. The Executioner accepted the statement at face value. "I didn't kill Komo Malua. But I thank you for talking with me first, regardless."

The doctor nodded thoughtfully. Bolan changed the subject. "I assume last night's siege was the reaction to Mr. Malua's death."

"Indeed. Many people are upset about it. Even those who are opposed to the Isolationist Movement are very angry."

"How was it done?"

The doctor leaned back in his chair. "Very efficiently. Someone managed to make his way past the sentries during a night meeting and shoot Malua between the eyes with a handgun. The assassin then managed to evade pursuit and escape. Malua's men found the empty gun where it had been dropped. The attack was…commando-like.

"There are a number of individuals in these islands who might match that description."

The doctor conceded the point. "That is true."

"A professional wouldn't leave his weapon behind."

"Mistakes, happen, Mr. Belasko, even among professionals."

"A professional would also be unlikely to announce his presence by shouting and giving away who he represented."

Tutarotaro folded his arms across his chest. "You believe these things were done deliberately to start an incident."

"It seems likely."

The doctor grunted as he shifted in his chair. "I have considered that as well."

Bolan folded his own arms. "What do you intend to do?"

Tutarotaro's eyes hardened. "What do *you* intend to do?"

The Executioner considered his answer. He believed the doctor was a brave and honest man, but he wasn't particularly an ally of the Americans or their cause in the islands. His personal beliefs would dictate his actions. Bolan decided on the direct approach. "I intend to put an end to the killing of American citizens in these islands."

The doctor nodded. "And what of USO Oil's bid for the development rights?"

"If the USO Oil crew can win them, I'll be happy, but that is not why I'm here."

Bolan let the exact meaning of that sink in for a moment. He looked at the doctor levelly. "What do you intend to do?"

Tutarotaro let out a long, slow breath. "I intend to speak with my people, at least to those who will listen. I wish to stop the killing as well. I'll tell them I don't believe you killed Komo Malua."

"You could get yourself in trouble taking our side."

The doctor nodded. "I'm in trouble by talking to you now. But I'm not specifically taking your side. It would be best for you to remember that. My allegiance is to my people. However, I'm aware of the French's behavior in our islands, and, like you, I have my suspicions about the Japanese. I want the killings stopped, and I want the man who murdered Komo Malua."

Bolan nodded and rose. "We both do."

Tutarotaro rose and extended his hand again. "That was a humiliating defeat you inflicted on our warriors. Most of them are glad to be alive, but they won't thank you for it. I don't think they'll attack your compound again, but as individuals, you and your men had best be careful when you are outside it."

"I'll keep that in mind."

Bolan left the doctor's office and found Racine sitting in

the back of the jeep. Across the street two native men were staring at him. Both men wore shirts and sarongs, but the garments didn't hide the brutal mottling of bruises purpling their arms and legs. The two men's eyes narrowed as Bolan emerged from the clinic, and they turned and limped away painfully in stony silence.

Racine turned to Bolan and shrugged. "I don't think we made any friends last night."

The Executioner glanced back at the clinic. "I think we might have made at least one."

12

Hayata Yoritomo stood at attention. It galled him to be taking orders from Raizo Tanaka. The man didn't come from a good family. Other than his loyalty to the Kanabo Corporation, which Hayata didn't question, Tanaka didn't strike him as a man of strict honor. He had allowed Mr. Ito to die, and for that the ninja would never forgive him. Tanaka had only one saving grace in Hayata's mind, though it pained him to admit it.

The man was brilliant.

He was also enjoying giving Hayata orders. Tanaka leaned back in the chair Hayata had once occupied in the command shed. "I want this American dead."

The older man nodded. "Yes."

Tanaka steepled his fingers in thought. "We don't have the time to wait for him to carelessly expose himself or make a mistake. Frankly, I don't believe he will do such a thing."

Hayata nodded again. He believed this much was obvious.

"Nor do I like the idea of attacking him in his own compound. I want the time and the place to be of our own choosing." He suddenly looked over at Hayata. "I believe we must create our own opportunity with this American."

Hayata considered that. "Perhaps we should use the Maitland woman. She was with him in the bar, and she was there when the compound was besieged by the natives. If he has grown attached to her, she could be used as a weapon against him."

"I have considered that as well, Yoritomo-*san*. Like us, this man is a professional. He is fighting for his country. Neither you nor I would allow a woman to interfere with our mission here. The thought is ludicrous. We must give our opponent at least as much credit as we give ourselves. This is basic strategy. I would've assumed you knew these things.''

Hayata's face didn't change expression, but he grew even more rigid in his stance. "You have a plan, Tanaka-*san*."

Tanaka scratched his chin. "As I have said, he's a professional. He's obviously here on a mission. To lure him out, we must give him something that he'll think is vital to accomplishing it. For that, he will come, and probably alone so as not to endanger his countrymen."

Hayata nodded. "That is undoubtedly true, Tanaka-*san*. Even so, as you have said, he is a professional and has proved himself highly capable. Even if he doesn't suspect a trap, he'll enter any situation relating to his mission in a high state of readiness."

"That is true. However, I have gone over the patterns of his movements on the island. I believe I have an idea as to how we might get to him. His state of readiness is immaterial to me." Tanaka suddenly locked eyes with Hayata. "If my plan works, and I can get this man to expose his weakness, I will simply rely on your superior skills to kill him, Yoritomo-*san*."

The ninja blinked, then instantly regained his composure. It would be a great honor for him to kill the American commando. Of course, Tanaka, as the commander of the operation, would take credit for the man's death. Hayata would simply be the sword with which he did it. But his actions would be noted, and to be the one who actually struck the killing blow to the man who killed Mr. Ito was a priceless gift.

Hayata nodded. "Tell me how you wish this to be done."

RENÉ SAUVIN STOOD BY the test derrick's rail and nodded into the phone as he listened. He was pleased with what he heard. He believed his plan just might work. ZeeZee sat behind him on the desk, finishing the reassembly of a .45-caliber Ingram

MAC-10 submachine gun he had been cleaning. He worked the bolt several times and grunted with satisfaction as the well-oiled action slid smoothly back and forth. ZeeZee was something of an expert with submachine guns, and he was particularly fond of the MAC-10. He liked its compact size and concealibility, and he was very fond of the big American .45-caliber bullets it threw. It wasn't a battlefield weapon, but in the kind of operations he engaged in, he found the weapon unsurpassed. The little Frenchman picked up the sound suppressor and screwed it onto the threaded barrel of the compact weapon. He glanced around at his commander.

After a moment Sauvin nodded into the phone. "Yes, excellent. We shall go ahead with the plan." The big man snapped the cellular phone shut.

ZeeZee looked up at him expectantly. "It's done?"

Sauvin slipped the phone into the pocket of his fatigue shorts and punched his fist into his palm. "It's done. We will be receiving reinforcements shortly. I believe you know Denys and Hubert."

ZeeZee smiled happily. He knew them well. They had served together under Sauvin in North Africa. "And what of our friend, the American?"

Sauvin folded his arms across his chest. "We have received permission to go ahead with our plan and find out whatever he knows. We're authorized to use whatever means we find expedient, short of maiming or killing him. We're warned to remember that America is still an ally of France." He raised a cautioning eyebrow at his right-hand man. "I want you to remember that, ZeeZee, and temper your enthusiasm during our interrogation accordingly."

ZeeZee put his hands to his chest and made a show of looking hurt. Sauvin snorted and waved a dismissing hand at him. "All right, just no blows to the skull if they can be avoided. We need his brains in his head if we're to learn anything of significance."

ZeeZee nodded and changed the subject. "Tell me, how soon may we expect to get our reinforcements. I don't like being short-handed like this. Those Japanese, they give me the creeps. I don't trust them."

Sauvin frowned. The Japanese made him uneasy as well. More so than he would care to admit. French Intelligence knew very little about Japanese covert operations and even less about their operatives. What he had learned about them in his briefing back in Paris wouldn't fill a brochure. Sauvin, himself, would be much happier when he had a full strike team armed and ready at his command.

"We can expect reinforcements within the week. Our men's papers must be in order as they are joining us as new workers for the derrick."

The little Frenchman suddenly grinned and exposed his missing teeth. "And when do we deal with this American?"

Sauvin grinned back. "Soon."

FATA LAHONA WEARILY DRAGGED his outrigger onto the beach. The day's attempt at fishing had been a joke. His whole body ached from the beating it had taken in the previous night's attack on the USO Oil compound. He had charged fearlessly through the gas and the horrendous beating of the rubber buckshot. He had reached the fence and begun climbing it with his father's war club slung over his shoulder and a Russian-made Tokarev pistol in his hand when the electrical current had hit him through the fence. His fingers and toes had locked in the chain link, and he had jerked and twisted uncontrollably five feet off the ground. He hadn't even realized the electricity had been turned off until he fell trembling to the sand. He had barely managed to rise to his feet when a hailstorm of rubber buckshot had beaten him senseless to the ground again. He had lain helpless for hours in the sand outside the compound among dozens of his stricken countrymen. Around three o'clock in the morning he had regained enough strength to crawl away into the darkness.

This day massive bruises covered his powerful limbs and torso, and his eyes were still red and puffy from the gas. The glare off the water gave him a blinding headache. His hands were still tender from the electrical current in the fence, and paddling his canoe had been torture. Lahona leaned a moment on his outrigger and took several pained breaths.

He rose and took his father's war club from the floor of the canoe and ran a hand down its polished length. It was nearly five feet long, with one end opening into the carved, paddle shape of the war god's snarling face. Lahona considered the demon visage. Perhaps he should go and speak with the doctor. Many in the Isolationist Movement discounted him. Some even spoke out directly against him. He gave medical treatment to foreigners and natives equally. But Tutarotaro was old and wise. He had been to Europe and the Americas. He counseled against violence. He had spread the word this day that he didn't believe the Americans had killed Komo Malua. At first, it had seemed an outrage, but as Lahona had thought about these things out on the water, the more it had made sense. He nodded to himself. He would speak with him.

Something moved in his peripheral vision.

A man had emerged from among the palm trees. He was a small man, much smaller than Lahona. He was clothed from head to toe in a garment of swirled khaki green and sandy hues. What caught the native's attention most was the black automatic weapon he held in his hands. The muzzle was pointed straight at Lahona's midriff.

Lahona was dead, and he knew it. He had lost his pistol in the battle with the Americans, and even if he still had it in the boat, he would never be able to reach it. This strange gunman could kill him whenever he wanted. Adrenaline filled Lahona, and he regarded his opponent with total scorn. The other night he had been prepared to die like a warrior. He found he was still prepared now, and that pleased him. As the hooded man raised his weapon to his shoulder, Lahona rose up on one leg in the first step of the war dance and raised his other leg gracefully before him. Balanced on one leg, he raised his father's war club overhead and widened his eyes and stuck his tongue out as far as he was able to demonstrate his power.

The gunman lowered his submachine gun and placed it

carefully on the ground. The man stood again and bowed deeply to him. It was then Lahona noticed the handle protruding from behind the man's right shoulder.

As the man stood, the sword came out of its scabbard with a swift rasp.

Lahona let out a thunderous roar and exploded across the sand.

HAYATA YORITOMO WAS FILLED with surprised delight as the big native bore down on him. Faced with imminent death, this half-naked savage had shown true bushido, the spirit of the warrior. Hayata had seen the natives dance and had known it was a dance designed for war. The man now charged him with all the grace, speed and power of the war dance in his every step. The man was also doing the ninja a favor. If he had to shoot the man, then he'd have to go to the trouble of butchering him to hide the gunshot wound. Now he could kill the man properly in honorable battle. Hayata took his stance with his sword high over his head in both hands and received the big man's charge.

The native man surprised him by skidding short and swinging his club low in a one-handed, extended sweep that scythed at knee level. The ninja leaped nimbly over the reaping attack and brought his sword straight down in a wicked arc. Hayata's own piercing battle cry rang out as he brought his blade down with immense precision and power directly to the top of Fata Lahona's forehead.

The blade sheared through Lahona's skull and nearly reached his jaw before it stopped. Hayata slid the blade free, stepped away and resheathed his sword before Lahona's body hit the ground.

Tanaka's plan was excellent, and it was working like a charm.

13

Mack Bolan knelt in the sand and patched into his comm link. He keyed in a few coded letters and numbers, and the brief-case-sized transmitter hurled its signal into space. A Pentagon communications satellite in high orbit over the Pacific Ocean received the signal and rebounded it across the arc of the planet's horizon. In Virginia, Barbara Price picked up immediately.

"Hello, Striker."

"What have you got for me?"

"Well, for one thing, the Man is pleased with you."

"He was watching?"

"No, he just read Hal's report. But most of us here at the Farm were. Even by satellite camera, it was very impressive. Though, to be honest, I didn't like the idea when Aaron told me what you were going to do. My vote was to extract."

"Thanks for the confidence."

"I'm sorry, Striker, but as mission controller here on the Farm, I don't see riot control as part of our operational agenda. That's—"

"What the Marines are for." Bolan chuckled softly for a moment, then his voice grew more serious. "What's the international situation?"

Price sighed. "Mostly, more of the same. The United Nations continues to wrangle over what to do. They're supposed to have some say in affairs around here, but they don't have any peacekeeping troops in the islands. As a voting member, France has vetoed the deployment of any multinational peacekeepers. However, their aircraft carrier the *Foch* should be steaming around the Cape Horn as we speak. Ostensibly for routine maneuvers around French Tahiti.''

''What about the Japanese?''

''They're being very quiet.''

''Listen, I need Gadgets here on the beach for about a day. Can you get me that?''

Price paused. ''We already bent the rules sending in half the Farm for your siege situation. I don't know how the boss will feel about deploying personnel again.''

The soldier drew a circle in the sand as he looked at the compound. ''I need him for one night, tops. The next time this place gets hit, I don't think its going to be by hordes of natives, obliging us by charging right down our gun sights. Japanese, native, or French, the next attack we take is going to be sneaky, and the USO compound isn't exactly Fort Knox. Anything Gadgets can design to beef up security would help the situation immensely. Besides, I thought you said the Man is pleased with me.''

Price snorted. ''All right. I'll get you Gadgets. I'll try to get him reinserted tonight.''

''Good. Has Aaron found out anything new?''

''He's had the whole team working night and day. Striker, he swears the Kanabo Corporation is involved, but he can't prove it. There is a labyrinth of dummy corporations and cut-outs between them and the Japanese oil development group working in the Pacific Trust Islands, but he says it's them.''

The combination of Aaron Kurtzman's analytical mind and the uncanny hunches he got was perhaps one of the greatest intelligence-gathering tools in the world. Kurtzman was seldom wrong. ''I'm having those same kind of feelings, and they're getting stronger all the time.''

''What have you got?''

''Nothing I can prove, but I'm working on it.'' The Executioner's voice grew cold. ''If I'm convinced the Japanese are killing American civilians, what actions am I authorized to take?''

Price's voice grew serious. "You're authorized to take any actions necessary to insure the continued safety of American citizens in the Pacific Trust Islands."

The Executioner stared across the Pacific. Those were nearly blank check parameters. He knew the catch but asked anyway. "And?"

Price's voice lightened. It was an old game they had played out many times before. "And you are on your own. If you are captured or killed, the administration will deny any and all knowledge of your existence."

BOLAN STOOD and snapped the comm link shut. Things could be worse. He had been dropped into a war on three fronts, and with luck he might just be down to two. He doubted whether this was going to make his life any easier. The Executioner turned as Chris Racine jogged across the sand toward him.

"You have a telephone call. It's Dr. Tutarotaro, and he says it's important."

Bolan nodded. "I'll take it in the conference room."

The Executioner examined the compound as he walked through it. The team had done an excellent job repairing the battle damage. The walls of the sheds now looked like modern art murals of sheet-metal patches and welds. Bolan glanced at the boat shed and couldn't help but grin. Howard Redland had run out of sheet metal, so he had taken tin snips and cut patches out of empty beer cans. It made for a very interesting looking wall. Bolan shook his head in admiration.

He walked into the conference shed, and Redland was waiting for him with the phone in his hand. He handed over the receiver and closed the door behind him as he left. Bolan leaned against the wall. "Hello, Doctor, what can I do for you?"

Dr. Tutarotaro's voice spoke quietly. "I have another body."

Bolan nodded. It was the kind of call he was expecting from the man. "What kind?"

"A murdered one."

"Who?"

The doctor sighed. "A native man named Fata Lahona. I didn't know him all that well. He recently moved onto the main island from one of the outer atolls and lives on the other side of the island from me. But I know of him. He was one of the leading warriors in the Isolationist Movement and was very vocal about how he felt and what should be done. I'm sure he was one of the warriors who attacked your compound. When I received his body, it was covered with blunt trauma from the riot rounds you used."

"I assume that his bruises weren't the cause of death."

"You assume correctly."

"Who brought him in?"

"A friend of his and his wife brought him in about an hour ago."

"How did he die?"

Tutarotaro's voice lowered even more. "In a way you and I have discussed before."

Bolan glanced at the wall map of the Pacific Trust Group. "What actions have you taken?"

"I have conducted a preliminary autopsy."

Bolan paused. "You haven't contacted the constable's office or the minister of security?"

Tutarotaro took a long, slow breath. "No. I have contacted only you. I have asked his family to keep quiet about what has happened and to allow me to hold the body for a day or two."

"You want me to take a look at it."

"I would appreciate it. I doubt whether you will disagree with my findings, but I would like you to look at it anyway. Then I believe you and I need to talk privately."

"I agree. What time?"

The doctor paused a moment. "I have had a steady stream of men trickling into the clinic today, most of them with heavy bruising and respiratory complaints. A few with burned hands, as well. I believe what we are going to discuss should be done after the clinic is closed. Let's say ten o'clock?"

"I'll be there."

Tutarotaro sighed. "Thank you, I appreciate it. One other thing."

"Yeah?"

"I don't know what purpose someone could have in killing Fata Lahona. I believe you should be very careful."

Bolan nodded. "Thank you, Doctor. I'll take precautions."

HAYATA BOWED AS HE ENTERED the command shed, and Tanaka inclined his head curtly in return. "How did it go?"

The ninja seemed pleased with himself. "Excellently. The man died well."

Tanaka shrugged. That was more of Hayata's throwback samurai thinking. It was of no importance to him. The success of the mission was everything. "How did you proceed?"

"I carried the man's body to a footpath close to his village. Within the hour, a man I had observed fishing with him came and found the body. He carried it into the village to his family's hut. A woman came out and was very upset. However, there were few people about. They wrapped the body with reed mats and carried it to the clinic. They entered through the back and stayed there for some time. They then left through the back without the body. I trailed them for some time until I was sure they were returning to their village. They didn't go to the constable's office, or contact anyone else."

Tanaka nodded and glanced up at the roof of the shed meditatively. He let Hayata stew for a moment. Tanaka knew he was eager to know what happened on the intelligence end of the operation. After a moment he glanced at the ninja.

"You are correct. They didn't contact the constable." Tanaka allowed himself a small smile. "But the doctor did call the American compound and spoke to the commando."

Hayata nodded.

Tanaka's first act on taking command had been to have the phones to the constable's office and the clinic tapped. The doctor was the key. It was a sign of Hayata's lack of imagination that he had written off the doctor. He was a native and spoke out against violence, so the older man had deleted him from his consciousness. Intelligence on the doctor prior to his arrival was scarce, but the pattern remained. Almost all of the bodies of those slain since the troubles had started had gone through the doctor's clinic, and twice the American had gone and spoken with him behind closed doors. Now the doctor had called him an hour after receiving a fresh body.

"What did they discuss?"

"Very little. The doctor said the man had been murdered in a way they had discussed before." Tanaka looked at him pointedly. "Apparently, this is not the first time your ruse of disguising your killings as the work of natives has failed."

Hayata blanched, and Tanaka continued. "It is of no matter. In fact, it has aided us in this situation. The two of them are going to meet in the clinic, tonight, at ten o'clock."

"What do you wish done?"

"I want the American killed. Do it quietly, in the clinic. The doctor, even if he isn't working actively against us, would still be a witness. Kill him, also. Take what men you feel are required, and use whatever means you feel are necessary."

Hayata bowed low to his commander.

"Tanaka-*san*, I will make the preparations immediately."

Tanaka nodded and waited until he had reached the door. "One other thing, Yoritomo-*san*?"

"Yes?"

"Bring me the American's head."

14

Gadgets Schwarz knelt on the beach and scooped up a handful of sand. He made a fist and watched with a bemused expression as the sand sifted between his fingers and drifted away onto the evening breeze. He looked up at the Executioner and grinned.

"That's the state of security in your compound, Striker."

"I'm aware of that. The question is, what are you going to do about it?"

Schwarz chewed his lower lip meditatively as he scanned the compound. "We don't have the element of surprise with the CS gas and the riot rounds anymore, and I doubt whether we can stop a second attack with those methods if they're determined. They know firsthand we've electrified the fence as well, so they'll probably just heave a tree trunk through it when they come." He shook his head slowly. "I don't think we could stop another native human-wave attack without going over to lethal methods."

Bolan frowned. "I believe that might be the least of our problems."

Schwarz raised an intrigued eyebrow. "Just who are we expecting for dinner?"

The soldier folded his arms across his chest. "French commandos or Japanese corporate ninjas, and they'll be coming in sneaky."

Schwarz scanned the perimeter of the compound and grinned up at Bolan again. "You have a problem."

The Executioner nodded. "I'm making it your problem."

The electronics expert nodded thoughtfully as he reexamined the area. "Well, my problem is this. On the landward side, the only tangible security you have is a chain-link fence that's seen better days. As for over there..." Schwarz waved a hand at the boat dock and shrugged. "Over there, we have the entire Pacific Ocean. Frankly, I've had better defensive scenarios to work with."

"You love challenges."

Schwarz nodded. "That I do. However, I wasn't exactly able to bring the whole toy store in the back seat of an F-14. You have to realize I'm working with limited resources."

Bolan accepted that. "All right. I'm authorizing you to steal anything on the U.S.S. *Sam Houston* that isn't bolted down."

Schwarz's eyes lit up. The *Sam Houston* wasn't a hunter-killer submarine or a boomer loaded with nuclear missiles. It had been converted to act as a delivery system for the United States Navy SEALs and their equipment. Compared to any other type of submarine in the Navy, the contents of its ship's stores could only be described as unique and interesting. He rose and dusted off his hands. "Well, that does add a new dynamic to the situation."

"I knew you'd be pleased."

Schwarz grinned again. "I suppose blanketing the area with mines is out of the question?"

Sowing the beach with land mines *was* out of the question. "Sorry, this one has to be purely defensive, from the perimeter inward."

Schwarz nodded ruefully. "You're deliberately making this difficult."

"I'm making it interesting."

"Can I get the rest of the team to help?"

"One man we can insert and extract fairly easily, but we're being watched by satellite and probably from the trees. I don't think we can sneak the whole team in a second time without being seen. We're already on thin ice on this one, politically."

"What if they stay under water the whole time?"

"I don't want to know about it."

"Know about what?"

Bolan glanced at his watch. "I have to go into town tonight and have a meeting with one of the locals. How soon do you think you'll have something?"

"I want to wander around the compound one more time, then I want to check out what the *Sam Houston* might have lying around. Give me two hours. By then I should be able to jury-rig something."

"Good. I'm counting on it."

Schwarz raised an eyebrow. "You're going into town alone?"

Bolan nodded. "Yeah."

"You want me to shadow you?"

The Executioner shook his head. "No. I'm the only person cleared to be operating outside of the compound. You see what you can do with this leaky sieve of a compound. I'll be back soon."

EZEKIEL TUTAROTARO LOOKED UP from the papers on his desk, and a massive revolver appeared in his hand. Bolan stood with his arms folded and looked down the gaping muzzle of a .455 Webley. The Executioner raised a questioning eyebrow.

"It's me."

Tutarotaro's shoulders sank, and he lowered the pistol. "I know that I'm old, but I wouldn't have thought I was that easy to sneak up on." He regarded Bolan ruefully. "You should have knocked."

Bolan shrugged. "I did."

The doctor grunted and rose from the desk. He tucked the big pistol into the waist of his sarong and pulled his shirt over it. Bolan nodded at the pistol as the doctor concealed it. "That's a grand old piece you have there."

"According to its serial number, it's as old as I am, and I assure you it is much better preserved."

"I gather the two of you have some history together."

Tutarotaro snorted bemusedly. "Oh, yes. We have been together for a long time. Though, it is only recently that I have removed it from my sea chest again.''

''You held on to it after the war?''

''Indeed, I did. Though, the way things are now, I'm starting to wish I had held on to my Sten gun and a few buckets of Mills bombs as well.''

The Executioner made a small leap of logic. ''You were a coast watcher.''

''You are a very clever man. Yes, I was, for the Australian navy. I was a young man when the Japanese invaded our islands in World War II. There was little I could do to stop them, but I was determined to fight. I fled to one of the neighboring atolls and then left the Pacific Trust chain. I joined the Australian navy as a coast watcher for the intelligence branch. They gave me a radio, my revolver and a pair of field binoculars, and I watched, and I reported. But, as I said, I was a young man, and my blood hungered to avenge the souls of my people the Japanese had slain. Watching and reporting wasn't enough. Soon after, I volunteered to fight with the commando units. Then they gave me a submachine gun, grenades and a fighting knife, and then I got my fill of the fighting I had so desired.''

The Doctor suddenly looked at Bolan and shrugged in embarrassment. ''But you aren't here to listen to an old man's war stories. Come with me. I have something I believe you should see.''

HAYATA YORITOMO WAS a shadow among shadows in the island night. He nodded to himself. The doctor was in his office. The light had been on. The American had arrived alone and gone in. Another source of light came on in another window. The ninja suspected the two men had gone downstairs. The street was abandoned.

The time to strike was now.

Hayata held up one hand and clenched it into a fist in the darkness. In the still of the night, an observer would have seen nothing. To men wearing night-vision goggles, Hayata was as plain as day at the edge of the trees. Honda had been in place on the roof for more than an hour, and he sharply nodded his affirmative. The man turned and made the same clenched fist at Kubo, who was concealed at the rear of the clinic. The ninja was pleased with his men. To his mind, they were samurai. The new samurai, the warriors of Kanabo. They wouldn't fail. Hayata checked his watch. Its luminous dial read 10:22 p.m. The American and the doctor should be deeply into whatever they were discussing.

Hayata pressed a single button on the communication rig on his belt. Back at the atoll, a single blip on a screen would tell Tanaka the attack had begun. He began to move in for the kill. Gichin shadowed him on his left without being told. They moved swiftly across the intervening ground between the trees and the front of the clinic. Hayata looked up and sliced his hand through the air. On the roof, Honda leaned forward and placed the blades of his insulated shears on the clinic's main electrical wire.

BOLAN GLANCED at the corpse.

The body had received numerous ugly wounds across its limbs and torso, but one stood out above the rest. No amount of hacking could disguise a blow that had neatly sheared a man's skull from the crown of his head to his palate. Anything else that had been done to this man after that blow had been window dressing.

Tutarotaro looked at the body distastefully. "A sword blow, you agree?"

Bolan nodded. "No machete did that. He was killed by a sword, and its user was very skillful." He looked at the doctor. "Do you have any idea why the Japanese would want to kill this man?"

Tutarotaro frowned. "I don't know. He was a member of the Isolationist Movement, of that I am sure. He spoke out against treating with the Japanese, but he also spoke out against the French and you Americans as well. It's puzzling."

"Do you know if any of the Isolationists attacked the Japanese lately? Or threatened them in any way that would make them retaliate like this?"

Tutarotaro folded his arms as he looked upon the body again. "No, none that I know of. I'm not exactly popular with the members of the Isolationist Movement, but I'm the local doctor around here, and I hear things. There have been no moves against the Japanese for some time. As you know, they have rented an atoll to do their research from, and no one has launched a canoe assault against it. The Japanese are very quiet. When they do come into town they move in groups, do their business and return to their compound. The French beat up a few of them rather badly early on, then some of the Frenchmen got killed. At first, I blamed this on the Isolationists, but as you have pointed out, some of the killings have not been what they seemed."

The doctor shook his head. "To my knowledge, no one in the Isolationist Movement has directly attacked the Japanese. For that matter, Fata Lahona had just received a severe beating and gassing at the hands of you and your men. I doubt he was in a position or the mood to launch an attack on anyone. I doubt he would have attacked any wandering Japanese he found on the beach, and I have grave doubts there would be any wandering Japanese on the beach unless they had an express purpose there."

"You believe they were there for the express purpose of killing Fata Lahona."

The doctor nodded angrily. "I do. I just cannot come up with an explanation as to why." Tutarotaro's eyes were very cold as he spoke. "But we're beyond explanations. I believe the Japanese have killed Fata Lahona. I believe they killed my friend, Komo Malua. I believe the Japanese will kill any of my people if it serves their purposes here in the islands. Long ago, the Japanese came to my islands and killed my people to suit their purposes. I fought them then. I am prepared to fight them now."

Bolan looked in Tutarotaro's face, and he didn't doubt the

man's resolve. His face grew grim. "I think I know why they killed Fata Lahona."

The doctor's white eyebrows raised. "Oh?"

"Yes. To kill us."

Tutarotaro looked at him dumbfounded. "How?"

The Executioner drew the Beretta 93-R from its shoulder holster and flicked off the safety. "We've been observed speaking together on more than one occasion. I suspect your phone and your office might be bugged. They killed Fata Lahona to bring us together again, in a way so that we would be alone and vulnerable to attack."

Tutarotaro seemed to grow before Bolan's eyes. As old as the man was, his formidable power was still evident as he drew himself up to full height. The doctor drew his massive Webley revolver. "Let them come. We aren't as vulnerable as they would like to believe."

"No. We aren't."

Tutarotaro glanced around the makeshift morgue. "It's been a long time since I have fought." He suddenly looked at Bolan directly. "I believe you have a great deal of recent experience in these matters. How do you wish to handle this situation?"

Bolan glanced around. "Let them come to us. I think they'll try to do this quietly, so I doubt they'll use explosives. Their plan is probably to shoot us with silenced weapons, then hack us into pieces to confuse matters."

The doctor nodded slowly. "A sound plan. How do you propose we stop them?"

The soldier peered around the corner and up the stairwell to the main clinic, then closed the door. He took a glass beaker from the table and leaned it against the closed door. "We kill them. Do what I say, when I say it. If you see something I don't, shoot."

Bolan turned as he heard the click of a cabinet door open and shut softly behind him. Tutarotaro stood with his Webley revolver in one hand and the ugly, razor-studded shark-toothed sword in the other. He smiled at the Executioner. "You may rely on it."

Both men froze as the lights went out.

Bolan had been expecting that. "How does the clinic get its power?"

The doctor's voice seemed very loud in the gloom. "From a cable on the roof."

The Executioner calculated. There was probably one man on the roof. The clinic had two doors, one in front and one in back. Bolan knew little of the Japanese corporate soldiers' mind-set except that they seemed to believe in subtlety. They would do this quietly. In such a situation, less would be more. Bolan figured at least three men to cover all the bases, though four would be more likely. "I figure at least four."

"There is an emergency generator by the cold storage unit. Shall I turn it on?"

"Not yet, but get over by the switch." Bolan counted from memory. There were three lamps in the room besides the overhead lighting. "Can you find the lamps in this room in the dark?"

"Of course."

"Aim them at the door, then get by the generator switch. When I tell you, hit it."

Bolan heard the doctor moving softly around the room and slight metal squeaks as he adjusted the flexible necks of his lamps. "It's done. I'm back by the generator."

"Be ready." The Executioner slid prone in the middle of the floor. People clearing a room would be expecting their trapped assailants to set up a cross fire from the corners. The Executioner pushed the Beretta 93-R selector switch to the 3-round-burst mode and lowered the folding foregrip into position.

They didn't have long to wait.

The glass beaker suddenly rolled across the floor in the darkness. Bolan roared. "Hit it!"

A hollow thrumming sounded through the walls and ceiling as the overhead lighting suddenly surged to life. Bolan's eyes slitted against the sudden brightness as he aimed the Beretta with both hands.

A man crouched in the doorway. He was clad from head to toe in close-fitting garments of a weird green-and-gray camouflage. Bolan recognized them as night-vision disruptive patterns. He squeezed the trigger of the Beretta. The man had been frozen for a fatal moment as his own night-vision was disrupted. The light amplification goggles he wore had solarized as he had suddenly been hit by the lights. Every cell in their detectors had overloaded and amplified the sudden light blindingly.

The Heckler & Koch sound suppressed submachine gun the hooded figure carried was damning enough evidence for Bolan. The Beretta snarled, and the man staggered as he took a 3-round burst to the chest. The Executioner raised his aim when the man didn't fall and fired another burst into his head. At the same time the doctor's Webley .455 boomed like a cannon in the confined space of the cellar. The hooded figure jerked and fell back.

Whispers hissed around both doorjambs, and two of the flexible lamps shattered as the Japanese shot them. The Webley roared again, and a huge chunk of the doorjamb splintered away. Bolan rolled sharply into a secondary firing position, bullets tearing a line in the linoleum floor where he had been. The Executioner brought the Beretta in line, and its front sight rested on the fore end of a black submachine gun. Bolan squeezed the trigger, and sparks shrieked off of the weapon. It fell to the floor.

The Japanese charged the room. Three men came in low and fast, the silenced weapons in their hands whispering deadly streams of bullets as they came. Bolan engaged the lead man, and he staggered as the 3-three round burst hammered into his stomach. The doctor's revolver boomed again and again as fast as he could fire it.

Bolan put a second burst into his target, then a third into his legs. The gunner staggered, and the soldier took him with a head shot. The man behind him carried no gun. His left hand trailed behind him dripping blood from where his submachine gun had been smashed from his hands. A sword rasped from its sheath behind his back as he charged forward. The blade glittered high overhead as Bolan's machine pistol clacked open on a smoking empty chamber.

The Executioner rocked back onto his heels and raised the empty Beretta. The sword whistled down, and its blade struck the Beretta 93-R between the barrel and the foregrip with numbing force. Bolan grabbed the snub-nosed Centennial revolver from its holster. As the glittering blade whipped up to strike again, Bolan aimed the revolver and fired.

The gun roared and bucked in Bolan's grip. Cold fire burned across the Executioner's left arm, but the blow had been diverted from its path as five .38 slugs struck the swordsman at point-blank range. The Centennial clicked on an empty chamber, and Bolan flung it into the swordsman's face.

The man staggered back. Blood ran down one leg and spread in a dark stain at his right collar. His armor had absorbed the rest. There was no time to reload and nowhere to retreat to. Bolan lunged upward and bore into the man as he raised his sword one-handed. The Executioner rammed into him with all the power in his two-hundred-plus-pound frame. The hilt of his opponent's sword crashed into the side of Bolan's head as the man yanked it down defensively, and the soldier saw stars.

The Executioner drove forward. He was much larger than his opponent, and the man lost his footing as he was driven backward. The two of them crashed into the wall with bone-jarring force. The Japanese took the brunt of the impact, and his breath came out in an explosive grunt. Bolan stepped back, picked up the Beretta and whipped the empty machine pistol into the side of his opponent's head.

The man absorbed the blow and kicked back off the wall. For a moment, the two men's balance was even, and the Japanese hooked one of Bolan's legs with an ankle sweep. The two of them toppled backward to the floor. The Japanese fighter relinquished his sword, and his good hand went to his belt. Bolan brought his knee up between the man's legs, and he cringed with the pain of a blow he couldn't ignore. The soldier used his strength and shoved the man off. His hand went to the fighting knife sheathed in his waistband as he rolled up on his heels.

His opponent struggled to rise. His right hand pulled forth a short, wickedly curved knife from his belt. Bolan lunged. The fighting knife skidded along the bloody collar of the man's body armor and sank into his throat. The Japanese shuddered and collapsed as the Executioner yanked the blade free.

Bolan got to his feet and breathed a ragged gasp of air. Three of the Japanese were down and not moving. One had managed to get to his hands and knees. His hand groped at his belt. Tutarotaro strode forward. The big Webley revolver lay smoking on the floor in front of him, and his right arm dangled uselessly at his side. Blood stained his shirt at his chest and shoulder where the automatic burst had climbed up his body. He walked forward and raised the shark-toothed club high over his head as the gunner managed to clear a small automatic pistol from his belt.

The war club crunched into the man's skull with an unmistakably lethal impact.

Bolan scooped up a fallen submachine gun and faced the door. Distantly, he could hear dogs barking their protest of the ruckus out on the street.

Tutarotaro leaned back against the wall heavily and sagged to the floor. The entire right side of his shirt and sarong were soaked with blood. He looked up at Bolan blearily.

"I knew I should have kept that Sten gun."

15

Gadgets Schwarz looked down at Ezekiel Tutarotaro. The doctor lay in the back of the USO Oil jeep and stared dazedly at the stars. Bolan had applied field dressings and shot him full of morphine, but Tutarotaro had taken on a deathly pallor, and his breathing had turned shallow and ragged. Schwarz grimaced. "He needs help, more than we can give him here in the compound. His left lung is punctured and has deflated. It's filling up with blood, and he's going into shock. The arm and the shoulder are more minor, but he can't afford the blood loss. He needs a qualified doctor, or he's going to die."

Bolan nodded. "I know. That's why you're taking him to the *Sam Houston*."

Schwarz gave Bolan a leery look. "I don't think he can take an underwater extraction, Striker. It would probably kill him."

"He can't. You're taking him out by boat. Now."

"Asking the *Sam Houston* to pop up in plain sight and take on a civilian casualty isn't going to make Washington very happy."

The Executioner's face was stone. "I don't care. They have the best medical facility within a thousand miles on board. Take the small boat. I want him patched up, and I want it done now."

"All right. I'm on it. I'll radio ahead to have the *Sam Houston* surface as close to shore as possible. Load him into the small boat, and I'll take him out." Schwarz looked at Bolan's arm critically. "You're bleeding all over the place."

The Executioner nodded, and Schwarz broke into a run to the main shack. Bolan motioned to Smitts, Redland and Racine. The four men took the corners of the blanket the doctor was lying on and lifted him out of the jeep. Racine and Smitts grunted with the strain. Ezekiel Tutarotaro was a very large man. They shuffled rapidly across the sand toward the pier. Bolan jerked his head at Smitts. "I'll take this end. Go warm up the boat." The soldier took the extra weight as the boat master ran to the pier.

Bolan looked down at Tutarotaro. The doctor was watching him through half-closed eyes, and his voice came out in a wet wheeze. "You're going to get yourself into trouble."

The Executioner's shoulders moved an inch as he shrugged with the doctor's weight. "Yeah, but in the end we'll both get medals."

Tutarotaro grinned crookedly, and blood flecked his lips and teeth. "Really?"

"Oh, yeah. Washington will fuss at first, but saving your life will be a major public-relations coup with your people. I need you to live long enough to tell your people the Japanese were the ones who did this. I figure between that and the Frenchmen's obnoxious behavior we have the oil development rights locked."

At the pier, the small boat's engine fired to life. Tutarotaro regarded Bolan dryly. "Not the most altruistic of motivations."

"You just stay alive."

Schwarz ran up to the pier and grabbed an end of the doctor's blanket-sling as they lowered him into the boat. "The *Sam Houston* will be half a mile offshore in five minutes. They sounded unsure about it, but I used every overriding security code I could think of."

"Get him out there."

Schwarz leaped into the boat and threw off the halyard. Tutarotaro's voice grew thick with shock and morphine. "I haven't been on a submarine in over fifty years."

Bolan nodded sympathetically. "They're much nicer now."

Tutarotaro's eyes were far away with the memory. "Thank God."

RAIZO TANAKA SAT at his desk and looked at his watch, which read 10:58 p.m. Twenty-five minutes since Hayata had begun his attack. No other signal had been sent. Minato Gosuke stood at attention by Tanaka's desk and tried not to show his nervousness.

Both men were beginning to fear the worst.

Both nearly jumped when the phone rang.

Tanaka picked up the secure line and spoke in unaccented English. "Yes."

"This is Otake reporting."

Tanaka recognized his man's voice. He had been stationed in the hotel across the street to observe. It wasn't good that he was phoning and not Hayata. "Report."

"I heard gunshots inside the clinic soon after Hayata made his attack. They were armed with silenced weapons. I'm assuming they met resistance."

Tanaka frowned his annoyance. "That is obvious. What have you determined?"

Otake paused for several long moments. His voice sounded very uncomfortable. "I believe Hayata and his men are dead."

Tanaka blinked. "All of them?"

"None of them exited. After some moments, a large Westerner, I'm assuming is the American, left the premises with Dr. Tutarotaro. The doctor appeared to be severely injured. They left in the American's vehicle."

Tanaka's eyes narrowed. "And the American?"

Otake paused again. "He didn't act as if he had been hurt."

Tanaka took a long, slow breath. "What is happening now?"

"Native constables have arrived on the scene, and a crowd has gathered on the street outside the clinic. I believe the bodies of Hayata and his men have been found. I have heard people shouting for the minister of security."

Tanaka shook his head wearily. It would take a great deal

of yen to smooth this situation out with Deputy Minister of Security Solomon Falahola, and, as greedy as he was, even he might not be able to squirm around investigating the situation. No amount of yen would rid them of the American. Only lead and steel would suffice. Yet the man had killed Hayata and three of his handpicked men. It was almost inconceivable. The old man wouldn't accept luck as an explanation. Neither did Tanaka. He had dealt with this American before.

He was the sort of warrior who created his own luck.

The situation was simple. One American commando and an ancient native doctor had slaughtered Hayata and his men. The mission had failed. Tanaka shrugged as he accepted what had happened. "Otake, continue to monitor the situation in the town. Report any new developments."

"Yes, Tanaka-*san*."

Tanaka hung up the phone and turned to Minato. "Patch me through to Tokyo immediately."

Tanaka leaned back in his chair as he waited for the secure satellite link. He wasn't relishing telling the old man of this latest failure. Tanaka mused on the situation. It didn't particularly sadden him that Hayata was dead. He had never cared for the sanctimonious lapdog's attitude. Tanaka's face twisted into a strange smile. He had likened the ninja to the sword that he, himself, had to wield. His stroke had missed, and the sword was now broken. Tanaka shrugged. Swords weren't his preferred weapon anyway. It was time to take care of the American once and for all.

Tanaka straightened in his chair as the light blinked on his phone console and Tokyo came on-line.

JEANINE MAITLAND GAVE Bolan a concerned look as she marched into the main shack. She frowned at the field dressing covering his upper arm. "I was right. You are hurt."

The Executioner sat on the conference table and raised a bemused eyebrow at her while he applied pressure to the wound. "You got here very quickly."

Maitland wrinkled her nose at the comment. "Chris let me

into your compound. My hotel is less than one block from the clinic. Everyone in town heard the gunshots. When I got there, the doctor was nowhere to be found, and there were four Japanese bodies lying on the floor and blood everywhere." She locked eyes with Bolan. "I had a feeling you were involved."

"You got there first?"

Maitland smiled wickedly. "I'm a good reporter, no?"

Bolan nodded. "So what happened?"

The woman shrugged. "The constables came and stole my camera and threw me out. But I saw the blood in the stairwell and on the stoop of the front door. As I said, I had a feeling it might be pointing in this direction."

The soldier gritted his teeth as she peeled away the field dressing, and her eyes flared at the wound. "This will require knitting."

"Stitches."

"*Oui*, stitches, whatever. Do you wish me to do it or not?"

Bolan looked at her with mild surprise. "Can you?"

She nodded. "Oh, yes. I was in school for nursing before I decided being a journalist would be more exciting." Maitland glanced around with a frown. "Where is your medical kit?"

He pointed to the storage-room door with his good arm. "In there. Top shelf."

"Take off your shirt. Keep applying pressure." The woman fetched the medical kit and broke out a sterile package of needles and thread. She took a medicated swab and wiped the wound clean. Her blue eyes gave Bolan's bare torso a once-over, then she smiled. "So, you were just going to sit on this table and bleed to death."

"No, I was about to do it myself when you came in."

She stopped swabbing and looked at him askance. "You were going to stitch yourself, by yourself?"

Bolan shrugged. "Dr. Tutarotaro is indisposed."

Her face grew somber. "Is the doctor dead?"

"He's in bad shape, but I expect he'll live."

She looked back at Bolan's wound unhappily. "He is one of the only native men who is nice to me. I like him."

"I like him, too, and I need him alive. But he's a tough one. I'm betting on him."

Maitland nodded. "I'm going to bet on him, too." She broke out a syringe of anesthetic and expertly worked around the wound. "I saw the bloody sword lying on the floor. Is that how this happened?"

Bolan nodded. There would be very little use in denying it.

She threaded a surgical needle and looked up at Bolan curiously. "If he was that close, how did you survive?"

"You ask a lot of questions."

"I'm a journalist."

Bolan nodded. "Ah."

"Well?"

"Well, what?"

"How did you survive being attacked with a sword like that?"

Bolan sighed tiredly. "I shot him five times, threw him against a wall, then cut his throat."

Maitland blinked and swallowed. "Oh."

He felt a slight tug as the needle pierced his numbed flesh. Her stitches were very neat. She was silent as she sewed up his wound. She clipped the thread on the tenth stitch and gave him a small smile. "Finished." She took a roll of bandages from the medical kit and swiftly rebound the wound and sealed it with surgical tape. "There."

"Very nice."

"I haven't lost my touch." She looked up at the clock on the wall. "What are you going to do now?"

Bolan shrugged. He was more exhausted than he cared to admit. "I was going to wait here for word on Dr. Tutarotaro."

Maitland glanced around the room again, and her eyes narrowed conspiratorially as she met Bolan's gaze. "May I wait with you?"

"Do I have to hold your hand again?"

"Oh, no. You are tired, and we don't want you to be ripping

your...stitches.'' She shrugged the straps of her dress from her shoulders, and the thin cotton garment puddled around her ankles. ''I can do most of the work.''

The Executioner admired the woman's form as she strode forward. As she put her hands on his chest, he found he wasn't quite as exhausted as he thought.

16

René Sauvin stood on the tarmac and watched as the small, twin-engined plane came rolling down the airstrip in the dawn light and ground to a halt. After a moment, the engines powered down, and the cabin door opened.

Sauvin grinned.

Large, rough-looking men began piling out of the plane. Each man carried at least one heavy nylon duffel that bulged at the seams. Most carried two, and two of the men lugged large plastic cases, as well. All of them wore khaki shorts and T-shirts with the French oil company logo emblazoned on the chest. Sauvin shook his head. He supposed there might be a few idiots who might mistake them for something besides trained killers, but it was difficult to imagine.

It had taken an ungodly number of francs to clear the way for these men and their equipment to make it on to the Pacific Trust Islands. Sauvin considered every *sou* well spent. It was good to have a full strike team. It was time to take the offensive.

Sauvin's grin widened as a man nearly as large as himself and just as burly walked up and saluted sharply. "Commander!"

Sauvin returned the salute, looking the man up and down with apparent disgust. "Look at you, you goddamned Gascon, and tell me you aren't the butt-ugliest thing standing on two legs."

The man stood rock still and stared straight ahead at parade-ground attention. "The only exception stands before me, sir."

He suddenly glanced back and forth out of the corners of his eyes for a moment. "Of course, I don't see ZeeZee anywhere about."

Both men burst out laughing, and Sauvin clapped him on the shoulder. "It is good to see you again, Hubert."

Hubert shrugged. "It is good to see you as well, sir. You wouldn't believe how boring North Africa has become." He glanced around again. "Where is the ugly little bastard, anyway?"

"ZeeZee is minding the shop, and he is uglier than ever." Sauvin frowned. "A troublesome American removed a few more of his teeth."

Hubert stopped in his tracks and looked at his commander in shock. "ZeeZee got beat?"

Sauvin nodded. "Beaten badly, and five of the roughnecks are in hospital. You and the men might actually have to do some real work on the derrick."

"Hard work never hurt anyone." He jerked his head back at the men pulling equipment from the plane. "These prima donnas of mine could stand to get their hands dirty. They're starting to believe their own reputations."

Both men grinned. Hubert became serious. "What are we to do about this American that is causing trouble? He is Special Forces, no?"

Sauvin cocked his head and sighed. "He isn't a hydrologist, of that much I'm sure." He smacked his fist into his palm and grinned. "However, ZeeZee and I are going to have a nice little chat with him very soon and find out."

Hubert nodded in satisfaction. In their organization, no blow was left unanswered. "And what is it you wish for me and the men to do?"

"At the moment, you are to beef up security and get the derrick running again. It has been idle for days. Also, I feel we might have some real trouble with the Japanese soon." Sauvin smiled. "However, after I have my talk with our troublesome American, you and I shall go and shut down the American facility, permanently."

MACK BOLAN'S EYES flicked open. A second later there was a knock at the door. He could hear Gadgets Schwarz clear his throat outside. "I have a communication from the *Sam Houston.*"

"I'm coming."

Jeanine Maitland made a small noise as Bolan disentangled himself and rose. He checked his watch with a rueful shake of his head. The sun had already risen about fifteen minutes ago. Bolan went to the door and opened it discreetly. Schwarz stood with his hands in his pockets and looked up at him innocently. "What's the situation?"

"The skipper of the *Sam Houston* says Dr. Tutarotaro is expected to live. They took two bullets out of him and patched up the hole in his lung. He lost a lot of blood, but apparently the old fellow is as strong as an ox. He's awake and lucid, and he wants to talk to you when you get the chance."

Bolan nodded. They had much to discuss. The soldier winced as he leaned against the doorjamb. His shoulder ached where the sword had cut muscle, and the stitches were already itching. He experimentally raised his arm over his head. There was a slight tugging twinge, but other than that he had free range of motion. He'd probably end up ripping the stitches anyway, but he could fight. Bolan yawned. "You shouldn't have let me sleep so long."

Schwarz shrugged. "I figured you needed it. You'd been in a fight, you'd lost blood, you had company and I was here to watch the store for you." He grinned. "I figured you could use some beauty rest."

"What have you come up with for our security situation?"

The Able Team commando warmed to the subject. "The *Sam Houston* has some very interesting ships stores and ordnance."

Both of them had been on the submarine before, and the SEAL delivery sub's ordnance and stores only got more wonderful as time went by. "I can imagine."

"Am I still limited to nonlethal countermeasures?"

"I'd like to have that option."

Schwarz chewed his lip thoughtfully. "I've looked at what the *Sam Houston* has, and I've given it some thought. I think I have a few ideas."

"What do you need?"

"I've already liberated most of the things I thought were useful. The skipper raised an eyebrow or two, but he didn't protest too hard. What I need is some netting. Heavy netting, and a lot of it. Do you think we can get that onshore?"

Bolan nodded. "I'm sure some of the locals can be convinced to part with some of their fishing nets. I'll draw Redland and Racine a blank check and send them into town."

Schwarz nodded. "Good. I think perhaps we can do something with this place after all."

Both men turned as Maitland cleared her throat inside. Bolan stepped aside as the woman walked past. She had a towel from the storeroom over one shoulder and nothing else on. She yawned casually. "It looks like a beautiful morning, and I'm going for a swim."

Schwarz did a very creditable job of maintaining eye contact with her. *"Bonjour, Mademoiselle Maitland. Comment allez-vous?"*

Maitland smiled delightedly. *"Bien, merci!"* She turned to Bolan and frowned at him. "You see? He is a man of culture."

Bolan and Schwarz watched her walk naked toward the surf.

Schwarz frowned and scratched his head. "You know, I don't think I've actually ever seen her with clothes on."

Bolan shrugged noncommittally. "Let's see about getting you that netting. I know just the place to try."

Schwarz seemed lost in thought. "You know, I still don't like the situation here. I can jazz up the compound a little, but you're still pretty far out on a limb here."

"I know, but I think I have an idea on how to improve our defenses dramatically."

"Oh? How?"

Bolan folded his arms across his chest. "Go on the offensive."

RAIZO TANAKA SAT RIGIDLY and listened to the phone.

Minoru Yabe wasn't pleased. The old man's voice rumbled like thunder across the secure satellite link. "I have considered your failure carefully."

Tanaka swallowed hard but kept his voice under control. "*Hai,* Yabe-*sama.*"

"You shouldn't have delegated the attack to Hayata. You should have overseen it personally."

Tanaka swallowed again, but this time with relief. Hayata was to receive most of the blame for the failure. Tanaka's own share of the blame would be for delegating too much authority. This wasn't good, but it was forgivable. It wouldn't be enough to put him back behind a desk in Tokyo, particularly if he accomplished his mission.

"*Hai,* Yabe-*sama.* However, Hayata's reputation in these situations, until last night, was unimpeachable. He had also been on the island much longer than myself. I believed it best to give him free rein to accomplish the mission. I apologize for my failure. It is inexcusable."

The old man grunted. Tanaka had apologized for his failure and made an excuse for it in the same breath. They both knew exactly what the situation was. Both knew that Tanaka was going to be forgiven and given a second chance. However, formalities had to be observed. "I'm not interested in your apology, Tanaka-*san.* I'm interested in the aims of this corporation. I want results, and I want the American commando's head set before me."

Tanaka cleared his throat. "How do you wish me to proceed?"

The old man's voice was cold and clear. "I'm tired of treading delicately with these Westerners. The Americans have delegated only one commando to the defense of their people. I believe if we kill this soldier, the American resolve in the Pacific Trust Islands will buckle with his death. Make his death a priority. I don't want you to cut him down in public, but don't shrink from the task for want of opportunity, either. Kill him. Quickly."

"*Hai,* Yabe-*sama.* Thank you for your faith in me."

For a moment there was a steely silence on the phone. Then the old man spoke. "Of course, Tanaka-*san.* I have the utmost faith in you and your capabilities." The old man's voice suddenly went cold. "Don't fail me again."

"Full Yabe-*sama.*"

17

The old woman stood behind her counter in the general store and stared at Bolan. Her dark eyes glittered shrewdly. "What you want so much netting for, big boy?"

The Executioner shrugged innocently. "To catch fish."

She folded her arms across her bare chest and rolled her eyes disbelievingly. "You think you gonna catch a whale or something, maybe?"

Bolan grinned. Knowing Gadgets Schwarz, they might catch all sorts of interesting things. "Maybe."

The woman exposed her massive front teeth. "I like you. You a crazy American big boy."

He leaned forward slightly and lowered his voice. "You're right. I am crazy. I'm crazy about spending American dollars. They're just so nice and green."

Her eyes suddenly sparkled. "I like you. Like way you think. I get you good deal."

"How soon can you get it?"

She sucked in her lower lip and frowned. "That much net. Don't have in store. Have to buy it from the fishermen. They make their own. Hard to find all at once."

Bolan nodded acceptingly. "I need it as soon as possible."

The woman scratched her chin. "How about by the end of the week? I'll ask around. Maybe I can do something for you."

"How about by tonight?"

The old woman snorted. "No way. You crazy."

"I really need it as soon as possible." He pulled a very

thick roll of one-hundred-dollar bills from his pocket and riffled its corners absently. "Money isn't an object."

The old woman swallowed hard. "How about tomorrow morning? Have some boys deliver it to your place of business first thing, okay?"

Bolan nodded. "Excellent. Whatever price the fishermen ask, I'll pay. Why don't I give you a thousand dollars up front, and another thousand on delivery."

The woman's eyes nearly bugged out of their sockets. For a moment, she forgot to haggle. Bolan took the opportunity to head her off at the pass. "I assume you can take a reasonable fee from the total for expediting the transaction? Fine by you?"

She blinked. Bolan would be surprised if she retained anything less than half, but that didn't worry him. Hard currency was always in short supply in the islands. He suspected if the main island's leading entrepreneur put out the word that the crazy Americans were handing out hundred-dollar bills for netting, there was going to be a long line outside her store before the sun hit noon. The old woman looked up at him and saw in his eyes that the price had been set. She nodded quickly in agreement. "Sure, sure. That be fine. Get you good net. All you can use. By morning."

Bolan smiled and handed her ten one-hundred-dollar bills. She kept a straight face, but her hand shook slightly as she took it. "And another thousand on delivery, right?"

She nodded vigorously. "Yes. Sure, sure. Right. Deal."

Bolan nodded. "Deal."

CHRIS RACINE WAS SITTING on the hood of the jeep watching the street as Bolan left the general store. A few people were walking about shopping and doing business in the relative coolness of the morning. He looked up and threw Bolan the keys. "Success?"

"I think we'll have everything we need by tomorrow morning."

Racine whistled appreciatively. "You sure can get things done."

Bolan climbed behind the wheel. Racine's eyebrows raised as he looked down the street. "Speaking of things you've done…"

The Executioner followed his gaze. Jeanine Maitland was walking toward them. They had dropped her off at her hotel ten minutes ago. The soldier's eyes narrowed. The woman didn't look happy. She walked with a halting, dazed gait. Her eyes were wide, and her face had an almost green cast to it.

She looked as if she was about to throw up.

Bolan slid out from behind the wheel. Outwardly, she didn't seem to be physically hurt. She kept walking forward looking straight ahead. He was standing in front of her, but he didn't think she was actively seeing him. Bolan stepped forward. "Jeanine, are you all right?"

She blinked as if seeing Bolan for the first time. She looked up at him and spoke haltingly to him in French. She was saying something about a message, but he couldn't quite understand it. Bolan took her shoulders in his hands and locked his gaze with hers. "In English, Jeanine."

She blinked again, then swallowed hard. Tears welled up in her eyes. "I have received a package for you."

"A package for me?"

She nodded several times. *"Oui."*

"Where did you receive this package?"

The tears overflowed her eyes and rolled down her face. "I…I found it in my hotel room. After you and Chris had dropped me off."

"You opened it?"

She blinked out more tears, and her shoulders shook. She nodded. Bolan let out a slow breath from between clenched teeth. It could have been a bomb. It still might be a bomb for all he knew. He shook his head slightly. "I wish you hadn't done that."

Maitland's voice quavered. "I'm a journalist! It was delivered to my room, I…" Her whole body shook. She seemed to be using every ounce of willpower to keep herself from breaking down and sobbing.

Bolan sighed. It was a little late for reprimands. He changed tactics. "So, now you're opening my mail?"

An awkward smile ghosted across her trembling lips.

"How did you know it was mine?"

She shrugged slightly. "Well, it said, For The American Commando, written in English, on top of the box. I figured that must mean you."

Bolan nodded. It was a fairly safe guess. "Was there anything interesting in it?"

The woman's shoulders shuddered under Bolan's hands. Her face went almost expressionless.

Bolan shook her gently, and his eyes never let hers look away. "Jeanine, what did you find?"

Her mouth worked up and down several times before words came out. "It was a head, a human head!" Maitland collapsed against Bolan and began sobbing uncontrollably. He glanced at Racine while she wept on his chest.

"Chris, was everyone accounted for at the compound this morning?"

Racine did some mental calculations. "Well, I mean, I think so. We don't exactly have a roll call every morning, but I don't remember anyone actually being missing or anything." He looked at Bolan. "But, I mean, I couldn't swear to it."

Bolan accepted that. Off of the top of his head, he couldn't be sure he had seen every member of the team that morning either. The Executioner's voice was calm. "Chris, stay with her, I'm—"

Maitland pushed off Bolan's chest violently. She looked up at him in wide-eyed terror. "No! I'm staying with you!"

Bolan shrugged. "All right." He handed Racine the keys. "Stay here. I'm going to take Jeanine back to her room and take a look at what we're dealing with. I should be back in a minute or two."

Racine nodded grimly and sat in the back of the jeep next to his tarp-covered carbine. "I won't move an inch."

Bolan took the woman's hand. "Let's go see what we have."

Maitland seemed to regain a little of her composure as they walked to her hotel. Bolan glanced around. It seemed quiet. No one was screaming, and no constables were standing around with submachine guns. "What did you do when you found it?"

She spoke in a tiny voice. "I believe the American word is 'puked.'" She looked up at him sheepishly. "I guess I'm not as tough as I thought I was."

Bolan gave her hand a consoling squeeze. "I mean, did you contact anybody?"

She shook her head. "No. I thought I had better find you first."

He nodded as they went into the hotel. A young native man stood behind the desk and smiled at them as they entered. Maitland squeezed Bolan's hand weakly. "I'm in room 12."

They walked up the stairs. The second floor was a narrow hall with doors on either side. Room 12's door was standing open. Bolan paused. "Did you leave the door open?"

She nodded. "Yes. I wasn't thinking rationally at the time." Bolan peered in without entering. The room was small and dominated by the single bed. A package approximately the size of a hatbox sat on the bed. Its twine had been cut, and the lid lay to one side. A small puddle of vomit was on the floor beside the bed. Maitland clenched his hand and froze. Her face looked terrible. "I think I'm going to be sick again."

"All right, stay here." He turned to the door, and his hand moved under his shirt to the grips of the Beretta pistol in his shoulder holster.

The Executioner staggered forward as Jeanine Maitland suddenly drove her shoulder into Bolan's back with all the strength in her body. Bolan's hands went up defensively as he went through the doorway. A booted foot came up at his face in a high round kick from around the doorjamb, and the soldier took the force of the blow on his forearms. Another boot came around the other side of the door fast and low. There was no way to block the blow, and the Executioner tensed his abdominal muscles and gritted his teeth as the reinforced toe of the combat boot slammed into his stomach.

Bolan didn't bother trying to stay up. He went with the momentum of Maitland's shove and hit the floor in a rolling dive. The Executioner felt the stitches in his shoulder pull, and the flesh around them tore with a searing burn as he rolled across the wooden floor and came up on his feet. There was no time to worry about his wound, and no chance to go for his Beretta. His assailants were on him in whirlwind of flying feet and clenched fists.

The Executioner sidestepped and momentarily put the bed between him and the big Frenchman. The smaller, ugly one hurtled in without hesitation, driving a second kick at Bolan's midsection. The man seemed to have target fixation. That didn't bother the Executioner. He was willing to exchange blows with him.

The soldier scowled as the blow hit him, then he was inside the man's guard. Bolan didn't bother hitting him as he came in. Instead, his hand shot out and clamped on the little man's throat like a vise. The Frenchman's eyes flew wide, and Bolan slammed his other hand hard into the man's crotch, ignoring the searing twinge in his wounded shoulder as partially healed flesh parted under the exertion. The Executioner bodily pressed the little Frenchman up over his head.

The big man rounded the bed and lifted his knee to thrust a kick into Bolan's solar plexus. There wasn't time to hurl his comrade at him, so Bolan simply dropped the little Frenchman before him as a shield. The big man's kick was already in motion, and his compatriot took the thundering heel kick in the kidney. The little man fell to the floor, writhing in pain.

Bolan stepped over his downed adversary and drove into his partner. The big man took a step back and raised his fists in a high guard, as a low kick was aimed at his shin. The big Frenchman lifted his leg to avoid the blow, and he and Bolan met. They locked collar and elbow, both of them tying up the other's arms and trying to position themselves for a blow. The

Executioner twisted his hips to avoid being kneed in the groin and rammed his head forward into his opponent's face.

The big man's head snapped back as his nose broke. Bolan brought his own knee up between the man's legs, and the Frenchman doubled over in agony. The Executioner opened his fist as he raised it overhead, then rapped the edge of his hand hard across the base of the Frenchman's head.

The big man fell as if he had been shot.

A foot slammed into Bolan's ribs brutally, and he staggered back a step. Jeanine Maitland arced her foot high at Bolan's head, and the Executioner barely managed to deflect the second blow. Her foot slammed into his shoulder rather than his head, and the rest of Bolan's stitches gave. She retracted her leg and blurred into a spin. The soldier stepped forward and swung.

Maitland wasn't a large woman. Kicking high for the head of a man as tall as Bolan had been a fatal mistake. It took her a split second too long to recover, and as she turned the Executioner could see the telegraphed spinning backfist coming. Bolan stepped inside the arc of her blow, and as her head came around his fist crashed into her jaw.

The woman reeled backward. Bolan was surprised that she wasn't knocked unconscious, but in this tiny hotel room, with three assailants, there was little room for mercy. Maitland tottered and tried to bring up her hands in a boxer's stance to defend herself. Bolan's fist opened, and he drove his stiffened fingers below her guard and into the pit of her stomach like a blunt spearhead.

Her body folded around Bolan's fingers, and she fell to the floor with a gagging wheeze.

The soldier saw motion out of the corner of his eye and he whirled. The Beretta 93-R filled his hand, and he pushed the selector switch to burst mode. The ugly little Frenchman was struggling to rise. He pushed up off the bed with one hand and managed to get his feet under himself. His hand groped under his shirt for something concealed under his left arm.

The cold steel slide of the Beretta 93-R laid the Frenchman's face open to the bone as Bolan pistol-whipped him with a backhanded strike. The little man's head jerked around, and he fell back to the floor in a bloody heap.

The Executioner stood among his fallen opponents.

The big man was unconscious. Maitland lay gasping and choking in a fetal position on the floor. The ugly one was curled in a semiconscious heap with blood pooling on the floor around his face. Bolan covered his battered assailants with the Beretta. For the moment, none of them were going anywhere, and he peered over at the box on the bed. Of course, it was empty. Bolan looked at the gasping woman. He had to give Jeanine Maitland credit. She was an excellent actress. He had just about bought her whole story. Forcing herself to vomit on the floor before summoning him had been an excellent touch. They had almost taken him down.

The Executioner dropped to one knee and patted down the big man. Under his shirt, he had a three-inch .357 Magnum Ruger in a shoulder holster and a double-edged commando knife sheathed in his waistband behind his back. Bolan took the weapons and threw them in the empty box on the bed. The little man groaned as the soldier searched him but he was in too much pain to resist. Bolan liberated his compact 9 mm Walther P-5.

Maitland attempted to struggle as Bolan patted her down, but she went limp as he put his knee between her shoulder blades and the muzzle of the Beretta against the back of her head. He raised an eyebrow as he looked in her purse. She was carrying a .45 Colt Combat Commander with two spare magazines, a compact 1100-volt stun gun, a silencer tube for the threaded barrel of the .45 and a switchblade knife large enough to skin an elephant. If she had just swung her purse at the back of his head to start with, she probably could have killed him.

But they hadn't intended to kill him. The knife, the stun gun and the method of their attack told him that. This was to have been an interrogation. The Executioner shook his head.

Nonlethal or not, he doubted he would've enjoyed the proceedings very much if he had lost the fight.

Bolan threw the rest of the weapons in the box on the bed and turned his attention to the woman. He took his knee out of her back and rose. He stood for a moment and decided the fate of the French.

Killing them would probably be inappropriate, particularly given the politics of the situation. France was still officially an ally of the United States, despite their conflict of interests here in these obscure islands deep in the South Pacific. He had also been seen entering the hotel with Maitland, and leaving three bodies in her room after he left by himself wouldn't do anything for his already tattered cover story. And he couldn't just execute these people in cold blood.

The attack had been nonlethal, which solidified his theory of what was going on in these islands. The French were his competitors.

The renewed throbbing of the sword wound in his shoulder told him all too well who his real enemies were.

Bolan scooped up the hatbox full of weapons and tucked it under one arm. Maitland's eyes followed the muzzle of the Beretta as Bolan stepped over her. Her expression was unreadable as she looked up at his face. The Executioner's smile didn't reach his eyes as he met her gaze.

"Have a nice day."

"HERE."

Chris Racine gasped as Bolan handed him a large box, then slid behind the wheel of the jeep. Racine held the box away from himself gingerly with his fingertips and gave Bolan a reproachful look.

"It isn't a head."

"No head?"

"No."

"Can I look?"

Bolan started the engine. "Be my guest."

Racine cracked the lid of the box slightly and looked at the guns, knives and implements inside. He blinked again. "What's all this?"

Bolan pulled the jeep around and pointed it toward the beach. "What do you think?"

Racine's jaw dropped. "It was a trap!"

"Red was right. You did go to college."

"Are they dead?"

"Killing them wouldn't have been appropriate."

Racine nodded in somewhat shocked agreement. "Well, what about Jeanine?"

"She's playing for the home team."

"Oh." Racine scratched his sparse beard and looked sad. He kind of liked having a fabulous naked French babe hanging around the compound all the time. "Are you sure?"

Bolan gave him a look. "Half of the stuff in that box is hers."

Racine's eyes flared. "You know, you're bleeding."

The Executioner nodded. He had packed the wound with paper towels from the hotel's lobby rest room, but they were soaked through already and his shirt was turning a dark crimson at the shoulder. The ripped stitches were going to leave an ugly scar. Bolan would've liked to get out to the *Sam Houston* and let her surgeon do the repair work, but he doubted he would get the chance. He shook his head ruefully. "Looks like Red is going to get his chance to play surgeon after all."

Racine looked at Bolan's blood-soaked shoulder greenly. "So what do we do now?"

Bolan frowned as he pulled onto the beach road. "Now we're going to have to deal with our Japanese friends."

18

Raizo Tanaka glanced at a satellite photograph of the main island. He glanced up as Minato Gosuke came in, followed by Ryuchi Taido. With Hayata and his handpicked men dead, Taido was the most senior field operative other than Tanaka himself. During his brief command, Hayata had relegated Taido to tasks such as base security and intelligence collation. A complete waste of his talents. Tanaka knew all too well how Taido felt. Hayata hadn't approved of him. Many in the Kanabo Corporation didn't. Ryuchi Taido was short, even by Japanese standards. He didn't come from a good family. His manners and speech were crude. He was hairy and had a short, full beard. With his long arms and heavy shoulders, Taido was almost simian in appearance. He undoubtedly had some of the old, despised, Northern Japanese aboriginal blood lurking in his family tree.

Tanaka liked everything about him.

"Greetings, Taido-*san*."

Ryuchi Taido grinned and nodded in an impudent stab at bowing.

Tanaka regarded him dryly. "I am making you my second in command."

Taido's inappropriate grin widened. However, he bowed fully at the waist to show his respect. "Thank you, Tanaka-*san*."

Tanaka grinned back. "You don't seem very surprised, my friend."

The younger man folded his arms and shrugged. "After

Hayata and his Bushido Boys got themselves slaughtered, it was only a matter of time." Taido covered his impertinence. "The old man should've put you in command in the first place, Tanaka-*san*. Then you and I could have dealt with all these foreigners properly. It would have saved the corporation a lot of time and trouble."

Tanaka shook his head at the man's shameless gall. "Taido, you're never going to make vice president."

The two men laughed. Minato smiled nervously as he looked back and forth between them. His superiors weren't behaving with proper decorum, but he wasn't about to mention this. Raizo Tanaka was his superior, and it wasn't his place. Ryuchi Taido simply scared the hell out of him.

Tanaka leaned back in his seat. "I can think of one problem."

Taido nodded knowingly. "The American."

"Yes," Tanaka agreed.

Taido scratched his chin and stared into space. "I have an idea about that."

"Oh?"

"Yes. I say we blow his head off."

BARBARA PRICE SOUNDED intrigued. "So the French weren't trying to kill you?"

Bolan swung his glance over at the hatbox and its contents as he spoke into the satellite link. "Well, I'm fairly certain they were intending to violate my civil rights."

"But you're sure it was only supposed to be an interrogation?"

Bolan nodded. "Pretty sure. They wanted information and probably wanted to make my life miserable enough to get me shipped off the island on a stretcher." Bolan paused. "What's the word on Dr. Tutarotaro?"

"We were in communication with the *Sam Houston* about four hours ago. The doctor is recovering nicely. I also understand Gadgets raided the sub's stores."

"He's installing some precautionary measures for me. We

got the netting earlier than expected. He should be done within the hour, and I'll have him extracted at nightfall.''

''Hmm…you know, Hal is having to do a lot of quick dancing on your behalf. You're playing very fast and loose with the President's guidelines for this operation.''

''Things are going to get a lot worse before this one is over. The Japanese made an attempt on my life the other night, as well as on Dr. Tutarotaro. I believe they killed Skip Porter, the former chief of operations. I also believe they have murdered a number of French nationals, other natives and were responsible for setting up the attack on the compound by the natives. I can't keep sitting around on the defensive and waiting for them to pick their next shot. Sooner or later, they're going to launch something that I won't be able to stop.'' Bolan's voice became grim. ''We have to go on the offensive.''

''You want Hal to tell the President that we are at war with Japan?''

''No. I want Hal to tell him we are at war with the Kanabo Corporation, and these islands are just one square on their chessboard. Tell the President he has two choices.''

''I'm not sure how Hal is going to feel about giving the President ultimatums.''

''It's not an ultimatum. It's just the way it is.'' Bolan paused. ''Tell the President if things go on the way they are, sooner or later most of the USO Oil team is going to wind up dead. He had better withdraw them or give me a free rein. We've been playing by the enemy's rules, reacting, when we should be acting. The choice is pretty clear. Either we start fighting back or we clear out.''

''The administration was hoping to keep things from escalating.''

Bolan ran a hand over the fresh stitches in his shoulder. Jeanine Maitland had done a far better job the first time than Howard Redland had an hour ago. ''One of our friends from the Kanabo Corporation tried to cut my head off the other night, Barbara. I respect the President's good intentions, and I'm aware of the politics of the situation. But we've dealt with the Kanabo Corporation before. We know they won't stop on their own."

Price's voice was calm. "The problem is, this situation isn't a direct threat to the United States per se. The President wasn't happy about having a Stony Man team deployed in the islands. What do you want to do if he won't commit more resources?"

The Executioner thought long and hard. The politics of the situation didn't interest him. They were simply a harsh reality he had to deal with. What it came down to was the men of the USO Oil team. They were sitting targets. Mack Bolan knew all too well that he was the only thing standing between them and professional assassins.

"Tell the President we can do this without committing more resources, but I have to have the freedom to move on this one."

"You think you can stop them by yourself?"

Bolan weighed his chances. "Maybe. But even if I can't stop them outright, I can make them wish they'd never started."

Price was silent for a long moment. "I'll have Hal contact the President."

RENÉ SAUVIN WINCED as he held an ice pack to the back of his head and sagged forward slightly in his chair. Hubert shook his head with renewed wonder and glanced over at ZeeZee. The little man sat rigidly on a folding chair while Jeanine Maitland bent over him and stitched the horrendous looking contusion wound that went from his nose to his cheekbone. Blood dripped down his chin as Maitland sewed his face back together. Hubert smiled slightly. Despite ZeeZee's obvious pain, he still had the wherewithal to keep his eyes focused down the front of the woman's dress.

Hubert ran an eye over the woman appreciatively. He knew Jeanine Maitland only by reputation. She was supposed to be a very good undercover operative, and she had a number of successful operations under her belt. She also reputedly had a number of confirmed kills as well, but who and where was on a need-to-know classification. Hubert's glance went to the side of her face. Massive purple bruising distorted the line of her jaw and her cheek below the ear. Her left eye was threatening to close.

Hubert shook his head again. It was unthinkable. One American had defeated Sauvin, ZeeZee and the Maitland woman in hand-to-hand combat, no less. Hubert frowned with after-the-fact wisdom. The commandant should have brought more men.

The commandant shouldn't have needed more men.

Hubert cleared his throat. "Sir, let me take some men and go kill this American for you."

Sauvin looked up at Hubert and smiled painfully. A few moments ago Jeanine had finished pushing his nose back into position and taping it in place. He wiped fresh blood from his upper lip. "Nothing would give me more pleasure, my friend, but, at the moment, we don't have clearance to terminate any of the Americans."

Hubert scowled. "And just what are our standing orders exactly?"

Sauvin's eyes flared. "Your orders, Sergeant, were to get the derrick operational. Just what kind of progress have you made?"

Hubert snapped to attention. He had overstepped his bounds. "Sir, the generators have been cleaned and tuned, and we have gotten the drill back on line. We're ready to restart sample coring. Sir!" Hubert snapped off a smart salute.

Sauvin rolled his eyes. "Oh, for God's sake. We're no longer in the legion, and you're giving me a headache." He sat up straighter and with an effort took the pained look off his face. "Listen, Hubert. I want an equipment check run on all of the diving gear, and I want all of the air tanks charged."

Hubert went from attention to at ease. "Of course. At once." He peered at Sauvin speculatively. "If we cannot kill the Americans, what is it we intend to do? We can't allow this to go unanswered."

Sauvin tossed the ice pack aside and rose to his feet. He squared himself and looked Hubert in the eye. "Success is the best revenge, my friend. If we cannot kill the Americans, we will kill their operation."

19

Gadgets Schwarz handed Bolan a remote control the size of a walkie-talkie. "Here you go. It's the best I can do with what's available. He pointed to an open suitcase from which wires trailed along the floor and out of the room. Inside the suitcase were several black boxes with dials and a bank of warning lights. "That is your security control suite. I've wired the outside of the perimeter fence with motion sensors and the first ten feet inside the fence with spaced pressure sensors under the sand. I've also changed the wiring so you can juice the fence, itself, with voltage from here."

Bolan nodded and took the remote. "How about on the sea side of things?"

"Well, the native netting is pretty strong stuff. They split fibers from one of the indigenous plants and wove it so that it has a rather strong tension. I've strung an arc of it from fence pole to fence pole at the water line. Then I wove some monofilament wires through it at fairly tight intervals. If someone cuts a hole big enough to send a diver through..." Schwarz pointed to the case. "Your console is going to light up like a Christmas tree."

"And then?"

Schwarz handed him a much smaller remote with a bank of small red switches. "And then you use your ocean-front countermeasures."

Bolan nodded in satisfaction. "I knew I could count on you."

The Able Team commando smiled with false modesty. "We

aim to please.'' He gave the compound the once-over with a practiced eye. "That's about all I can do, given the parameters of the situation. So what are you going to do now?"

"So far, I don't have clearance to go on the offensive, and I don't care for waiting in the corner and covering up while someone measures us for the next punch."

"You have a plan." It was a statement, not a question.

"Well, I have three missions here. One is to defend the USO Oil crew, and, thanks to you, we've got the compound secured as tightly as possible. Two is to find out who is killing Americans. I've done that, and now that information is being run through the political machine in Washington."

Schwarz cocked his head. "What's the third?"

"Well…" The Executioner shrugged with false helplessness. "I'm also supposed to see if I can keep the oil exploration going."

"Ah. And what is the first thing on that agenda?"

The Executioner looked out across the water. "I think it's time to take one of the boats out on a test ride. See if it's still in operational trim after all this downtime."

Schwarz smiled. "Want some company?"

Bolan shook his head. "No. I want you to stay here and hold the fort until dark, then I want you to extract to the *Sam Houston*. See if Dr. Tutarotaro is up to coming ashore. I have a feeling I'm going to need his influence."

"You got it. Try not to stray too far off course on your little boat ride."

"The South Seas can be treacherous. You never know quite where you'll end up."

MINATO GOSUKE RAN into Raizo Tanaka's office. The two men inside looked up from their beers and the map on the table as Minato bowed breathlessly. Tanaka inclined his head and raised an eyebrow at his designated intelligence officer. "Report."

"Satellite intelligence shows the Americans have launched one of their boats from their compound."

Tanaka frowned. The USO Oil team had shut down nearly eighty per cent of their operations since the troubles had started, and the American commando had turned their compound into an armed camp. That was acceptable. It prevented them from achieving their goals. The fact they were launching their oil exploration platforms again wasn't a good omen. "Which way are they headed?"

Minato bit his lip. "They have taken a somewhat meandering course, Tanaka-*san*."

Tanaka nodded. If they were mapping the bottom with sonar or taking magnetic readings, they might follow the signs wherever they led them. "Give me a general direction."

"East."

Tanaka blinked.

Minato swallowed and wiped the sweat from his brow. "If one were to draw a straight line that intersected their weaving, the line would lead directly to our atoll."

Taido finished his beer and looked at his superior without comment. His expression spoke volumes. The Americans were probing them. Very daring. Very foolish. Tanaka turned to Taido. "Taido-*san*, take one of the boats and what men you might require." Tanaka searched for the right word. They would have to play the situation by ear. "Go...reconnoiter the Americans."

"*Hai*, Tanaka-*san*." A frightening grin split his furry face.

MACK BOLAN STOOD on the flying bridge of USO Oil's boat, *USO Oil 735*. The boat was essentially a highly modified, deep-sea, sport-fishing craft. Most of its interior cabin space was taken up with magnetometers and sonar equipment. It had been converted into a shallow water survey ship and was ideally suited for poking around the plateaus and reefs on which many South Sea island chains rested. It had a winch in the bow that could lower a ground-penetrating radar to the plateau floor and had facilities to accommodate several divers and their equipment in a modified cabin. The craft was small and cramped with its job-related gear, but it was very efficiently equipped.

Someone had painted the name *Scrappy* on the side of the hull beneath its official designation. Bolan had smiled at that. He hoped it was a good omen.

Howard Redland stood beside the soldier and manned the wheel. Chris Racine was belowdecks with Smitts. They ran tests on the equipment and occasionally fired off the terrain-mapping sonar to make it seem to any listening submarine they were just out mapping the bottom. Bolan peered through his laser range-finding binoculars. In the distance he could see the atoll where the Japanese had been allowed to set up camp.

Redland gnawed on the stump of an unlit cigar and grinned. He liked being out on the water. "So, how do you like our little boat?"

Bolan lowered his binoculars. "*Scrappy* is a fine craft."

"USO did a fine job with her, didn't they? From what I hear, they bought her at a government auction. She used to be owned by some drug dealer in Florida until the Feds confiscated her in some sting operation. She fit the small boat specifications and the budget, as well. USO got it at a ridiculously low price."

Bolan clicked on the intercom. "Chris, how are the engines?"

There was a pause, and then Racine came on. "Running like champs."

The vessel had a pair of massive twin diesels. Whoever had first owned her had wanted *Scrappy* to be able to scramble in an emergency. "How does the equipment check out?"

The intercom squawked fuzzily. "Everything seems to be A-OK despite the layoff. The only thing bellyaching seems to be this goddamn intercom. I'll get the bastard working, don't worry about it."

Bolan and Redland looked at each other. The Texan grinned. "Geez, give the boy a rifle and put him out to sea, and he just goes all salty on you."

The Executioner shrugged as he brought his binoculars back

up to his eyes. "I don't know who he gets it from." The banter died on his lips as he scanned the eastern horizon. A craft was coming around from the far side of the Japanese atoll.

"We have company."

"What kind?"

Bolan adjusted the binoculars and looked at the flag on a small commercial vessel slightly larger than *Scrappy*. The flag featured a red, rayed ball with a white background. It was the flag of the Rising Sun.

The Japanese flag of war.

Bolan lowered the binoculars. "The vengeful kind."

RYUCHI TAIDO STOOD beside the cutter's helm and looked across the water through his binoculars. He lowered one of his oversized hands and scratched his jaw as he examined the American boat's lines. He suspected it was faster than it looked, though he was still willing to bet he could run it down. He had eight men armed with 9 mm Uzi submachine guns. He could probably just board the vessel, give anyone on deck a well-deserved beating, then scuttle the tub to the bottom of the sea where it belonged.

Taido sucked on his lower lip reflectively. The problem was that it was the kind of action that might cause an "international incident." Very embarrassing. The paper shuffling toads squatting behind their desks in Tokyo wouldn't like that. Taido really didn't care about that too much. However, he wasn't about to disappoint the old man. He was certainly not going to make him lose face internationally.

Taido considered the problem as they chugged toward the Americans. He glanced at the long green crate on the deck behind him. He could just blow the hell out of them, but he doubted that could be explained away satisfactorily either. Taido suddenly brightened. The best way to save face in this situation was to lose it.

An embarrassing accident would be ideal.

The Kanabo Corporation cutter was longer and heavier than

the American boat, and it had a welded steel hull. It would be a terrible misfortune if they were to inadvertently bump its steel nose into the American vessel amidships at high speed. It might just have the terrible consequence of breaking the American boat's back and killing its crew. A terrible tragedy. How could this have happened? It had to have been that incompetent ape, Taido. Who put him in charge of a boat? So very sorry. He will be punished. He won't be promoted to vice president. We will send him to Thailand. We will force him take care of Kanabo Corporation business there. We assure you he will be utterly miserable. Please, Kanabo Corporation will be happy to pay for damages and compensate the families of the bereaved.

Taido nodded to himself with a happy grunt. He turned to the helmsman, a half-Korean named Si who was excellent with a semiautomatic shotgun. Taido himself had trained him. "All ahead full."

Si looked at Taido expectantly, and Taido suddenly jerked his head in a single, grinning nod. "Ram them!"

BOLAN LOWERED THE BINOCULARS. In a few moments, the Japanese were going to be close enough so that they wouldn't be necessary.

"Here they come, Red."

Redland looked at the oncoming Japanese cutter in amazement. "What do you think their intentions are? Think they'll try to board us?"

Bolan considered the question for about a second. "I think they intend to smash us to pieces." He glanced at the oncoming cutter. They had raised the international signal flag for "boat out of control, stand clear." They were covering all the bases.

"Red, what kind of speed could you get out of a boat like this with normal engines?"

"About twenty knots."

"Take her up to that and one knot over. I want them to think we're making an all-out attempt to run."

"You got it." Redland took the throttle up to two-thirds, and *Scrappy* lurched ahead through the water with a surge of power. Still, it wasn't going to be enough. The Japanese cutter was closing rapidly. The Executioner still had a card to play. His gaze swept the horizon. To the west, there was a reef with calm water behind it and a small island. If he could get to it, he might be able to accomplish something. The only problem was that the Japanese were right in their path.

The Executioner made his decision. "Red, I'll take the helm."

The Texan stood to one side. "Right."

Bolan took the intercom mike. "Chris, Smitts, either jump now or grab on to anything solid. Be ready for a possible collision."

Redland's cigar stub fell out of his mouth. Bolan clicked off the mike without waiting for a reply. *Scrappy* belched black smoke and her twin diesels roared as Bolan went to three-quarter throttle and brought her around. The boat lurched, and the bow came around to point straight on at the oncoming Japanese vessel. The vessel shuddered as she rammed through the water at speeds her hull had never been designed for. The Japanese cutter still bore down at them, and both boats now had a combined closing speed of over forty knots as they knifed through the water straight at each other.

Bolan kept the bow aimed straight at the Japanese cutter and the throttles full ahead. The Executioner spoke to Redland matter-of-factly without taking his eyes off of his target.

"If you're going to jump, you'd better do it now."

TAIDO GAPED at the American boat as it bore down on them. It was utterly ridiculous. The Americans couldn't hope to survive a crash with a steel-hulled cutter. They would be smashed to pieces. Of course, at their combined closing speed, the cutter's bow would be damaged, but it should still be seaworthy. It would be a futile and suicidal trade-off for the Americans. Taido looked through his binoculars at the American boat's bridge. A large, powerful-looking man stood behind the wheel.

Taido had seen the intelligence photographs. There could be no mistake. It was the American commando. He stood staring straight at Taido as his boat bore down. The American was obviously insane.

He was also a dead man.

Taido punched the intercom. "All hands, brace for collision!" Taido grabbed hold of the rail and braced himself as he shouted at Si over the thunder of the engines. "Be ready!"

"*Hai!*" Si's knuckles whitened on the wheel, and he took a braced wide-legged stance. The American boat loomed as it closed in.

THE EXECUTIONER'S FACE was expressionless as he kept his course straight at the Japanese cutter. They were at one hundred yards and closing fast. The sleek white bow of the cutter knifed toward them like the fin of a shark. They would collide in seconds.

"Hold on, Red!"

At twenty-five yards Bolan went to full throttle.

The twin diesels thundered and blasted out blue smoke in a roar. *Scrappy* vibrated from bow to stern as Bolan yanked the wheel savagely to starboard. The vessel sheared away from the collision with about ten feet to spare and shot past the cutter. The Japanese boat burst through her wake and plunged through a wall of water. Bolan kept at full throttle and ran for the reef. He shot a look over his shoulder and saw the cutter beginning its turn to chase them. They would be too late. *Scrappy* would make the temporary safety of the reef.

Redland was in awe. "God, you cut that close."

"Had to." Bolan jerked his head at the deck. "You'd better get your rifle. This isn't over yet."

TAIDO SHOOK his head in disbelief. The American boat's wake had broken over the cutter in a thick curtain that had soaked the open bridge. Taido wiped his face with the back of his fist and grinned with outraged delight. Oh, this American. He was a wily one. However, he had played his ace. Taido now knew his boat had a powerful engine, but it still wouldn't be enough to outrun the cutter. They both knew that. That was why the American was hiding behind the reef. Taido's grin spread. The foreigner had dropped the gauntlet now, and he was seriously outengined and outgunned.

"Take it to one-quarter ahead."

Si dropped the speed as they cruised toward the reef. The American boat was cruising slowly in the shallows with only three hundred or four hundred meters separating them. Taido keyed the intercom. "I want the fire team on deck, now."

Instantly, eight men armed with submachine guns burst onto the deck and took position along the gunwales. Taido considered the situation. They were probably being watched by satellites. He ran the scenario in his mind. He had come out to investigate. The American had turned and tried to ram them. From above, it would look plausible. Now, if he used force to destroy the Americans, he could argue that he was simply defending himself and insuring the safety of Japanese lives.

Taido sliced his hand through the air. "Fire!"

Submachine guns opened up, firing in long bursts. Taido bent to the green case and flicked the clasps. He lifted the lid and grinned at the contents. Inside lay a Russian-made RPG-7 rocket-propelled grenade launcher and four 85 mm rockets. Taido selected a rocket and slipped it into the launch tube.

It was time to rid the Kanabo Corporation of this irritating American once and for all.

"GET DOWN!"

Bullets began to strike the hull of the USO Oil boat as the snarl of automatic weapons' fire echoed across the water. Bolan knelt behind the molding of the bridge and observed. Many of the bullets were short, striking the water, and those that hit weren't penetrating. The Executioner listened carefully. He had heard the firing signatures of most common small arms many times, and he was fairly sure they were being fired at with Uzis.

At close to four hundred yards' range, the 9 mm bullets had lost much of their velocity and dropped to subsonic speeds. They couldn't penetrate the hull of the boat. The USO Oil team's .30-caliber carbines were only slightly more efficient. He clicked on the intercom. "Chris, Smitts, get on deck. Stay low."

"Roger." Racine and Smitts crept out of the cabin, cradling their carbines, and peered up at the bridge. They ducked and flinched as occasional bullets smacked into *Scrappy*'s hull. Bolan jerked his head toward the Japanese cutter. "Let's return fire. Set your sights for their longest range."

Racine, Redland and Smitts pushed the rear sights of their carbines all the way back, then looked up at Bolan hesitantly. It was the first time they had ever been in a shooting fight, and they were unsure of themselves. Bolan gave them a smile of encouragement. "Gentlemen, remember Pearl Harbor!"

Redland grinned approvingly and slid the barrel of his carbine over the railing. Bolan spoke low and calmly as the Japanese continued firing. "Aim high. Fire semiauto."

The Texan squeezed off a shot. A second later there was a small splash of water by the Japanese cutter's hull. Bolan nodded. "Aim a little higher."

Redland lifted the muzzle of his carbine slightly and fired again. Bolan saw the sudden yellow flash of a bullet ricocheting off metal from the cutter's steel hull. "Excellent. Fire at will."

Redland, Racine and Smitts began emptying their carbines as fast as they could aim and pull the trigger. Bolan scanned with his binoculars. Yellow flashes were erupting all along the cutter's hull. There was no way the little M-2 carbines could damage the cutter, but being fired on seemed to be infuriating the Japanese. They began firing off entire magazines on full-auto in response, and most of their shots were now falling short or flying wide. Bolan looked at the men under his command. It was little more than skirmishing, but it was tremendous for USO Oil morale. For the first time, the team was actually fighting back. They aimed and fired their carbines with fierce determination.

Bolan stiffened. A man had popped up suddenly on the cutter's deck. He held a long green tube across his shoulder, and he seemed to look straight at Bolan through his optical sight. The weapon's protruding conical warhead was unmistakable. The Executioner rammed the throttles to full.

"Hit the deck!"

Scrappy lurched forward blindly with a diesel roar. Across the water, the RPG-7 rocket hissed out of the launcher and zoomed through the air. The rocket streaked by only ten yards off port and continued on to the island a hundred yards beyond. It smacked into the sand and detonated in a blast of orange fire.

Smitts stared in horror. "Jesus Christ! They have bazookas!"

The Executioner's voice roared out in the unmistakable tone of command as he stood up and grabbed the helm. "Chris! Smitts! Return fire! Try to keep that bastard down!"

Racine and Smitts began firing their carbines again. A second rocket shrieked through the air and slammed into the water a few yards off the bow. Water geysered into the air as the five-pound, high-explosive warhead detonated and steel shell fragments hissed out of the water and slammed into the hull.

"Red! Take the helm. Keep us moving and get us as close to the shore as you can without beaching us."

The Texan nodded and crouched behind the wheel. Bolan leaped from the flying bridge onto the deck. Racine and Smitts glanced at him quickly. The soldier nodded at them. "Keep firing."

Bolan went into the cabin and retrieved a long, thin, hard plastic case that leaned against the sonar panel. He laid it on the floor and flipped the latches open. As he raised the lid, the bolt-action .378 Weatherby Magnum sniper rifle gleamed dully. Bolan picked up the precision weapon and worked the bolt. It was smooth as glass. Cowboy Kissinger had done his usual excellent job with the rifle. The Executioner broke open a package of hand-loaded .378 Magnum ammunition and began feeding steel jacketed solids into the top of the big rifle.

Something struck the bow, and the boat shuddered. The forward cabin window shattered as steel fragments ripped through at shoulder level. Bolan slammed the bolt home and dropped an extra five rounds into his shirt pocket as he rose. Out the shattered window he could see the tip of the boat's bow had been blown off. So far, they had been lucky. But soon enough the opposition was going to put a rocket through them amidships, and they were going to be sunk.

Bolan crouched as he went out on deck. Racine was still firing. Smitts was crouched behind the gunwale and was trying to slip a fresh magazine into his carbine with shaking hands.

The Executioner snapped the Weatherby to his shoulder and peered through the eight-power scope.

On the cutter the man had risen and was handing the rocket launcher operator a fresh rocket. Bolan's eyes narrowed. The rocking boat he stood on wasn't an ideal firing platform, but the water was relatively calm and the range was under five hundred yards.

He put the crosshairs on the rocket loader's chest and fired.

The big rifle recoiled against his shoulder, and half a second later the man was flung from the view of Bolan's scope as the steel-jacketed .378 Magnum bullet swatted him across the deck of the cutter.

The Executioner worked the rifle's bolt as the rocketeer dropped out of site. He swept the cutter with his telescopic sight. The Japanese craft was built along the lines of a fast attack boat. He examined the open bridge.

No one was visible. Bolan glanced up at Redland. "Take us close to the reef and head in an opposite course from the cutter. See if you can get me an angle on her bow.

The Texan peeked up over the bridge as he turned the wheel. "Can do."

Scrappy moved sideways away from the Japanese boat.

The cutter's engines roared as they realized what Bolan was doing, but they were too late. They had put themselves too close to the reef to turn their bow toward him. The only way to cover their rear was to momentarily expose it as they turned the other way.

Bolan began firing rapidly as the stern of the cutter's engine housing was exposed. The soldier aimed a foot above the waterline, and the thin metal of the engine compartment twisted as the heavy rifle bullet tore through. Bolan fired again. The bullet smashed home, and even at three hundred yards he could hear the cutter's engine shriek as the steel-jacketed bullet plunged into its inner workings.

The cutter desperately continued its turn, and Bolan caught a flash of the open bridge. The arm and shoulder of a crouching man were visible in the Executioner's scope as someone held the wheel from behind cover and blindly kept the cutter turning. Bolan moved his crosshairs two feet and snapped off a shot. The bullet ran into the fleeting target.

The hand and shoulder disappeared. Blood spattered the white paint of the helm's control panel as the cutter suddenly slewed about without control in its turn.

Bolan fired a second round into the engine housing at deck level, and black smoke oozed out of the exhaust as the cutter howled. Bolan put a third round lower into the engine compartment, then a fourth. The engine screeched as its workings broke apart at high speed, and smoke began to seep out of the bullet holes as well. The sound of the cutter's engine suddenly died.

The Japanese vessel moved through the water another fifteen yards from its own momentum, then slid gently to a stop. Nothing moved on its decks as it bobbed in the waves that broke against the reef.

Bolan slid fresh cartridges into the Weatherby's magazine and flicked the bolt shut. He raised the rifle to his eye and scanned. The situation was a standoff. The Japanese couldn't move, but he didn't have the men or the firepower to board her. They still had their RPG-7, but the individual who exposed himself to use it was a dead man. Bolan lowered the big rifle. The Japanese had lost their communications and their engine.

He hoped they would have a nice swim back to base.

Bolan glanced up at Redland, where he was crouched at the helm. "Take us home."

20

Redland looked amazed as he examined *Scrappy*'s bow while Smitts tied her off to the compound pier. The nose of the boat simply wasn't there. The RPG-7 warhead had blown it off, leaving only a blackened three-foot triangular hole. The starboard side was riddled with bullet holes, and long ripping gouges scored her from the flying shrapnel.

Bolan clapped the big Texan on the shoulder. "Looks like the old girl is going to need a new coat of paint."

Redland nodded grimly.

Racine was irrepressible. He slapped the boat's battered hull affectionately. "We kicked their butts!"

"We won that round," Bolan told him.

The Texan added with a laugh, "We did. But it's going to take more than beer cans to patch up this one."

Racine was undeterred. "She's still seaworthy, and besides..." His grin went nearly from ear-to-ear as he repeated himself. "We kicked their butts!"

The college kid's enthusiasm was infectious. Redland turned to Bolan. "So what's the plan now?"

"Why don't you and Chris go see about rustling up some food. I'm going to check in. After we eat, we'll start on repairs. As of tomorrow, I want USO Oil back in business."

"Can do." Redland jerked his thumb at Racine. "Come on, Rambo, let's go get you some raw meat."

Racine happily followed his colleague down the pier. He looked up at Bolan as he passed and nodded his head up and down earnestly. "We kicked their butts, didn't we?"

"Yes, Chris, we did."

TAIDO WOULDN'T MEET Tanaka's eyes as his motor launch came alongside. Tanaka's eyes narrowed as he glanced about the stricken cutter. Bullet strikes smeared the sides of the hull. Two of the windows had been shattered. The communication antennas leaned sadly and wobbled in the breeze at a forty-five-degree angle. The shut-down engine still smelled of burning oil and overheated metal. Tanaka had seen the gaping holes in the engine housing as he had approached. One of Taido's operatives, a man named Mas, lay on the deck with a ragged hole in the center of his chest where his soft body armor had been defeated. Tanaka had little doubt that the man had been killed instantly. The helmsman, Si, sat with his back against the helm. The bridge around him was spattered with dried blood. Si appeared to be missing several fingers. The rest of the men stood dejectedly at attention on deck.

The commander turned his gaze on Taido, who examined the toes of his boots with great care.

Tanaka spoke in a very calm voice. "Taido. Report."

Taido flinched. He would have much preferred it if Tanaka had been screaming at him and foaming at the mouth while he struck him about the face and neck. However, his boss simply regarded him with an icily condemning calm. He considered his words carefully. "*Hai*, Tanaka-*san*. We ran into the American commando."

Tanaka nodded. His face remained expressionless. "I can see that."

Taido glanced up from under his heavy eyebrows, and then quickly fixed his eyes back down at the deck. "Well…" He shrugged helplessly. "He had an extremely large rifle."

Tanaka blinked incredulously. "That is your report? You encountered the American, and he had an extremely large rifle?"

Taido wished Tanaka would just shoot him and get it over with. He sighed and drew himself up to his full height, which was still nearly a head shorter than his superior. He looked up and down the crippled and bloodstained cutter in response, then met Tanaka's gaze. "*Hai,* Tanaka-*san.* I believe that sums up the situation very accurately."

For a moment, the older man was speechless. A part of him almost had to respect Taido despite this monumental failure. Even in the face of his own possible death, the hairy ape remained impudent. Tanaka kept his face impassive. "Taido. You have failed."

Taido flinched as if he had been struck. He swallowed hard. "*Hai,* Tanaka-*san.*"

"You engaged the American boat. What happened?"

"We engaged in maneuvering. I attempted to ram him. The American boat surprised us with powerfully modified engines and managed to escape. However, our boat was still faster than theirs and stronger. I had more men, automatic weapons and the RPG-7. I believed we could defeat them in battle."

Tanaka nodded. "So, then, how did you fail?"

Taido looked down glumly. "The American managed to put the reef between us. He then used a high-powered rifle with a telescopic sight to force us under cover. Then he picked apart the communications system and disabled the engine." Taido sighed. "I'm deeply sorry, Tanaka-*san.* I'm not a ship's captain. I know little of naval tactics. I'm a field operative by training."

Tanaka's voice broke into a low snarl. "You are an incompetent ape, Taido, and you've failed in a most miserable fashion. I'm actually beginning to believe that you're genuinely as stupid as you look. This failure is intolerable. Only your notable past service to the Kanabo Corporation is preventing me from obeying my better judgment and having you killed."

Taido's face set. He pulled a short, double-edged fighting knife from a sheath on his belt and extended the little finger of his left hand. He raised one eyebrow questioningly.

Tanaka spit on the deck in disgust. "You're an idiot, Taido. We aren't Yakuza gangsters. I don't accept your apology. I accept only results. I want the American killed. I want the

USO Oil operation shut down. Do these things, and perhaps I'll forget your idiotic naval engagement.''

Taido bowed very low. *"Hai,* Tanaka-*san."*

"Have one of your men tie a tow rope to the launch. We will haul your worthless hides back to the atoll."

Tanaka turned without another word and leaped from the cutter down to the deck of the launch. He thought Taido had taken his dressing down rather well. He believed the man was actually repentant, and he had no doubt that with a simple nod Taido would have removed his little finger without blinking. Tanaka shrugged. He needed the man, and he needed all ten of Taido's thick fingers in place if they were going to accomplish their mission and kill the American. Tonight he would have a conference with Taido about killing this troublesome American.

Tanaka believed it was about time to take the direct approach.

THE MOON WAS WANING as René Sauvin checked over his armament and equipment one more time. Seven men, including himself, stood under the lights on the boat dock of the French test derrick. The men wore black wet-suit vests and knee-length dive shorts for the tropical waters. Their exposed limbs were smeared with gray-and-black streaks of camouflage grease, and each had a bubbleless rebreathing apparatus strapped to his back. Their munitions were sparse. Each man carried a sound-suppressed 9 mm Glock 18 pistol sealed in heavy plastic and a fighting knife. Their mission wasn't an all-out assault. Tonight's action was to be quick and clandestine. Sauvin glanced at the two waterproof demolition bags where they rested on the dock's metal deck.

Each package contained two limpet mines with ten pounds of high explosives. They were small charges. They wouldn't be enough to blow up USO Oil's two exploration boats, but when they were properly placed along their hulls they would be more than sufficient to break the small exploration vessels' backs and scuttle them to the bottom. With their boats sunk and the delicate equipment inside them under ten feet of water, USO Oil would be finished in the Pacific Trust Islands.

Sauvin would have preferred to go ashore and kill the Americans in their beds, but orders were orders. Sauvin shrugged nonchalantly. It mattered little. He rather liked sinking other people's boats. It was satisfying work, and it might be enough of an injury to draw the big American out into a situation where Sauvin could kill him without breaking orders.

ZeeZee shrugged into the straps of his air tank. He grinned at Sauvin through the bruises and stitches in his face. Swimming so soon in the ocean would probably make his face hurt worse, but the little man wouldn't stand being left behind. He was also the best demolitions man on the strike team. "Good fun tonight, huh, Commandant?"

Sauvin grinned. "Yes, ZeeZee. Just like old times."

Hubert heaved his breathing unit onto his massive shoulders, which bulged out of his swim vest. "Just remember, ZeeZee. These won't be a bunch of vegetarians waving signs and whining about the rights of whales this time. It'll be American oil men, waving guns, and their commando friend will undoubtedly be lurking about. Try not to blow yourself up. If you get any uglier, no one will be able to stomach working with you."

The rest of the team laughed as the little Frenchman exposed his gap-toothed smile. "Don't worry, Hubert. I'll be very careful with the explosives. We both know that your wife would weep if I lost any of my fingers."

Hubert snorted as the rest of the men roared and clapped ZeeZee on the back. Sauvin nodded with satisfaction. Morale was high, and the mission should be an easy in and out. After the beatings they had taken recently, it was a testament to his men that they were salty and ready for action. Sauvin checked his watch, then glanced at his men. They looked back at him expectantly. He folded his arms across his chest.

"Gentlemen, the operation is fairly simple. Hubert and Denys will scuttle the large boat. ZeeZee and Peter will take the smaller one. Marco and I will take covering positions."

He turned to the edge of the deck where Nicholas was half submerged in the water, giving the Dolphin the final once over. "How are we?"

Nicholas gave Sauvin the thumbs-up. The Dolphin swimmer delivery vehicle was little more than a dark blue torpedo with a saddle, a steering wheel and a small navigation console in the middle. Three sets of steel tow bars sprouted along its sides, each of which could accommodate a pair of divers. Most of its surface was covered with cleats to hold various weapons and equipment fits. Nicholas threw a leg over the saddle and saluted as he gunned the engine. "Any time you are ready, Commandant."

Sauvin checked his watch. It was 2:30 a.m. He figured about an hour to transport themselves outside of the USO Oil pier, ten minutes to affix the charges, then another ten minutes to get away before the detonations. His men were eager. The equipment had been checked three times already. There was no point in waiting around. "All right. Into the water."

The men pulled their diving masks onto their faces and slid smoothly off the metal deck into the ocean.

"Bon voyage!"

Sauvin glanced at the catwalk. Ten feet up, Jeanine Maitland smiled and blew the team an expansive kiss. The men in the water grinned and saluted back. She motioned Sauvin toward her, and he stepped closer. As he looked up at her, he could still see the massive purple bruising that distorted the left side of her face. She leaned over the railing and spoke low. "Hey, Sauvin."

He raised a questioning eyebrow. "Yes, Miss Maitland?"

She smiled at him winsomely. "You think maybe you can do me a favor?"

Sauvin shrugged. "If I can."

Maitland's smile grew very cold. "If you should happen to see my boyfriend…" She stuck out her fist and extended her forefinger and raised her thumb. She pointed her finger directly at Sauvin and dropped her thumb like the hammer of a gun. "Send him my love."

Sauvin slowly nodded, then smiled back. "Given the opportunity, I'll give him your regards."

She gave him a casual salute. *"Bonne chance, Commandant."*

Sauvin saluted back. *"Merci."*

The big man slid into the water and took his position on the leading tow bar of the Dolphin. He jerked his head at Nicholas. "Let's do it."

The Dolphin moved away smoothly from the dock, and Nicholas pulled the diving planes down. The swimmer delivery vehicle slid below the surface in a shallow dive. In moments, there was no trace of the strike team except for the already dispersing triangle of their wake under the moonlight.

21

Bolan spoke into the secure comm link. "So, is the Man still pleased with me?"

Nine thousand miles away Barbara Price sighed in a bemused fashion. "Well, he's irritated, but in an amused sort of way. The administration is very concerned about having a messy international incident, but I think they're secretly pleased with you." She paused for a moment. "Your little naval engagement this afternoon raised some eyebrows, though."

Bolan shrugged. "I'm pushing it. But we were in international waters, and it was the Kanabo boys who started the Pirates of the Caribbean routine. I just finished it. Why? Has the Kanabo Corporation filed an official protest?"

"No, and short of us nuking their installation, I don't think they're likely to. They're even more leery of international attention than we are. The members of the Pacific Trust Islands' provisional government might be going to the highest bidder, but even they weren't too pleased about the attack in the hospital clinic. The heavily armed Japanese bodies strewed about were kind of hard to explain away."

"You'd be surprised what a few million yen can do."

"I'm afraid you might be right. But there is some good news."

"Oh?"

"Yes. While you were out on the high seas, the Navy doctor on board the *Sam Houston* pronounced Dr. Tutarotaro's condition stabilized, and they brought him ashore on one of their inflatable launches. He's resting comfortably in his clinic with his own personal honor guard of heavily armed Isolationists. The shootout has caused quite a stir locally. Tutarotaro is a popular man, and even people who opposed his views respected him highly. Plus, I don't think any of the islanders are too pleased about having one of their few trained doctors attacked. They are proud that he shot it out with his attackers and won. When the United Nations confers nation status on the Pacific Trust Island group, he might become their first official national hero. The fact that it was Americans who whisked him off when he was wounded and kept him alive has probably bought us some significant brownie points with the locals."

"He's a good man. What did he say about my involvement?"

"Not much. He's expressed gratitude to the *Sam Houston*'s medical team, but from what we hear on our end he's being kind of vague about how he got on the sub and who, if anyone, helped him. According to Gadgets, the doctor would like to speak to you at your earliest convenience."

"I'll go see him first thing in the morning."

"It's already morning there, isn't it?"

Bolan stifled a yawn at the reminder. "Close to 3:00 a.m. Has Aaron dug up anything new?"

"Hmm. Not much. He—"

Bolan suddenly cut her off. "Hold on a moment."

On the console next to the comm link was the control panel of Schwarz's jury-rigged security suite. A tiny speaker peeped plaintively at the Executioner, and a little red light began to blink.

The Executioner rose and picked up his M-4 Ranger carbine. He checked the load in the carbine, and in the breech of the M-203 grenade launcher mounted beneath it. "Keep the line open. I'll get back to you."

Price's voice showed her concern. "What is it?"

The Executioner pressed the button on the console to trigger the alarms in the rest of the compound, then flicked the

M-4's selector to the 3-round-burst mode. "I think I have company."

RENÉ SAUVIN EASED through the netting in the murky water. He had tested it gingerly, and on close examination it had turned out to be the local heavy fishing net woven from plant fibers. The serrated edge of his fighting knife had parted it with ease. Nicholas had parked the Dolphin five hundred yards out, and Sauvin and the rest of his team had swum in the rest of the distance.

The French leader moved out to cover the right flank as Marco slid through the opening and swam to the left. Both men cradled the plastic-sealed Glock pistols. ZeeZee and Peter swam through with their demolition packages, and a moment later the larger forms of Denys and Hubert moved through the netting. The men floated in place for a moment as Sauvin rose through the water and silently broke the surface.

The USO Oil compound was quiet. The lights were running, but no one appeared to be moving. The situation seemed normal for 3:30 a.m. Sauvin watched for a few moments more and descended again. The water was dark but clear, and the moon was very bright. The men could see one another as murky shapes. Ahead of them, the lights of the complex made a dim refracted glow in the water near the beach.

Sauvin joined the underwater huddle and stuck his fist in the middle of his assembled men's diving masks. He stuck his thumb up and nodded once vigorously. The men gave the thumbs-up back and split into their teams. ZeeZee and Peter swam quietly toward the small boat. Denys and Hubert trailed them slightly off to the left and diverged toward the bulk of the larger craft. Marco had moved to the other end of the net's perimeter to take point. Sauvin rose again with his weapon in his hands. He broke the surface and watched the USO Oil compound.

Nothing moved.

With luck he and his men would be in and out within five minutes.

MACK BOLAN CROUCHED behind the boat shack with an open suitcase on the concrete step in front of him. Racine and Redland knelt beside him with their carbines ready. The rest of the team was positioned behind the other three shacks in two-man fire teams.

Bolan glanced at the display on the security suite. The Texan spoke in a hoarse whisper. "What's going on?"

"When my friend set up the netting, he wove some monofilament wires through it. They're very thin. Anyone cutting through the net underwater at night would never notice them, particularly if they were being stealthy and not using any lights. If the filament is broken, it sends a signal to our security box."

Red nodded. "And?"

Bolan pointed to the little blinking red light on the miniature console. "And I believe Charlie may be in the wire."

Racine swallowed. "Are you sure?"

Bolan's eyebrow raised just a fraction. "No, I'm not positive. It could be a shark or a dolphin got caught in the net and snapped some of the filaments." The Executioner kept his eyes on his readouts. "But I think we'll know one way or the other in a moment."

Redland frowned. "Like when they come out of the water and start lobbing in grenades?"

Bolan smiled ruefully. "Give me a little more credit, Red. We do have a backup system."

"I'm glad to hear that. What is it?"

"My friend set us up a magnetometer and put detector strips into the sand fifteen yards out from the beach and around the pier area."

Redland looked puzzled. "Magnetometers? You mean like the kind you use to find ore samples?"

The Executioner nodded. "It's the same principle, but in the military application you set them along your perimeter and they detect any significant sources of metal that pass over them."

Redland still frowned. Racine looked smug. "Bad guy frogmen would have scuba tanks and guns, Red."

"You guys are catching on," the soldier stated.

The Texan had been around the block, but this big guy never stopped teaching him things. "So we wait?"

Bolan's eyes narrowed. "No. Chris, hand me the detonator."

Racine's eyes widened. "What's happening?"

The Executioner gestured at the console. The magnetometer's receiver panel had a bank of six tiny green lights. The fifth and sixth monitored the pier area not twenty feet from where Bolan and the two USO men crouched. The little green light was blinking in a perturbed fashion. Bolan took the detonator from Racine and rose. He flicked up the plastic safety shield over the remote detonator's trigger buttons and pressed the first button.

"They're going for the boats."

SAUVIN STARTED IN ALARM as the pier lit up from under the water with intense, bright white light. A split second later, a second flare of duller orange light followed it. The water around the pier seemed to fall in on itself, then it suddenly erupted into a geyser that shot thirty feet into the air. Twenty yards down from the pier, the water lit up again, then again twenty yards farther. The shock wave from the first explosion hit Sauvin and rolled him in the water violently as geyser after geyser blew up into the air in a line of blinding white explosions.

Sauvin thrust out his limbs to try to stop his cartwheeling and held on to his pistol with grim determination. The shock waves rolled over him continuously, and he snarled as he tried to keep his head above water. They had been detected, and the Americans had set concussion charges in the water. God help his men who were under the water near the charges when they went off. Beneath the surface, the shock waves would brutalize them. They could possibly kill them. Sauvin had seen the orange secondary explosion by the pier, and he knew that was one of the strike team's high-explosives detonating. The USO Oil boats were rocking violently in the water, but they showed no signs of sinking.

Sauvin doubted the charge had been in place when it had gone off.

The hollow thump of a grenade launcher sounded from within the compound. Sauvin squinted as the night lit up under the harsh white glare of a burning magnesium flare. Sauvin glanced about desperately. It seemed almost as bright as day, and his men were surfacing. ZeeZee was dragging Peter behind him in the water lifeguard fashion. Hubert lay on his back in the water thrashing weakly. Like himself, Marco had been above the water on point and was unharmed. Denys was nowhere to be seen.

They were sitting ducks.

Sauvin roared. "Dive! Dive!"

ZeeZee swam toward him, towing Peter. Sauvin realized his men had been deafened by the concussions and couldn't hear him. He ripped open the packing on his pistol and spun the suppressor tube off the barrel. He thrust the pistol into the air and held down the trigger on full-auto. The Glock sent a strobing stream of fire into the air. His men focused on him. Sauvin pointed at Marco, then at Hubert. Marco nodded and swam hard toward his stricken comrade. Sauvin pointed at ZeeZee and jerked his thumb down at the water. ZeeZee kicked his swim fins up into the air and dived, dragging Peter with him.

Sauvin kicked and dived.

He prayed fervently that there were no more lurking explosive charges as he slid down into the darkness.

THE EXECUTIONER STOOD on the pier and watched the last frogman swim toward a body and pull it under the water with him. Bolan flicked the selector switch of the M-4 Ranger carbine to full-auto and sent several long bursts into the water over the netting. He kept the shots at too high an angle to go in the water and hit anybody, but anyone passing through the net would know they were being fired on.

Racine and Redland stood beside him as he lowered his weapon. Bolan turned to Racine. "Go give the others the all-clear."

The younger man cradled his carbine. "Are we going to chase them?"

Bolan slid a fresh magazine into the M-4. "No. I have a better idea."

Redland looked out across the water as the magnesium flare slowly drifted down on its parachute. "Damn, the Japanese sure hit back fast."

Bolan shook his head. "It wasn't the Japanese. It was the French."

"How do you know?"

"I think the Japanese would have come up from the beach and from the pier in a two-pronged attack, and they would have come to kill us. So far, the French have kept their she-nanigans brutal but nonlethal. Our friends in the water wanted to sink the boats and put us out of business. I believe the Japanese want our heads."

"So you're going to let the French get away?"

"Yes and no. We're going to let them get back home, but I want to give them something to remember us by."

"What are you going to do?"

Bolan slung the M-4. "I'm going to make a call."

GADGETS SCHWARZ STOOD in the attack center of the U.S.S. *Sam Houston* next to the captain. His obvious love of every unclassified mechanical device that the crew could show him had endeared him to the entire boat's complement. The chief sonar operator was a stout young man named Lawrence. He swiveled in his chair and checked his watch.

"Five minutes since last explosion, Captain."

The submarine had been a few miles off shore, listening passively, when the explosions had begun at the USO Oil site. On passive listening, it had sounded like World War III, and Lawrence had confirmed that the explosions had taken place below the surface. They had steamed in slowly and quietly to half a mile from shore and had sat to listen again at periscope depth.

The captain nodded and turned to Schwarz. "Apparently, someone put the stores you commandeered to some good use."

Schwarz nodded thoughtfully. The captain peered at him. "If the compound is under attack, I can have a SEAL team onshore in ten minutes."

The Able Team commando shook his head. "No. I believe if the compound was under direct attack or in danger of falling we would have heard from them." He checked his watch. "Though, I believe we should hear something any minute."

On cue, the radio operator swiveled about in his chair. "I have a scrambled satellite communication." He paused for a moment and looked at Schwarz. "It's for…Mr. Gadgets."

Schwarz took the headset. "Yes."

"This is Striker."

"What can I do for you Striker?"

"We've just repulsed an attack on our pier. I think the divers were French, and they intended to scuttle our boats."

"Can you confirm?"

"No. That's what I'd like you to do, if the captain is willing."

"The captain is a swell fellow. We're getting along famously. What would you like us to do?"

"I don't think the French swam seven miles from their derrick. I'd be willing to bet they used a swimmer delivery vehicle to insert. It's been about five minutes since the fireworks stopped. They should be underway. See if you can detect them and find out where they go."

"Will do, Striker, but there is a French hunter-killer submarine lurking somewhere in the island chain. If the French sent in a strike team, it wouldn't surprise me if their sub was hanging around somewhere close keeping an eye out for them."

There was a slight pause. "Use your best judgment."

"Will do. Over and out." Schwarz handed back the headset

and turned to the captain. "We may have a swimmer delivery vehicle in the water, heading outward from the USO Oil site. We're betting it's heading for French territory."

The captain scratched his jaw thoughtfully. "That vehicle would have a small screw, and it would be optimized for quietness, but we should be able to pick it up." The captain turned to the chief sonar operator. "Lawrence, see if you can scare up something small and French, heading west, going quietly."

Lawrence swiveled back around and listened intently in his headphones. Long moments passed, and he seemed to go into a trance. Schwarz checked his watch. The bridge had been almost silent for three minutes. Lawrence suddenly spoke. "Something, Captain."

"What kind of something?"

Lawrence cocked his head. "Nothing I recognize off the top of my head, but it's small. Quiet. I'd say a single screw."

The captain nodded. "Let's follow it. Conn, ahead one-quarter speed."

The *Sam Houston* slid ahead through the water after its quarry. Lawrence nodded to himself and wrote in his log. "Closing in three minutes, Captain."

"Close to a thousand yards, then shadow them." The captain stood in front of his map panel as they closed in and smiled at Schwarz. "You have good sources. Unless they peel off their projected course, it takes them right to the French test derrick."

Lawrence started in his seat. "Captain! Unidentified submarine! Bearing zero-six-three. Speed eight knots. On intercept course!"

The captain's poker face slid on as he leaned on the bridge railing. "Can you identify?"

Lawrence cocked his head again. "It's diesel, two screws." Lawrence's eyes peered into the beyond as he listened to the sonic fingerprint of the oncoming submarine. "I'd say it's French, Daphné class, an attack boat."

The captain nodded. "Speed and bearing?"

"Unchanged sir. Still closing." Lawrence bolted upright. "Captain! They're opening their outer doors and flooding their torpedo tubes!"

Schwarz scratched his chin. "They seem to be rattling their saber."

The captain's brow knitted. "Yes. And I'm afraid under the circumstances I'm going to have to back off. My orders are rather explicit about international incidents. I believe sinking the sub of an ally of the United States might qualify."

Schwarz nodded sagely. "Well, we still can't be absolutely sure it was a French swimmer delivery vehicle."

The captain regarded Schwarz dryly. "It is my opinion that if it was a Japanese swimmer delivery vehicle, the French would be all too happy to let us blow it up or follow it to hell and back. It is also my opinion that since the unidentified vehicle is heading toward a French base and a French hunter-killer submarine has intercepted us, there might be a ghost of a chance that the French have tipped their hand in the matter, and, frankly, I'm unwilling to exchange salvos of torpedoes over it at this point in time."

Schwarz shrugged. "Still, you can't be absolutely sure about the swimmer vehicle."

The captain looked at Schwarz with exasperated disbelief and finally shook his head. "No. I guess we'll never be totally sure."

Schwarz examined his fingernails critically. "Well, you could ping them. Just to make sure. There's no law against it."

The captain's mouth worked up and down for a moment before words came out. "You're a devious bastard, you know that."

Schwarz feigned shock. When a submarine was pinged, it sent out a massive pulse of sound through the water. The returning echoes of that pulse gave a much more exact reading of how big something was, how fast it was going, and where it was exactly. The U.S.S. *Sam Houston*'s BQS-4 sonar dome was nearly twenty feet in diameter and took up almost the entire bow of the submarine. It could generate immensely powerful pulses of sound. Sound transmitted much more powerfully through water than through air, and the pulse of the BQS-4 was almost a solid wave of force as its energy moved through water. The effect of being pinged on divers in an open submersible would be horrendous.

The captain turned to the chief sonar operator. "Mr. Lawrence, please go active, and ping the unidentified craft for identification purposes."

"Aye, aye, sir." Lawrence scribbled quickly in his log and looked up. "How many times should I ping them?"

The captain pushed away from the bridge railing and folded his arms across his chest. "Repeatedly."

RENÉ SAUVIN CHECKED the luminous dial of his watch in the murky depths. The Dolphin towed them along back toward the derrick. His men had taken a terrible beating. The concussion charges had thrown them about like rag dolls. ZeeZee had used hand signals to tell him that Denys was gone. It seemed he had been directly over one of the charges when it had gone off, and he had been carrying twenty pounds of high explosive at the time.

According to his watch, the team was about two kilometers from the derrick. Sauvin considered surfacing and checking his team. Hubert was still alive, but he was obviously hurt. Sauvin reached up to poke Nicholas and tell him to surface when an immense hand suddenly slapped the Dolphin, and the hand clapped like thunder as it hit.

The delivery vehicle lurched as the solid wave of sound struck. A second hand slapped them, then a third. Sauvin flinched and jerked as the sound hit them. They were being hammered on the anvil of God. Pulses of light flashed under Sauvin's squinting eyelids, and each pulse sent screaming agony through his eardrums into his head. The Dolphin lurched and shuddered under the sonic beating. Sauvin reached up and managed to grab Nicholas's arm as he swayed in the submersible's saddle. Sauvin yanked his arm and pulled his head closer. Sauvin shoved his hand in front of Nicholas's mask and pointed upward. Nicholas leaned over the controls and yanked up on the control yokes. The Dolphin pulled into a steep ascent.

The submersible shuddered as it climbed. The hammering was continuous, and Sauvin could taste the copper of blood in his mouth as his nose started to bleed and the blinding pain in his skull mounted. Sauvin forced his eyes open and could see the water becoming brighter. The Dolphin suddenly broke the surface nearly vertically and fell back like a breaching whale. Sauvin lost his grip and was knocked away from the submersible as were most of his men. But the surface was blessedly silent except for the painful ringing in his ears. Sauvin suspected that would last for several days. He pulled off his mask and swam weakly back to the Dolphin.

Nicholas sat doggedly in the saddle, and ZeeZee and Peter had already remounted. Marco swam up with Hubert in his grasp. Sauvin spoke but found he couldn't hear his own words. He wearily grasped his tow bar and raised his hand. He waved toward home. Nicholas restarted the Dolphin's engine, and Sauvin could feel its mechanical hum vibrate through the tow bar as they pulled ahead through water. They were sitting ducks on the surface, but Sauvin didn't care.

If the American had wanted to kill them in the compound, he could have. Of that Sauvin was certain. Whoever had hammered them just now could have killed them. He realized that from start to finish he and his team had never stood a chance. They had gone out to make mischief, and the Americans had spanked them as if they were unruly children. Sauvin sagged with exhaustion on the tow bar.

It was the worst defeat of his life.

LAWRENCE WATCHED his sonar screen attentively as the last echoes of the pings faded from hearing. "Captain, the submersible vehicle has surfaced." He paused as he listened for several more moments. "Screw noise has resumed. They have resumed original heading toward French test derrick. They're remaining on the surface."

The Captain nodded. "What are their pals doing?"

Lawrence listened for the French hunter-killer submarine. "They've come to a complete halt. Maintaining position, Captain. Six thousand yards to starboard."

"Have they changed course or speed?"

"Not yet, Captain."

The captain turned to Schwarz. "What do you think?"

Schwarz gave it a moment of serious thought. "I suspect there is a great deal of swearing going on in French."

The captain grinned. "I concur. Helmsman, we're done here. Take us back to our patrol area. Ahead one-third."

22

Mack Bolan walked into the island clinic with a package under his arm. Four native men armed with French MAT-49 submachine guns and machetes stood at the doorway. Being so blatantly armed was a criminal offense in the islands, but Bolan doubted any constables were going to argue the point with the hard-eyed men guarding the clinic. They peered at Bolan warily but made no effort to stop him as he walked in. The doctor sat in a wheelchair in the clinic's little day room and stared out the window. The big man had lost weight. His eyes seemed sunken, and his saddle-leather complexion was noticeably paler. However, his eyes were alert, and the deep lines in his face rearranged themselves into a smile as Bolan entered the room. "I thought perhaps you had forgotten about me."

"No, you're a pretty memorable character." He handed the doctor a cardboard box. "Here, this is for you."

Tutarotaro opened the box and peered inside. The men on the USO Oil team often received care packages from home. Bolan had passed the hat and come up with an assortment of candy bars, a couple of back issues of *Playboy* and a pint of half-decent Scotch whiskey. The doctor peered up at Bolan with mock suspicion. "You are trying to corrupt me with the decadence of Western civilization."

"You're right. So, how are you?"

"Much better, thank you. I'm expected to make a full recovery."

"How do things stand with your people?"

The doctor looked at Bolan levelly. "I have spoken with

many of the big men, including the leaders of the Isolationist Movement."

Bolan nodded. "I noticed your honor guard."

The old man smiled. "Yes, I can't even go to the bathroom without at least two or three of them lurking about." His face grew serious again. "Many of my people weren't pleased when I told them what happened in the clinic. The Isolationists, in particular, wish to attack the Japanese atoll in force."

"Many of your people would be killed."

Tutarotaro nodded grimly. "That's what I told them. I also told them that if they load their canoes and attack the Japanese en masse, the United Nations would probably take action, and we might not receive nation status for years to come. I believe we must attempt to drive them out through our provisional government, but many yen have changed hands. Our current leaders are weak and corrupt. I fear they will take no action."

Bolan looked Tutarotaro hard in the eye. "Perhaps it's time you had new leaders."

Tutarotaro met Bolan's gaze. "You aren't the first person since my return to suggest that. However, that isn't as easy as it sounds. I don't believe we can go back to the old ways. Our population has grown too much to support itself by fishing and growing taro alone, and we have grown dependent on many technologies." The doctor's face grew grim. "If we are to truly be a nation and not another United Nations welfare state, I believe we will have to choose sides. I feel I owe you a great deal, Mr. Belasko, but not enough to simply hand over the future of my people."

Bolan shrugged. "I'm not a politician. I can't make you any promises, save one."

"What is that?"

The Executioner's voice was as cold as the grave. "The Kanabo Corporation is killing people. I'm going to put an end to it. Whatever happens after that is up to you."

BOLAN PULLED UP SHORT as he walked down the steps of the clinic. Jeanine Maitland had assumed the position with her hands on the hood of his jeep and her feet spread apart. Two native men were pointing submachine guns at her head, while a third was patting her down. She was wearing only a pair of cutoff khaki shorts and a scoop-necked T-shirt, but Bolan knew from experience she liked to go heavily armed. A moment later, the man frisking her produced a tiny Browning .25 automatic pistol and a long, slender folding knife. The faces of the two men covering her hardened. All four of them looked up as Bolan approached.

The natives had watched Bolan silently when he had entered the clinic. Now they grinned. The man who had frisked Maitland spoke. "This woman say she want to see you." He held up the knife and the gun. "She a friend of yours, Mr. Belasko?"

Bolan regarded Maitland. She looked at him with an irked expression from where she was bent over his jeep. The left side of her face was still deeply bruised, though the swelling had gone down considerably since he had last seen her. Her composure finally broke as she snarled, "Are you going to tell them to let me go or what?"

"Let her go. I'll talk to her."

The men simply walked away from the vehicle and resumed their vigil on the clinic steps. The leader handed Bolan the pistol and knife as he passed. "You be careful, Mr. Belasko."

Bolan nodded. "I will." He climbed into the passenger seat and pointed his thumb at the driver's seat. "Let's go. You're driving."

She frowned. "Where are we going?"

"You said you wanted to talk. I'm not willing to go anyplace you suggest. We're going to take a friendly drive."

Maitland's face went expressionless for a moment as she considered that. Her hand went unconsciously to her face. "Give me back my stuff."

Bolan handed her back the pistol and the knife. The little automatic went down the front of her shorts, and she slid the knife down the rear. She took the wheel, gunned the engine, pulled out onto the road and headed toward the beach.

"We have a problem."

The Executioner smiled coldly. "You're right, and the next time you or your friends try something I won't pull my punches."

The woman glared. For a moment they were both silent as they drove along the beach. "That isn't what I mean, and I'll tell you, we lost a man last night."

Bolan nodded. "I know. Chris found a swim fin with a foot in it this morning floating under the pier."

Maitland blinked, then continued. "We both know my people attacked your compound last night and tried to scuttle your boats. Between you and me, I won't deny it, though, officially, my government will deny everything. But you must also admit that though our methods have been rough, we have, as you say, pulled our punches with you, as well."

He frowned slightly. "It's been nonlethal between us so far, but things change. Swimming into our compound with high explosives can do that."

Maitland shook her head. "We didn't intend to kill anybody."

Bolan stared at her expressionlessly.

"Listen, the Kanabo Corporation is a mutual enemy of ours, you agree, no?"

The Executioner nodded. It was true enough. "Yeah, I believe they've killed both Frenchmen and Americans."

"Good, because I have been authorized by my government to offer a deal of mutual assistance in this matter."

Bolan's face remained expressionless as he considered this. "Go on."

The woman took a deep breath and pushed her bangs out of her eyes. "We're going to take out the Japanese atoll. We believe your assistance would be invaluable in this endeavor."

"I hope you won't be insulted if I don't immediately take your word on this."

"I would rather hope you'd confirm this through channels before you agreed."

The Executioner ignored the comment. "You intend to take them out?"

"Yes. By night assault."

"What about the Japanese oil workers and crew?"

Maitland smiled. "I will tell you something for free. We both know that the Mitsuko Geothermal Development group is a front for the Kanabo Corporation. Our intelligence shows that the Mitsuko personnel have undergone heavy rotation in the islands in the past two weeks. We believe that few, if any, real laborers are on the Japanese atoll at all. It is now a paramilitary camp, and it will continue to launch attacks against you and us until the French and Americans have been driven from the islands and the Kanabo Corporation has secured the oil development rights in the Pacific Trust chain. That is why we are offering a deal of mutual assistance. The Kanabo Corporation is going to a full clandestine war footing."

Bolan suspected everything she said was true. "And you want to hit them immediately."

Maitland squinted from the glare off the sand. "That would be ideal. We are sure the Japanese have a sub in the area and are watching the islands with satellites. They must know we attacked you last night. They won't expect to be attacked immediately, much less by our combined forces."

The Executioner looked at her hard. "Why do you want me along?"

"To be honest, we need you. You put several of our men in hospital, and as I told you, we lost Denys last night. There isn't time to bring in more men, and if we do the Japanese will undoubtedly detect it. Our strike team is under strength, and you, Monsieur Belasko, have already proved your capability. If we combine our forces and strike now, we can win."

Bolan folded his arms and leaned back in his seat. "And then?"

She shrugged indifferently. "And then whatever happens, happens. The United States and France will still be competing for the oil development rights here in the islands. Someone will win, and someone will lose. But the killings will be stopped, the competition between our two countries will be on the level and the Kanabo Corporation will be out of the game.'' She grinned at him winningly. "It is best for both of us, no?''

Bolan looked out at the ocean. "I'll run it by my people.''

HAL BROGNOLA ANSWERED the call. "You've been approached by the French?''

Bolan looked out the window to where Racine and Smitts were repairing *Scrappy*'s bow. The RPG-7 hadn't been kind to her. "Yeah. Are they on the level?''

"The French military attaché in Washington walked into CIA headquarters first thing this morning and dropped it in the director's lap. I think they're dead serious.''

"How does the Man feel about it?''

The big Fed was quiet for a moment. "He's authorized it.''

"Exactly what am I authorized to do?''

Brognola's tone turned professional. "You are authorized to participate in concert with French agents in neutralizing Kanabo Corporation paramilitary forces in the Pacific Trust Islands. Logistics and tactics will be up to you and the French commander as the situation develops.''

Bolan let out a long, slow breath. That was about as straightforward as orders in his line of work ever got. "We'll go in tonight. Striker out.''

23

Mack Bolan sat across the table from René Sauvin. The big man still had a band of surgical tape across the bridge of his nose from when Bolan had hit him. The ugly one, ZeeZee, sat at his right hand. The little man got more repulsive each time Bolan saw him. Jeanine Maitland sat on Bolan's right and drank bottled water. The rest of the French strike team stood around the table. A blown-up satellite photograph of the Kanabo Corporation's atoll held everyone's attention.

The atoll was a small ring of coral barely three-quarters of a mile across that nearly encompassed its own little lagoon. From the satellite's view, two parts of the ring were open. One part was a cleft that boats could pass through, and to the north, part of the atoll was submerged and formed a barrier reef. Sometimes the reef was exposed by the tide, and sometimes not. It was much too shallow for boats to cross. Barrier reefing also fringed most of the atoll along its perimeter. There was really only one entrance to the lagoon for boats of any size.

Sauvin pointed at the cleft. "The plan is simple. We take the Dolphin straight down their throats and assault. They won't expect it."

Bolan shook his head. "We detected you at USO Oil when you tried that, and I suspect the Kanabo installation is more heavily defended and has much more sophisticated security. There's a Japanese submarine lurking around somewhere as well. We have to assume it's listening. If their boat happens to be close by, its sonar will hear your submersible's screw noise. Surprise is our best weapon. I don't think we should be willing to give it up so easily.''

Sauvin frowned. ''I'd personally rather insert from our submarine, but it would have to surface for us to find it and once we went out to it I believe we would be detected. The Dolphin is our only choice.''

Bolan shook his head. ''It's too easily detected by a wary enemy. I don't like the idea of swimming through the cleft. We have to assume they have magnetometers and passive listening devices. The cleft is a death trap.''

Sauvin's frown deepened. ''Perhaps you would prefer crawling over coral in the dark during the tide.''

''I think we should make a surface approach.''

ZeeZee snorted. ''Suicide! If their satellite is watching, they'll see us coming from miles away! Any boats we have would be detected from miles away as well.'' The little man shook his head derisively.

Bolan shrugged. It was time to start playing some trump cards. The Stony Man team had been furiously doing homework for him all day. ''You're partially right. My sources say there's a Japanese telecommunications satellite that passes over the South Pacific, and it's in a position to observe the Pacific Trust Islands. But it only has about a five-hour window of observation starting from 8:00 p.m. our time, and then its orbit takes it over the horizon around 1:00 a.m. There's also another Japanese satellite farther north. Its view isn't as good, and its window is 4:00-6:00 a.m. That gives us a three-hour attack window when we can't be spotted by their satellites.''

Maitland tapped a finger on the table in thought. ''How do you expect to get boats close enough without being detected? And we still have to swim into the lagoon. If they have passive listening devices and magnetometers as you say, they will still detect us, no?''

Bolan shook his head. ''No. Not if we use native canoes.''

Sauvin blinked. ''Canoes?''

The Executioner nodded. ''Small, two-man native outriggers. We can ride them in with the tide right over the reef.

Passive sonar won't detect us. The boats are made of wood, and without scuba gear, our only sources of metal will be our personal weapons, and they'll be spread out in several canoes. I doubt any magnetometer will pick them up, and if they do, the signal will be very weak and dispersed. It'll appear to be an anomalous reading. The prevailing currents will take us to the atoll almost without us having to paddle. No submarine will detect us floating on the surface unless it is actively pinging."

Several of the Frenchmen winced involuntarily at the word "pinging." Bolan continued. "Inside the lagoon, we paddle only enough to steer, then let the tide take us right up to the sand. With luck, we hit the beach dry, undetected, and ready for immediate action."

Hubert stood behind Sauvin and nodded. "I like it."

Sauvin folded his massive arms across his chest. "It's very clever. It could work." He glanced around the table. Maitland's finger lazily traced the perimeter of the atoll on the satellite photo. "*Oui*, it is good."

Sauvin looked at his right-hand man. "ZeeZee?"

ZeeZee looked at the satellite photo for a long moment, then nodded at Sauvin. He looked at Bolan and grinned his gap-toothed smile. "Yankee ingenuity, no?"

The woman leaned forward and looked Bolan in the eye. "You can get the canoes?"

Bolan smiled slightly. He thought Dr. Tutarotaro might just be persuaded to scare up some outriggers for him. "I think so."

Sauvin nodded. "Good." He leaned over the satellite photo. "Then we'll attack tonight."

RYUCHI TAIDO WAS ALMOST beside himself with glee. Tanaka gave him a suspicious smile. "You have found a way to redeem yourself." It was a statement, not a question.

Taido nodded. "I have had a thought, Tanaka-*san*."

"Oh?"

"Yes, why don't we just kill all the Americans, including the commando, and get back to business."

Tanaka blinked at him. "Just kill them all and get back to business?"

"Yes, Tanaka-*san* I believe that would solve our problems nicely."

The Japanese leader put his chin in his hand and peered at Taido speculatively. "So you're just going to kill them all, including the commando, that easily."

"Yes, I will."

The men looked at each other. Taido's grin widened. "Ah! I suspect you would like details!"

Tanaka looked at his subordinate with bemused irritation and idly considered beating him to death with a chair.

Taido knew he had pushed his impudence as far as he could. He smiled and shrugged. "Nerve gas, Tanaka-*san*. With your permission, I'll contact Tokyo and have them acquire the necessary equipment and air drop it to us tonight. Then we insert an attack team to the main island. We'll take a portable 81 mm mortar and assemble it in the tree line outside of the USO Oil site and lob a pattern of nerve-agent mortar bombs into their compound. This will circumvent any security system they have implemented along their perimeter or their ocean flank. It would be incredible if they had any kind of chemical warfare masks and suits in their inventory, much less be able to put them on before the gas killed them. They'll all be killed, and they'll never see it coming until death is among them."

The older man nodded. Taido's reputation for innovation was well founded. "And then?"

"We'll use a quick dispersing agent. Within an hour, most of the airborne gas will have dispersed or degraded, and we should be able to enter the compound safely wearing only gas masks. We then collect the bodies and put them in their main shed and burn it. The USO Oil team will have died in a tragic fire. Suspicious, perhaps, but there will be no bullet-ridden or mutilated bodies and no evidence of our involvement. After that, I suggest we try it on the French." Taido exposed his horselike teeth. "I understand oil-rig fires can be spectacular."

Tanaka couldn't help but smile. Ryuchi Taido was perhaps the most genuinely devious man he had ever met. "An excellent plan, Taido-*san*. Go find Minato and see to the logistics of it immediately. When I see the American commando lying twisted and dead in his own vomit, you may consider yourself redeemed."

Taido bowed low. "*Hai*, Tanaka-*san*. I will implement the plan at once."

Tanaka leaned back in his seat. When he returned to Tokyo and produced the American commando's head with its face frozen in a rictus of agony and set it before Mr. Yabe, he would be redeemed, as well.

MACK BOLAN DIPPED his paddle into the water, gently propelling the canoe along. Four outriggers moved across the open sea between the main island and the Japanese-held atoll. There was no moon, but there were no clouds, either, and the sea of stars above were more than enough light to navigate by. Off to the left, Bolan could see the dark bulk of the sister island, and he could hear the waves breaking off its reef where he had battled the Japanese cutter. He mentally calculated that the atoll would be four or five miles ahead.

In front of Bolan, Jeanine Maitland dipped her paddle into the water. The current was in the strike team's favor, and they had fallen into an easy, ground covering rhythm. Maitland's rifle was slung across her back. The French team was rather well-armed. Each member carried a Steyr AUG assault rifle. With its green plastic body and built-in telescopic sight, it looked like a prop from a science-fiction film. Bolan was intimately familiar with the weapon, and he had the utmost respect for its capabilities. Sauvin had smiled and told him that the rifles had been destined for the Australian army but had been "lost in shipment." Each member of the French team also carried a small assortment of Belgian-made rifle grenades.

Bolan suspected that the high-explosive munitions had "magically" disappeared from their original consignment as well.

The exception was Sauvin himself. He carried a Browning semiautomatic sporting shotgun with the barrel shortened to a brutal eighteen inches. In a shoulder holster, he carried a four-inch Smith & Wesson Model 29 .44 Magnum revolver.

Sauvin apparently believed in maximum stopping power.

The rest of the French team carried a hodge-podge of personal handguns, fighting knives and Russian black-market offensive and defensive hand grenades. All of it was untraceable. Bolan had to admit the French strike team's equipment was extremely functional. All of them wore black raid suits, knit caps and body armor.

Since they weren't swimming in, Bolan had on his full war load. The M-4 carbine with its attached 40 mm M-203 grenade launcher rested across his knees as he paddled. The .44 Magnum Desert Eagle pistol and the Beretta 93-R rode in their respective holsters under his left arm and at his right hip. A Tanto fighting knife was strapped upside down in his web gear on the front of his body armor. The snub-nosed 9 mm Centennial revolver rode in a holster on his right ankle, and a slender skeleton-handled stiletto rode in his left boot. Spare ammunition was strapped all over his web gear.

Bolan considered the last communication he had received from Stony Man Farm before the strike force had set out. A plane had been tracked flying over the Pacific Trust chain earlier in the evening, and its path had intersected the Japanese atoll. Kurtzman suspected it had dropped somebody or something into their compound. Bolan agreed with that, but he had also agreed with Sauvin when he had run the information past him. It wasn't enough to scrub the mission. They would attack as planned.

Bolan kept his paddle stroke in rhythm with Maitland. Out in the gloom ahead he could see the darker smudge of the Japanese atoll on the horizon.

24

Ryuchi Taido barked at his men. "Again!"

The men scrambled forward with the components of the broken-down mortar and began rapidly assembling it in the trees outside of the Kanabo compound. To one side sat a long green crate with its lid open. Inside it lay six 81 mm chemical agent bombs.

Taido didn't believe in taking chances. In the uncertainty of combat, men would fall back on their training. So Taido was making sure his men would know what they were doing. Taido was also making them drill wearing gas masks, body armor and carrying their 9 mm Uzi submachine guns with six spare magazines.

The men weren't happy about it, but no one grumbled. Wearing masks in the dark made the relatively simple task of erecting the mortar difficult. The heavy-weapons man was a short fellow named Goro who Taido knew only by reputation. Goro suddenly looked up from the sighting apparatus at Taido.

"Sighted in and ready for firing, Taido-*san!*"

Taido nodded curtly. "Fire!"

Goro's loader was a thin man named Chitose. Goro nodded at him. "Fire!"

Chitose dropped the training bomb down the mortar's 81 mm launch tube, and the weapon shuddered on its base plate and thumped loudly as pale yellow flame shot out of the muzzle at a ninety-degree angle into the air. The other three men stood with their weapons ready to cover the team in case of attack. There was a distant smacking noise as the weighted plastic training bomb hit the sand a hundred yards away. Moments later Minato Gosuke's voice spoke in Taido's headset. "Direct hit, in the middle of the compound."

Taido grunted with satisfaction. The operation was likely to go off without a hitch. He grinned at his men. "Very good. Now, once more, just for luck!"

The masked heads shook with disbelief, then quickly began to break down the mortar for another practice run. Taido grunted to himself in satisfaction as his men sweated in their masks. Sweat in training saved blood in combat. He believed an American had coined the phrase, but that didn't prevent him from embracing it wholeheartedly.

Just before dawn they would go out and kill the Americans.

MACK BOLAN RAISED his paddle as the canoe ground to a halt in the sand. The Kanabo compound lay two hundred yards west on the curving beach of the inner atoll. Their lights were bright, and there was little activity. Bolan had to agree with Sauvin. He doubted very much whether the Japanese expected an attack tonight. He doubted whether they expected to be attacked at all. In the battle for the Pacific Trust Islands, they had dominantly been the aggressors.

The canoes had slid over the barely submerged reef barrier with only inches to spare. Once past the reef the lagoon was as smooth as glass. Bolan and Maitland jumped from the outrigger and dragged it onto the beach. Canoes beached on either side of them as the rest of the strike team hit the sand.

Maitland unslung her Steyr AUG rifle and fitted a high-explosive rifle grenade over the muzzle until it clicked onto the launching fins. She reached to her hip and cocked a .45 Colt Combat Commander pistol similar to the one Bolan had taken from her in the hotel. Sauvin jerked his head silently, and the strike team moved out.

The plan was simple, and Bolan had no problem with it. They would break the force into two-man fire teams and attack from the side and the rear. There was no way to know if the fence was wired with an alarm or electrified, so they would simply blow their way through it with rifle grenades and assault weapons.

Bolan and Maitland moved toward the side of the compound, shadowed by Sauvin and Hubert to their right. ZeeZee and the other three men moved inland and began to skirt toward the rear. Bolan and his teammate stopped and knelt fifty yards from the fence. They would give ZeeZee and the flanking teams sixty seconds to reach the rear of the compound. The soldier counted down mentally, while Maitland looked over at Sauvin in the starlit gloom. As Bolan hit sixty, the French commander sliced his hand through the air.

Maitland's rifle boomed, and she rocked back with the recoil as the grenade launched off the end of her rifle barrel. Bolan was already moving before the grenade hit. With a flash of orange fire, the high-explosive rifle grenade hit the fencing. The entire perimeter fence shook on its poles as the links came apart in a ragged four-foot circle. A second blast from Hubert's weapon detonated next to it, and there were similar explosions at the rear of the compound.

Bolan could hear Maitland hard on his heels as they charged across the sand, and off to his right he could see Sauvin and Hubert moving at a dead run. The soldier hunched his shoulders as he went through the blackened hole in the fence and raised his M-4 carbine.

RAIZO TANAKA JUMPED from his desk at the sound of explosions. Taido wouldn't be so stupid as to accidentally use live mortar bombs for his training session. The sudden ripping snarl of an assault rifle firing on full-auto solved the question for him.

They were under attack.

Tanaka went to his cabinet and pulled out a 9 mm Heckler & Koch MP-5 submachine gun and his web gear with six loaded magazines. He racked the bolt as Minato ran into the room. "Tanaka-*san!* We're under attack!"

Tanaka nodded and shoved a second weapon and ammunition bandoleer into Minato's hands. "Get to the barracks and get the rest of the men moving." Two more men raced into the room with Uzis in their hands.

"You have your weapons. Good. Follow me." Tanaka scooped up his hand radio and pushed the transmit button as he moved to the back door. "Taido, we're under attack. Come back at once."

BOLAN THREW HIMSELF down as the window of a long shed suddenly smashed outward. A gun muzzle protruded and began to spit flame in his direction. The Executioner rolled and leveled the Ranger carbine. The thirty yards between him and his target was point-blank for the M-203, and he simply aimed the weapon without using the sights and fired. The M-203 boomed, and the fragmentation grenade flew through the window and detonated with a yellow flash and a concussion that blew out the rest of the windows in the shed as well.

The enemy submachine gun suddenly fell silent.

Men began to spill out of the prefabricated buildings, and the strike team cut them down in the withering cross fire. The estimate was that the Kanabo Corporation had anywhere between twenty to thirty men on-site. If French Intelligence was correct, almost all of them were combat operatives. The strike team had speed and surprise on their side. High-explosive weapons didn't hurt, either. At least half a dozen of the Kanabo operatives were down already, and that wasn't counting those who had died in their buildings. Bolan reloaded the M-203 and fired a frag grenade through the window of the long barracks to his left. The rest of the windows blew out as it detonated. Muffled screams came from within.

Behind Bolan, and to his left, Maitland's weapon boomed as it launched another grenade at a small metal shack that someone was firing from. The grenade slammed into the side of the shed, and there was a flare of light. The woman had fired an antiarmor munition. Its shaped-charge warhead had struck the shed and sent a jet of molten metal and white-hot gas into it. The shed listed as it sagged and burned.

Bolan moved forward and took cover behind a stack of

crated machine parts covered by a tarp. Maitland quickly jumped beside him. Sauvin and Hubert had reached a storage shed and were crouched with their backs to it. Bolan loaded a high-explosive round into the breech of the M-203.

The door of the central shack flew open, and the flame of several automatic weapons strobed from the darkened interior. Bolan launched his grenade at the black rectangle of the open door. Someone slammed the door shut, but the high-explosive grenade blew it in two and sent the pieces flying inward.

The Executioner rose from cover and advanced.

TAIDO DIDN'T LIKE what he saw. Men in raid suits were moving purposefully through the compound. They were heavily armed and had explosive projectiles. Taido extended the stock of his 9 mm Uzi and aimed. With a scowl, he lowered the weapon. The range was too great, and it would announce his presence. He had been clever enough to leave Goro and Chitose with the mortar. The other three men of the attack team looked at him. They wondered why he was waiting to attack. Taido clicked on his radio.

"Tanaka-*san!* Tanaka-*san!*"

After a moment Taido's radio squawked. "Taido! Where the hell are you!"

"In the trees! Listen! Take your surviving men, and go to the far west of the compound. I'm going to use the mortar on the attackers!"

Tanaka's response was immediate. "Do it!"

Taido called Goro. "Set your sights for the eastern quadrant of the compound and fire immediately! Chemical munitions!"

"*Hai!*"

Taido put the radio back on his belt and nodded at the three men with him. They began creeping forward into range with their submachine guns.

THE EXECUTIONER FROZE. The hollow thumping sound was unmistakable. Someone from outside the compound had fired a mortar. Bolan hurled himself to the sand and roared at the top of his lungs.

"Incoming!"

Bolan could see ZeeZee and his men on the other flank of the central shack. Sauvin and Hubert were moving forward as the soldier and Maitland covered them. Sauvin hit the sand, but Hubert kept moving forward. He hadn't heard Bolan over the roar of the automatic rifle in his hands. Sauvin screamed at him in French, and Hubert lunged at the ground. Ten feet from Hubert's head the sand erupted as something struck it. The big Frenchman froze for a moment, then jumped up and began to move. Bolan rose to one knee and jerked to a halt.

Hubert stiffened and the assault rifle in his hand went off in a continuous burst as his finger clamped on the trigger. His back spasmed, and he fell to the ground twitching and shuddering. The Executioner's blood went cold. He had seen that effect before, and it still made his spine crawl. The Kanabo Corporation hardmen were using nerve gas, and none of the strike team had chemical masks or suits.

Bolan jacked a white phosphorus grenade into the breech of the M-203. He could see the canister where it lay imbedded in the sand. In the sudden silence, he could hear it faintly hiss as it released its deadly toxins. The sudden cessation of gunfire told Bolan that the Kanabo operatives were pulling back from the area and repositioning themselves. He gritted his teeth. Hubert was already a dead man. He had no gas mask, and the team had no atropine to administer. To save the rest of the team, he had to act now.

Bolan aimed at the gas canister and fired.

Yellow light flared as the white phosphorus grenade blasted the gas canister apart in a ball of fire. Hubert's twitching form disappeared inside the opaque smoke. Streamers of burning phosphorus shot into the air like a Fourth of July display, and a cloud of superheated white smoke billowed forth.

Bolan racked another phosphorus round. The nerve agent was a complex liquid chemical agent, and the canister delivered it like an aerosol spray into the air. Being exposed to the burning phosphorus would break it down chemically, and the superheated smoke would dry and disperse any of it that was already airborne.

Theoretically.

The soldier knew he couldn't sit and shoot skeet with the incoming mortar rounds. If they pulled back and went to the canoes, the Japanese would get in one of their motorboats and slaughter them at will. There was only one alternative. The Japanese wouldn't gas their own people. They had to go forward. The Executioner rose, and his voice rang out across the field of battle in the unmistakable tone of command. "Attack! Go! Go! Go!"

Bolan charged forward. Out of the corner of his eye, he saw Sauvin rise as well. Out in the trees, the hollow thump of the mortar boomed, and Bolan broke into a dead run. He squinted and gritted his teeth as he skirted the white phosphorus smoke cloud. Suddenly, he was through, and ahead lay what looked like an equipment shed. Off to his left ZeeZee led Peter, Nicholas and Marco around the other side of the cloud.

Automatic weapons opened from the shed, and others began firing outside the fence perimeter. Peter and Nicholas fell in the cross fire. ZeeZee and Marco ran forward. The only cover was a parked open-top Land Rover. The vehicle shuddered under the sudden onslaught and the two men dived behind it. ZeeZee and Marco hunched together to keep the thick metal of the winch and the engine block between them and the hail of gunfire.

Bolan aimed the M-203 into the middle of the strobing muzzle-flashes outside the fence and fired. He turned to Maitland, but she was already on the ball. She had fitted another grenade to her rifle, and she fired it at the shed. The round shot through the thin metal wall, and the structure came apart as the high-explosive grenade detonated inside. Outside the fence, the palm forest lit up with white-hot smoke and streaks of burning phosphorus. Men screamed.

The Executioner moved onto the burning shed.

RAIZO TANAKA ROSE shakily to his feet. A moment ago he had been firing from behind the shed. It had swelled outward and smashed him in the face. He wiped the blood from his mouth. Minato lay charred and dead a few feet away with his head at a disjointed angle from his shoulders. Ishikawa sat on his heels and shook his head dazedly. The tool shed was smoldering and had crumpled to half its original height. Its rear wall was gone. Tools lay scattered all around them. Tanaka scooped a pair of heavy-duty shears and yanked Ishikawa to his feet.

"Cut the fence! Quickly!"

Ishikawa nodded and took the shears.

Tanaka keyed his radio and was relieved to find it still functioned. "Taido!"

Static crackled.

Ishikawa shouted. "Tanaka-*san!*"

Tanaka turned. Ishikawa had snipped a four-foot slit in the fence and was holding it open. Tanaka dived through it and turned to cover Ishikawa as two men rounded the burning shed. Ishikawa was halfway through when he shuddered and collapsed as he was stitched with automatic rifle fire. Tanaka put a burst into one of the charging men, and his head snapped back as he was hit. The Japanese commander rolled into the trees as the second man dropped prone and squeezed off a long burst. He walked on his knees and elbows deeper into the brush as he whispered into the radio.

"Goro! Use all the remaining gas bombs! Blanket the compound!"

MACK BOLAN HEARD the mortar fire again as he reached the shed behind ZeeZee. Sauvin and Maitland followed quickly behind him. ZeeZee lay prone, firing quick bursts into the darkness. He glanced around at his reinforcements and spoke rapid French. Bolan caught enough to know that Marco was dead and at least one man had gone through the fence. The other Japanese lay hung up in the wire links. The Executioner jerked his head toward the fence.

"We have to get out, now!"

Sauvin glared. "There could be an ambush out there! There are only the four of us left!"

The mortar fired again. "Then stay," Bolan told him.

Sauvin took his meaning. They each took a limb and yanked the dead Kanabo man out of the hole in the fence. Behind them they heard the smack of the mortar round impacting. It was only twenty yards away. Bolan snarled as he held the slit open. "Move!"

ZeeZee, Maitland and Sauvin piled through the fence. ZeeZee and Sauvin grabbed it from the other side and yanked it open wide as Bolan pushed through. They ran into the trees as the gas canisters hissed behind them. Twenty yards in, the Executioner halted as the mortar thumped again and he grabbed Sauvin's shoulder. "There!"

Sauvin nodded. They had both seen the pale puff of yellow flame through the palms. Bolan guessed the range at seventy-five yards and jacked a fragmentation round into the M-203. ZeeZee and Maitland both fixed grenades onto their rifle muzzles. Two seconds later, the thump and the flame repeated itself. The three of them aimed high and arced their munitions into looping trajectories. Bolan moved ahead to put more distance between them and the gas. The French followed.

Moments later the detonations of their grenades lit up the palm forest as they exploded one after the other. Bolan loaded a frag into the M-203's breech. He whispered harshly, "You three, spread out, head for the fire. I'll flank wide." Sauvin nodded, and ZeeZee and Maitland fanned out toward the burning palms in the distance.

Bolan headed out into the darkness.

TANAKA THREW HIMSELF to the ground as he heard the grenades launch. Moments later, the palm forest erupted. The grenades had fallen right on top of the mortar position. Tanaka rose and ran ahead. He reached the burning circle. Goro and Chitose lay dead. The mortar tube was twisted on its base plate. Tanaka's shoulders sagged.

He had lost.

The commander surveyed the scene. Soon, they would be coming for him. If he kept on, he would come to the end of the atoll in half a mile. He'd be flushed out and killed. Tanaka's eyes flared as they saw the mortar bomb box. Two bombs still lay inside. Tanaka unslung his Heckler & Koch submachine gun and tossed it aside. He drew his Walther P-5 pistol and knelt by the ammunition crate.

He had one last card to play.

BOLAN EDGED CLOSER to the burning palm trees. The flames were dying, and in the red glow he could see Sauvin, ZeeZee and Maitland approaching warily. Three bodies lay on the ground. The mortar was out of commission.

As Bolan started to rise out of his crouch, one of the bodies rolled to its feet.

"Freeze!"

Maitland was between Bolan and the man, and he couldn't see why the French hadn't simply shot him. Bolan circled around in the darkness as the man shouted, "Drop your weapons! Or we all die together! Do not doubt me!"

None of the French budged an inch. Sauvin's fingers opened, and his shotgun fell to the sand. ZeeZee's and Maitland's rifles quickly joined it. It seemed no one doubted the man. Bolan continued to circle, then froze. The man was Japanese, and he was holding a cylinder with fins crooked in one arm. It was one of the nerve agent canisters. In his other hand, he held a Walther P-5 pistol with the muzzle pressed against the mortar bomb.

The nerve agent was an aerosol, and it was held under pressure in the canister. If the man put a bullet through the thin casing, it would burst and spray concentrated nerve gas in all directions. Bolan found he didn't doubt the man, either. He had dealt with agents of the Kanabo Corporation before. The man would take them all to hell with him. The man grimaced as the weapons fell to ground. "Your side arm! Use two fingers! Drop them! Now!"

Sauvin dropped the big .44 Magnum revolver to the ground. ZeeZee's 9 mm Hi-Power fell next. Maitland's open hand hovered over the grips of her .45. She glared bloody murder at the Kanabo operative. Bolan knew she was fast, but he doubted she could draw and fire before the Japanese simply squeezed his trigger. Sauvin's voice was a strangled snarl.

"Maitland! Drop your weapon!"

She glared at her commander, then back at the Japanese. Her hand curled into a shaking fist, then her thumb and forefinger pinched the .45's grips. She slowly drew the pistol and let it fall.

Bolan edged around through the trees until he faced the Japanese. The man glanced with a sneer at the French operatives. "On your knees, and hands behind your heads if you want to live!"

None of them were going to live and they knew it, but they knelt in the sand and put their hands behind their heads anyway. They knew one thing the Kanabo man didn't, and they were betting their lives on it.

Out in the darkness, an American was lurking.

Bolan could kill the man right now and risk killing the rest of the French team and possibly himself when the canister exploded. The safer bet would be to kill him once he started shooting the French, but again, some of his allies would probably die. Bolan raised the Ranger carbine to his shoulder. The orange light of the burning palm trees flickered and brightened as dead palm leaves suddenly ignited overhead. In the flare, Bolan saw one thing clearly.

The Japanese agent's pistol wasn't cocked.

The Walther P-5 was a double-action pistol. It didn't have to be cocked to fire, but it lightened the trigger pull immensely. A dying man might spasm and touch off a cocked gun. Bolan doubted his finger would pull through a 12-pound double-action trigger pull.

The Executioner put the M-4's front sight between the man's eyes and fired.

The man stiffened and jerked back. The mortar bomb slid

out of his arm and fell to the sand. Bolan put a second round in his chest, and the man fell forward onto his face.

The Executioner emerged from the trees.

"Are you all right?"

Sauvin scooped up his shotgun and rose. He peered at Bolan narrowly in the firelight. "It was a close thing. He might have killed us all."

Bolan shrugged. "His gun wasn't cocked. He probably didn't want to accidentally shoot the canister."

Sauvin blinked and suddenly grinned in understanding. "Ah! The trigger pull. You are very clever." He whipped the muzzle of his shotgun around at Bolan. "Too bad you died heroically in the fight."

The Executioner swung up his carbine as Sauvin's shotgun roared. The carbine shuddered and twisted painfully in Bolan's hands as a solid 12-gauge slug smashed into the weapon. Sauvin brought the sawed-off shotgun out of its brutal recoil to fire again. Bolan hurled the mangled carbine into his face and dived back into the trees. Rifle bullets streaked into the brush after him as ZeeZee and Maitland tracked him. The soldier continued to roll and yanked the Beretta 93-R clear of its holster. He fired off several bursts to keep the French down and suddenly fell three feet down a sand embankment. The sonic cracks of the rifle bullets flying overhead snapped through the air. Sand rained on Bolan as Sauvin probed his position with his shotgun. The Executioner groped at his belt, and his hand closed on a grenade. Its cylindrical shape told him it was one of the two CS tear-gas grenades he had brought in case the Japanese had managed to stockade themselves. He pulled the pin and hurled the bomb over the embankment.

Bolan drew the .44 Magnum Desert Eagle with his free hand.

He heard the pop and the hiss of the CS grenade and Sauvin's guttural shout in French. *"Gaz! Gaz! Gaz!"* The shotgun roared again, and sand spilled down on Bolan.

The Executioner heard the thud of boots, then rifle fire opened up again over his head. One rifle. Two members of the French team were flanking him while the other one kept him pinned down. Bolan rolled up tightly against the embankment as ZeeZee rounded the palm tree to Bolan's left.

Bolan fired a burst from the Beretta, and ZeeZee staggered. The little Frenchman's Steyr rifle ripped into life, and sand spouted into the air as bullets struck the embankment over Bolan's head. The Executioner raised his aim and fired. The 3-round burst walked up ZeeZee's chest and finished at his throat. ZeeZee fired his rifle again, and the bullets flew high over Bolan's head. He put a third burst into the Frenchman's face, and he fell dead to the sand.

The soldier rose to one knee and whirled at a sound behind him. It had taken him too long to kill the little Frenchman. As Bolan raised the Beretta at the dark form in the trees, the night lit up with orange fire.

An immense weight smashed Bolan in the chest and knocked him backward. The shotgun roared again, and the tree to the soldier's right shuddered as it was struck. His armor had absorbed the buckshot, but it had felt like being kicked by a mule, and Bolan blinked from the flash blindness of staring straight into the shotgun blast. He rose half-blind to one knee and raised the Beretta.

Something hard and heavy struck him in the face. Bolan rocked back on his heels and fired the Beretta into the darkness. Part of the soldier's mind still worked with the cold efficiency of battle.

Sauvin hadn't picked up his revolver back at the mortar sight, but he was coming for Bolan. The Executioner began emptying both pistols in the direction he had last seen Sauvin. Above their roar, he felt the thud of boots in the sand nearly on top of him to his right. As Bolan whirled, a heavy body slammed into him and bowled him over. Cold sharp steel burned across his arm as he covered himself, and a knee slammed into his thigh as it aimed for his groin.

Bolan dropped the Desert Eagle and grabbed Sauvin's knife arm. His left hand was jammed between them, so Bolan shoved the Beretta's muzzle into Sauvin's stomach and fired.

The Beretta fired a 3-round burst into Sauvin, and 9 mm hollowpoint slugs punched against his armor. Sauvin grunted at the blows, as the Beretta clacked open on empty. Bolan felt the Frenchman's knife slam into his side and snag in his armor. The soldier dropped the spent pistol and brought his right knee up between them. His fingers curled around the grips of the Centennial revolver in his ankle holster.

Sauvin ripped his knife free and drove it at Bolan's face. The Executioner yanked his head aside, and the knife plunged into the sand. The revolver came free with the ripping sound of Velcro, and Bolan shoved the muzzle under Sauvin's chin and fired.

The big Frenchman went limp and fell on top of the Executioner, who shoved the corpse off him and rolled to one knee wearily. Blood ran down his arm as he scooped up the Desert Eagle.

Jeanine Maitland was still out there.

Bolan pulled his second CS tear-gas grenade and peered over the embankment. Out in the distance, he could see the dim glow of the burning buildings in the Kanabo compound. The trees by the mortar emplacement flickered orange as the flames died down. Under the palm trees, it was all gloom and silence.

Behind the mortar barrier, something flickered orange for a split second. Bolan's eyes flared. It was a reflection. Maitland's Steyr AUG rifle had an integral optical sight. Its lens had reflected the firelight as it scanned for him. The Executioner rose and hurled his hand grenade.

The Executioner dived down and rifle bullets stitched the top of the embankment as Maitland caught his movement. A moment later, Bolan heard the pop and hiss of the grenade, then the woman's strangled gasp. He rose to a crouch and ran to his left to flank her. He could hear her choking, and her rifle ripped off a long burst toward the embankment. Bolan saw the muzzle-flash and moved in.

She fired another burst, and her rifle clicked open empty. She staggered away from the spreading gas and fumbled for a spare magazine. She dropped the rifle and went for her .45 as she heard Bolan's footfalls.

Bolan put the glowing front sight of the Desert Eagle in the middle of her dark form and fired. Maitland staggered as the .44 Magnum bullet hit her. She tottered on her feet and tried to aim her .45, but fell forward onto her hands and knees.

She made a retching noise as her hand groped for the .45. Bolan stalked forward and leveled the big .44 Magnum at her head. The canopy overhead was clear, and in the starlight Bolan could see tears streaming down her face from the gas, and blood oozing from her broken nose.

Maitland's body armor had saved her from the bullet, but the big .44 Magnum round had still delivered over half a ton of muzzle energy. Her breath came in ragged gasps as she stared up at the Desert Eagle muzzle.

Bolan looked down at her coldly in the twilight. "I'm assuming this was a personal vendetta and not the orders of the French government."

She wiped the back of her hand across her bloody lips and glared. Her voice was a hoarse croak from the tear gas. "Go to hell."

The Executioner extended his arm, the muzzle of the Desert Eagle was less than a foot from her face. Maitland flinched and squeezed her eyes shut. Bolan's tone was matter-of-fact. "Get up."

Maitland gritted her teeth. "Go ahead and shoot me."

Bolan exposed his teeth in an unfriendly smile. "Get up or I will."

She stared up at him. "You aren't going to kill me?"

"Not unless I have to. You're useless to me without a pulse."

"What do you mean?"

Bolan glanced back toward the compound. "It's seven miles back to the USO Oil site. A lot of it against the current. You're going to paddle."

Maitland spit a stream of high-voltage obscenities in French. They cut short to a yelp as Bolan sank his hand into her hair and yanked her to her feet. He shoved her ahead of him. She stumbled a step or two and whirled with her fists clenched.

Bolan recalled René Sauvin's tattoo and smiled at her as he spoke. "*Marcher ou mourir,* Jeanine."

EPILOGUE

Dr. Tutarotaro was still in his wheelchair, but his hands were steady as he stitched the knife cut in Bolan's forearm. He raised a bushy eyebrow. "You made her paddle?"

Bolan rubbed his forehead where Sauvin's shotgun had struck him. "I was tired."

Tutarotaro shook his head in wonder. So did his bodyguards. The American had defeated all of the Japanese warriors and all of the French, as well. The Polynesians had a word for personal power, called *mana*. This man seemed to be loaded with it.

Bolan changed the subject. "So what's going on in local politics?"

One of Tutarotaro's bodyguards, a young man named Samu, piped up gleefully. "We are going to make Ezekiel Tutarotaro the first governor of the Pacific Trust Islands!"

It was hard to tell under the saddle-leather skin, but Bolan was almost sure that the doctor was blushing. Tutarotaro cleared his throat as he wrapped a bandage around Bolan's arm. "That remains to be seen. I won't allow myself to be given the job." The doctor refused to meet Bolan's eyes. "However, if I'm nominated, perhaps I'll run in a free election."

Samu folded his arms and grinned triumphantly. "Damn right! We're going to freely elect Ezekiel Tutarotaro for first governor of the Pacific Trust Islands!"

Bolan frowned slightly. "What will the United Nations and the provisional government have to say?"

It was the doctor's turn to frown. "The United Nations and their provisional government can go to hell. The Pacific Trust Islands will have free elections. If the UN would like to help, we would be grateful. If they don't, we'll have them, anyway. The world can recognize us as a nation or not. We don't care. My people will decide their own destiny."

Bolan smiled. He had no doubt he was looking at the first governor of the Pacific Trust Islands. Tutarotaro looked at Bolan's grin and grinned back sheepishly. "I don't mean to preach at you." He changed the subject. "You'll be pleased to know that whoever wins the elections, I believe the Japanese lease will be revoked."

Bolan nodded.

"And, if my people choose to develop our natural resources, I doubt we'll look to the French."

"Red will be glad to hear that."

Tutarotaro rose from the wheelchair and extended his hand. "I would like to thank you for your help."

Bolan took the doctor's hand and shook it. "I'd like to thank you for yours, as well. We helped each other solve a mutual problem."

"Take care of yourself, Mr. Belasko."

RYUCHI TAIDO SAT despondently by the shore and waited for the submarine. His hands had been blistered and burned by a streamer of white phosphorus. He had dropped his smoldering submachine gun and watched the rest of his men get killed by shrapnel and burned alive. He had been unable to hold a weapon, so he had crawled away into the underbrush and hid. He had seen the big American and the woman walk to the beach and get in a native canoe and paddle away.

Taido had spent the morning walking dazedly around the atoll. Tanaka was dead. Minato was dead. Everyone was dead. He looked down at his blistered hands which were awkwardly swaddled in cloth. He suspected they would require extensive rehabilitation. That, however, was the least of his problems.

The old man wouldn't be pleased.

Taido's shoulders sagged. He had been chewed out before and demoted. But the Kanabo Corporation needed operatives like him, and both he and the old man knew it. Taido was a hunter and a killer. The Kanabo Corporation was a conglomerate that spanned the globe. Its network of resources was unbelievably vast. They would find this American commando, and Taido would kill him. He smiled grimly.

He would swear it to the old man's face.

James Axler

OUTLANDERS™

OUTER DARKNESS

Kane and his companions are transported to an alternate reality where the global conflagration didn't happen—and humanity had expelled the Archons from the planet. Things are not as rosy as they may seem, as the Archons return for a final confrontation....

Book #3 in the new Lost Earth Saga, a trilogy that chronicles our heroes' paths through three very different alternative realities...where the struggle against the evil Archons goes on....

An enemy within...

Stolen U.S. chemical weapons are believed responsible for attacks on Azerbaijan and on a merchant ship in the Caspian Sea. While all indications point to Iraq, Bolan and the Stony Man team are sent to track a much more insidious enemy....

Available in July 1999 at your favorite retail outlet.

Shadow THE EXECUTIONER®
as he battles evil for 352 pages of heart-stopping action!

SuperBolan®

#61452	DAY OF THE VULTURE	$5.50 U.S. ☐ $6.50 CAN. ☐
#61453	FLAMES OF WRATH	$5.50 U.S. ☐ $6.50 CAN. ☐
#61454	HIGH AGGRESSION	$5.50 U.S. ☐ $6.50 CAN. ☐
#61455	CODE OF BUSHIDO	$5.50 U.S. ☐ $6.50 CAN. ☐
#61456	TERROR SPIN	$5.50 U.S. ☐ $6.50 CAN. ☐

(limited quantities available on certain titles)

TOTAL AMOUNT	$
POSTAGE & HANDLING	$
($1.00 for one book, 50¢ for each additional)	
APPLICABLE TAXES*	$ _____
TOTAL PAYABLE	$ _____
(check or money order—please do not send cash)	

To order, complete this form and send it, along with a check or money order for the total above, payable to Gold Eagle Books, to: **In the U.S.:** 3010 Walden Avenue, P.O. Box 9077, Buffalo, NY 14269-9077; **In Canada:** P.O. Box 636, Fort Erie, Ontario, L2A 5X3.

Name: _____

Address: _____ City: _____

State/Prov.: _____ Zip/Postal Code: _____

*New York residents remit applicable sales taxes.
 Canadian residents remit applicable GST and provincial taxes.

GSBBACK1